About the Author

Jeri Lynn Stone lives in a small Arkansas town with her husband. She works at a large manufacturing plant in the Quality Assurance Department as an ISO Internal Auditor and Quality Assurance. Her and her husband love to camp and fish. They live in the center of four beautiful lakes and each are within twenty-five miles from home. They love going to antique car shows, gardening and Mother Nature. She has enjoyed writing novels, from historical to chick lit to mystery for about twelve years, now. She's currently working on the fourth novel in her Detective Crime Mystery "Tara" series.

OTHER BOOKS BY JERI LYNN STONE
'TARA' DETECTIVE CRIME MYSTERY SERIES
TAUNTING TARA
TEACHING TARA
TANGLE WITH TARA

COMING NEXT
TERRORIZING TARA

I0592494

Shadow's Justice

ISBN/SKU:9780692193532

ACKNOWLEDGEMENT

I would like to thank my wonderful husband, my loving family, friends, and the talented writers' community for the helpful support they've given me all of these years. I'm very grateful and honored to have everyone in my life.

I would also like to thank my terrific critique partners. They keep me on the straight and narrow path in my writing career.

And, to my fans. You are the greatest. I appreciate you all.

You have my deepest gratitude.

Thank you,
Jeri Lynn Stone

SHADOW'S JUSTICE

A Romantic Suspense Novel

by

JERI LYNN STONE

CHAPTER ONE

Two long, agonizing days after the State of Louisiana wrongly executed her father for murder, Shadow McClane bought a gun and sought justice. It also happened to be the day her stepbrother's best friend, Raven Deveroux pissed her off.

* * *

After her father's funeral Sunday morning, Shadow stood alone on the wide, pillared veranda of his home with eyes as dry as the southern summer skies.

She was too damned angry to cry.

Glancing over the long, circular driveway, she watched more friends and relatives arriving to give their condolences. Her father's widow Rose, his two stepson's, John and Michael Tolliver and herself had been busy for hours greeting each one and accepting their calculated sympathy. Until, she broke free from the growing crowd.

"Damn vultures," Shadow muttered and swore beneath her breath. She tapped her toes encased in her favorite black, three inch-heeled sandals and pushed the loose tendrils of her shoulder-length hair from her face while she watched another well-wisher approach.

She cursed the new arrival and every one of the bald-faced hypocrites who had the nerve to waltzed in front of her and her family offering their false condolences. Their greedy eyes passed right over her, lingering on her family's wealth of the antique furnishings and objects d'art inside the older, white-stuccoed mansion.

She visualized the drool dripping from their lips, the dollar signs in their eyes and jealousy's ugly head rearing over her father's self-made fortune.

Shadow brows narrowed as she watched the woman making a beeline toward her. She glanced over her shoulder looking for an avenue of escape. She needed time alone to grieve before her tough facade disintegrated.

She'd struggled a long time to be strong for her father after his arrest for the murder of a prominent banker, but that ended when they lowered her father's casket into the ground.

One bullet shot pointblank to the brain ended Judd Tucker, the banker's life and destroyed two families. The top it off, the murder weapon belonged to her father.

Watching her father give up hope after years of struggling to find the truth devastated her. She couldn't save her father's life, but come hail or high water, she would clear his name.

Shadow spun around to bolt away from the approaching visitor and her inconsolable thoughts. She plowed head-on into Raven Deveroux, Michael's long time friend. She stepped back and stabbed him with a glare before she moved to walk around him.

Raven placed both hands on her shoulders to stop her. He turned her to face him. "Are you okay?" She saw the concern in his eyes, but she was in no mood to be civil. Not to him.

She jerked away from him and snarled. "No, I'm not okay. I won't be until I find the real killer and shove him and the town's corrupt court system right smack into their self-righteous faces."

"Shadow, I'm not going to argue with you about this right now. This is not the time or place." His deep sigh expressed his fatigue.

"There's nothing to argue about. You've refused to help me, so I'll do it alone."

He shrugged. "Then, you're a fool. I'm not going to help you throw yourself into an early grave. The murderer still roams the streets a free man. You'll be putting yourself and your family in danger if you stir up anymore trouble. The law considers the case closed. There's nothing more you can do. Leave it alone." Raven pinned her with a fixed glare before turning and walking away.

Shadow watched his back disappear through the front doors. "That's where you're wrong, Buster. There is something I can and will do," she whispered.

* * *

Honorable Judge Ben Adams grinned around his Cuban cigar. His superiority glance swept around the rich and elegant office in his home. He met and held the gaze of both men sitting at the large round table taking up half the room. He raised his glass of fine brandy in salute. "It's over, gentlemen."

* * *

Five days later, the late evening breeze blew soft across Shadow's hair. She stood on the veranda sipping from a glass of wine with a profound lethargy she'd been unable to shake since her father's death.

She brushed the loose tendrils back from her face and glanced toward the end of the long veranda and studied Raven and her stepmother, Rose sitting on the swing beside him.

Still pissed at Raven, Shadow's stormy thoughts calmed somewhat since the day of the funeral. She reflected on everything she knew about him. First and foremost, he was a frustrating jerk at times.

Only a few months older than her thirty-two year old stepbrother, Michael, Raven had survived a harsher life. His training with the U.S. Special Forces led him to the secret life of a mercenary. The only information she'd found out was that he led small groups into enemy territories and retrieved 'items' belonging to the United States and large companies. He also worked for the family's business McClane's Construction Company. He steadily brought in new clients he met in his extensive travels and locally.

Shadow brought her thoughts back to the scene before her. She took a sip of her wine and watched as Raven held her stepmother secure with a comforting arm wrapped around her. He spoke softly into her ear while she cried beside him. He glanced up and caught her bold gaze.

She controlled the unwanted shiver running through her from that one cool, assessing look of his. A look that missed nothing.

She took another long sip, almost a swig, from her wine glass. Her hand shook.

She'd watched him enough over the years to know about his soft heart and good deeds behind his tough exterior. She'd witnessed on several occasions the unhidden desire showing as clear as day on other women's faces when they met him. Looking at him now, how could she not respond as a woman to his military cut, black-as-night hair, his jade green eyes, dimpled cheeks, dark tan or his 'made-for-women's pleasure' body outlined beneath his clothes?

In the life she'd led before her father's unjustified imprisonment, Shadow pursued those erotic details. She'd considered his good looks, erect military manner and his hands-off attitude a challenge to her femininity. But, not now. She was no longer the same gullible woman who saw good in all people, loving, charitable, laughing at life and living the fast lane to the fullest.

In fact, she'd become the very opposite of her youth. Her latest ex-boyfriend had called her a hard-boiled, streetwise with a kick-ass attitude bitch. And, he was right, she admitted. No more emotions, therefore no more pain.

Shadow turned away from the man staring at her. Her father once told her that her eyes expressed every dream and emotion spinning inside her. She had a sinking feeling the man who assessed her from across the veranda was a pro at finding the hidden passages to a woman's soul.

* * *

Raven gauged Shadow's nervous actions as she crossed the veranda and entered into the kitchen. She'd developed into a human time bomb ready to explode. A little over five feet tall, Shadow had a petite, curvy figure and an innocent face that could make a man sizzle and moan. Beautiful and dangerous. Add her blonde hair and blue, bedroom eyes to the picture and she became a volatile combination best left alone. Which he had. He'd spent many restless nights because of it.

Raven felt Rose's hand trembling on his arm and his thoughts of Shadow and what he had given up years before vanished. He looked down in concern at the only mother he ever knew after his own mother had died when he was a baby. His father died soon after his eighteenth birthday.

Rose appeared so pale and tears continued to fall from her reddened eyes. Strained from worry and pain, her face looked as if she'd aged ten years since the funeral.

"Rose, the guests are leaving soon. I wish you'd lie down and rest for awhile after they leave. You're exhausted."

Rose smiled up at him. Her hand came to rest on his cheek. "I will. I promise. First, I want to talk to you. I'm so glad you could come, Raven."

"I wouldn't be anywhere else."

"I know. I don't know what I would've done without you here. You've always been the strong one. Not that Michael and John would do any less for me, but you've always been more mature than your age. That and your immense experience is why I want to ask a big favor of you. This matter is very important to me or I wouldn't be putting you in this position."

Raven leaned down and kissed her on the forehead. "You know you can ask anything of me, Rose. But only if you promise to rest." He grinned, relieved to hear her slight laughter.

"That's bribery, son. But, I promise. I'll go straight up after we talk." Amusement fled and she sat in silence for a moment thinking on how to begin.

"Shadow is like a daughter to me. I love her as much as I do my own boys and you."

"I know that, Rose. She loves you, too."

Rose smiled and nodded. "Yes, she does." Her face grew serious. "I'm very worried about her, Raven. She eats, drinks and sleeps her father's case. Her mind is on this one track and no matter what I say, she's determined to find the killer. She's stirring up a hornet's nest and I'm scared she's going to be hurt. She doesn't realize what she's getting into."

"Do you want me to talk to her, again?"

Rose shook her head and looked him straight in the eyes. "No. I want you to help her."

CHAPTER TWO

Shadow closed the door to her father's office. She leaned heavy against the solid frame taking deep gulps of air into her lungs. Damn. Damn. Damn.

She couldn't lose it. Not now. With a clenched fist, she wiped away a tear sliding down her cheek. She would always mourn the loss of her father and live with the horror of the family's ordeal, but she couldn't let that stop her from searching for the truth. Her father would want her to stay strong and continue the investigation. That was the least she could do for him.

With a stronger resolve, she pushed away from the door and walked over to her father's desk. She sat down in his chair and smelled his favorite musky cologne still lingering on the leather.

She glanced around the familiar room. Everything looked like her father just stepped out and would be back at any moment. Blueprints rolled up in tubes lay in shelves lined up against one white wall categorized by the name of the building. On the wall facing the desk was a large framed picture of her father's last construction job. He'd stood in front of a substantial, luxurious, four-star hotel and casino shaking hands with the new owner.

Shadow's Justice

In one corner of his office stood a drafting table laden with drafting pencils, erasers and drafting paper. Next to it were tall bookshelves holding technical construction books and manuals.

She loved it. She had warm memories of spending long hours with her father in this room. It was where they talked and where they dreamed.

Shadow was jerked from her deep, soulful thoughts by a hard knock on the door. Guessing who it was, she glared toward the sound. "Go away."

The door opened and Raven stood in the doorway. "Hiding out, Shady Lady?" He strolled into the room.

Shadow rolled her eyes. "I knew I should've locked the door. Why can't you call me Shadow like everyone else and didn't you hear me say "Go away"?"

Raven shrugged his shoulder and sat down on the edge of the desk, his long leg swinging back and forth. "I heard you. Since when do I take orders from you?"

"So, bite me, 'Raven Lunatic'."

He laughed. "Tsk. Tsk. Tsk. That's no way for a lady to talk."

"Since you've always thought of me as a slut instead of a lady, it really doesn't matter." Shadow fumed, but refused him the satisfaction of knowing. It hurt too bad.

Raven stared her down, his quiet voice seared her heart. "You know that's not true."

Shadow eyed him up and down before responding with an 'I don't give a crap' shrug. Another lie. If he knew the truth, he'd run like hell.

Shadow shook her head. Just like that, her wayward thoughts rushed back to the night of her sixteenth birthday party. Getting Raven hot and bothered while pinning him up against the wall and plying him with a full-fledged tongue in mouth kiss hadn't exactly gone the way she had planned. He had taken her by the shoulders, pushed her away and told her to quit acting like a slut. These were long ago memories she would like to forget.

Shadow leaned her head back against the chair and sighed. She cringed inside every time she thought about that night. It almost killed her love for him. Almost. "What do you want, Raven? I'm really not in the mood for any more of your lectures."

Raven's expression softened. "I know, and I didn't come in here to lecture you. Actually, I need to get away for a while. What would you say to a long drive in the country and then a quiet Italian dinner afterwards? I doubt you've eaten anything all day. What do you say to us calling a truce for today?"

Shadow showed him the first genuine smile she'd smiled in days. Hell, in years. Getting away for a couple of hours was just what she needed and she was getting hungry. For that, she could put up with Raven's company. She stuck her hand out to seal the deal. "Truce. Give me ten minutes to change and I'll meet you out front."

Ten minutes later on the dot, dressed in her peach strapless dress and sandals, Shadow slid in beside Raven in his 1962 Corvette Roadster convertible.

Minutes later, she smiled as the car ate up the miles into the country. The wind whipping around them blew her hair into an unmanageable mess making it impossible to carry on any kind of conversation. She sat back and enjoyed the freedom. For the first time in ages she felt the tension draining from her shoulders. God, how she needed this sense of a normal life, if only for a short while.

The scenery passed by in a blur. She felt the power and excitement vibrating beneath her feet each time Raven shifted gears. The car was just like its owner, sleek, beautiful and dangerous if not handled carefully. She glanced toward him and noticed his wide smile matched her own.

Long before she was ready, the exhilarating ride was over. Raven eased the car into a parking place at Luigi's Italian restaurant filled with the Friday's crowd. They entered and the hostess escorted them to a table adorned with a white tablecloth and one rose standing in a vase placed in the center. Soft Italian music played in the background of the small intimate room with romantic candlelight on each table as its only source of light.

The waiter took their wine order and brought their drinks to the table while they waited on their meal to be prepared.

Shadow raised her wine glass to her lips and sipped. Setting her glass down, she smiled at Raven. "Thank you for getting me out of the house for a while. My nerves were about shot. If I'd spent one more second around those lingering vultures, I would've started waving my arms and hollering 'shoo'. I didn't think they would ever leave to catch their flights home."

Laughter burst from Raven's lips. His eyes twinkled. "Coming from anyone else, I would think they were joking, but I actually believe you would have."

Shadow grinned. "Rose told off on me again, didn't she?"

"Well, she has mentioned some of your little

escapades."

"Such as?"

"Such as the time you pushed the paralegal on Jack's case into the pool for losing some documents."

Shadow's smile disappeared. "They could've been very important to Father's case. Now, I'll never know."

Raven leaned forward and clasped his hands on top of the table, all teasing gone. "Rose is very worried about you, Shadow. She's afraid you won't let it go."

"I won't."

He reached out and covered her hand, deep sympathy evident in his eyes. "Your father is dead. Trying to find the killer and getting yourself killed in the process will not bring him back."

Shadow jerked her hand back and all but snarled. "No, but it will give me great satisfaction to know the bastard ends up in hell. He's not going to win. I won't let him. I will clear my father's name if it's the last thing I ever do."

"It may very well be the last thing you ever do if you keep on. Believe me, this killer is no amateur. Only a professional can cover his tracks as well as he did. In all of these years, there hasn't been one substantial clue found pointing toward the real killer. Nothing. What makes you think you can find anything, now? Hell, the killer's probably long gone or dead by now."

Shadow was thankful the waiter picked that moment to bring their food. Fuming, she sat back while the dishes were set in front of them. Picking up a fork she began to eat, giving herself time to decide how much she could tell Raven.

She glanced up to see him watching her as he ate.

She swallowed the bite of food and put her fork down. Taking a sip of wine she set it back on the table before finally answering. "The killer contacted me on the day of Dad's funeral and warned me to back off."

Raven's fork clattered to his plate. He exploded. "Why in the hell haven't you said something before now? That does it. No more playing Nancy Drew. Are you crazy, woman?" His voice rose.

"Shhhhhhhh." Shadow gave a quick look around the room of strangers. "Why don't you tell the whole world?"

Raven took several deep breaths. His glare spoke volumes. He clenched his fists as if he wanted to reach across the table and strangle her. Instead, he picked up his wine glass and took several large gulps of the calming liquid before he leaned back and continued. With clipped words he asked, "Exactly, what did he say?"

Shadow had gone through a full day and night of worry and fear after the dreadful phone call, but her nerves had settled somewhat. She was able to think about it without wanting to throw up.

She answered. "He told me if I didn't back off he would make sure he dealt me a fate much worse than what he had my father and then he hung up."

"Did you recognize the voice?"

"No. It was very muffled and distorted."

"Did you call the police?"

"Ummmmm. No."

"Shadow. What have you done?"

"Relax Raven. I've done nothing more than to take measures to protect myself and my family."

She could tell he didn't want to ask. He didn't want

to know. He really didn't.

"Shadow?"

"I bought a gun. Okay?"

"Gaaaa....damn!"

CHAPTER THREE

Gripping Shadow's hand thirty minutes later, Raven all but dragged her into her father's study and locked the door behind them. He pulled her across the room. "Sit." He pointed toward the cushioned straight-back chair against the wall. Thankfully, she obeyed without a fuss.

His hand ran over the stubbled hair on top of his head as he stood over her. "What in the hell do you mean you bought a gun?"

Her eyes blazed. "If you'd quit manhandling me for a minute, I'd tell you. If you were anyone else right now you'd be rubbing your bruised balls for jerking me around like that."

Raven glared down at her. "I haven't hurt you and you know it. Start talking."

Shadow crossed her arms over her chest and glared. "I'll spell it out for you. I applied for a gun permit days ago and picked the gun up yesterday."

Raven's eyebrow rose as her mind-boggling words sank in. He held his hand out. "Let me see it."

"Go to hell."

"Shadow." He took a warning step forward.

"Okay. Okay. Chill out." She reached into her

purse and pulled out a gun and handed it to him barrel first.

Raven turned the piece over in his hand and took a long look from one end of the pistol to the other. "Nine millimeter, stainless steel, single-action Smith & Wesson. Nice. Planning on blowing the bad guy away, do you?"

"I don't plan on playing tiddly winks with him."

One brow rose as Raven's attention turned back to Shadow. He sighed and shook his head. He knew her tough façade revealed nothing more than a cover up for her fears. She's tough, he would give her that. She had to be to go through the hell of her father's trial, the publicity and his funeral.

He ached from the pain she was experiencing. He loved Jack himself. He could only imagine how he would react if his real father suffered in prison for years and then executed.

"Rose thinks I should continue helping you." Raven announced as he handed the gun back to her.

Shadow's white teeth nibbled her lower lip. She studied his face. "What do you think?"

Raven walked toward the chair beside her and turned it around to face her. He straddled the chair backwards, his arms crossed over the top rung. His slacks pulled tight against his legs. He stared her down. "I don't have a choice. I promised Rose I would help you and keep you safe even though it's against my better judgment."

Shadow bristled. "I can take care of myself. I don't need your help."

"Oh yeah, honey. You do. But, it will be by my rules. If I help you, you will do everything I say and nothing more."

She sat up straighter, ready to argue. "You're crazier than hell if ...."

He held his hand up to stop her. "If, nothing. This is my field of expertise, not yours. That's the way it will be. Take it or leave it."

Shadow's eyes narrowed. She stared at his unsmiling features. She needed his help and he had her over a barrel. "I'll take it."

Reluctant, but powerless, Raven made up his mind to believe her. He reached out and shook her hand to seal the deal. "All right."

"What do we do now?"

"We get down to business." He stood and pushed his chair to the desk and sat down. "Let's make up a list of what we do know even if we think it's not important. We've been overlooking something, so I suggest we scrap all the notes from before and start over."

Shadow nodded and jumped up to find a pad and pencil for both of them. She sat back down behind her father's desk and scooted one of each across the table.

"All right. I'll start with the obvious." She began writing her notes as she spoke. "Number one. Tucker was shot and killed only minutes after the bank closed and his employees went home. The doors would've been locked and I don't see him opening the doors for anyone. He had to know this person well enough to not suspect him of any wrong doing."

Raven tapped his pen against the table as his mind worked through several possibilities. "Or, the killer never left the building in the first place. Maybe he hid out in the bathroom or an empty office until everyone left. The trial cleared all of the bank's employees with solid alibis, but I still want their names on the list along with the other suspects who were never investigated."

Shadow frowned. "That's a big order. Judd Tucker had a lot of enemies. He was notorious for turning down loans for the needy, including my father when he was first starting his construction business twenty-five years ago. I've heard talk of several farmers who went to him for a loan to keep their heads above water and he turned them down."

With a wry laugh, she added. "If you weren't already filthy rich you didn't stand a snowball chance in hell of getting a loan from that man. From what I hear, his son Steve isn't any better after he took over. He was so tight with money that he squeaked when we were in school together."

"I remember the family. Never liked them." Raven scribbled a note on his notepad in front of him. "First thing in the morning we'll try to get names of the ones turned down for a loan and start paying them visits. Is your friend Stacy still a reporter for the Gazette?"

"Yes. Why?"

"Call her in the morning and ask her to come by for a visit. We'll need her help and resources if she's willing. I don't want anyone to know she's stopping by for any reason other than comforting a friend. We don't want to raise suspicion. What time will Collins be here tomorrow to read the will?"

Shadow finished scribbling herself a note to call Stacy. "Eleven o'clock."

"Good. I want to ask him a few questions and see if he'll let me look over some of his files on Jack's case." And if he doesn't, I'll look at them after his office is closed for the night.

Shadow nodded. "Can I ask you something?"

Raven glanced up, surprised she even asked permission. "Sure."

"You have a life and a business that you're neglecting. Don't you need to get back to them?"

"I have a group of professional people working for me who are more than capable of carrying out any assignments we're hired to do. As long as I have my laptop, internet and a phone I can give the orders from here." His eyes hardened. "I'm not going anywhere, Shadow."

The bastard made the mistake of threatening his loved ones. He would live to regret it. The case was closed. Eyes would no longer closely monitor his actions. Well-guarded evidence and secrets would be thought safe. False security would grow. And, that's when he would hit.

Raven glanced down at his watch. Midnight. He watched Shadow trying to cover a yawn. It had been a long, exhausting day for both of them. He pushed his pad and pencil back and stood up. "I vote we get some sleep. We can get an early start in the morning before we have to get back here for the reading of the will."

* * *

For once, Shadow didn't argue. Exhausted, she covered another yawn. Telling him goodnight, she grabbed their notes and carried them up to her room.

Entering her haven, she walked to her window and looked out into the darkness. She knew her deep, troubled thoughts would keep her from sleeping right away. She leaned her head against the cool pane and sighed.

Working with Raven everyday would push her hate/love relationship with him to the forefront, but she didn't have a choice. She needed his help to find the real murderer.

Living for the most part of her twenty-eight years in Hell City, Louisiana or as it was written on the map and history books, McClane Ridge, Louisiana named after her paternal grandfather had evolved her into a woman with a mission.

It wasn't the beautiful small town of McClane Ridge surrounded by lakes and rivers, huge oak trees and old historical buildings that damned the area. Instead, the money-hungry, self-elected, so called leaders of their community who destroyed everything dear to her heart captured her blame for not doing more. And, they would pay. That became her heart's desire, not the man downstairs.

* * *

Saturday morning, Randall Collins stood in front of the bay window of the large family room the next morning, his hands stuffed into his expensive, designer business suit. Bright sunlight cascaded over his silver hair giving him a distinguished and authoritive air about him. At sixty-five years old, he was still a very handsome man. His wife died two years earlier in a car accident and he'd become a well-sought after, rich and eligible bachelor.

Shadow studied him from the doorway. Randall was a dear friend to her family as well as her father's lawyer. He'd put in long hours on their case and dined in their home often.

Shadow smiled and crossed the room to where he stood. She wrapped an arm around his waist and leaned her head against his shoulder. "Thanks for coming, Randall. Everyone should be in any minute and then you can get started. Can I get you something to drink?"

Randall Collins smiled down at Shadow and wrapped his arm across her shoulders. "No thanks. I have a lunch appointment as soon as I leave here, so I'll wait on the drink." He took his fingers and raised her chin. He frowned in concern when he saw the dark circles underneath her eyes. "You didn't sleep at all last night, did you?"

"Not much."

"Why don't I call your doctor and see if he'll prescribe some medicine to help you sleep? You're going to make yourself ill if you don't start getting some rest." He gently brushed her hair back from her brow.

Shadow shook her head and smiled up at him. "I'll be fine. Really."

Before he could argue, the door opened and Rose, her two sons and Raven entered. Greeting each other, everyone took a seat waiting on Randall to begin.

Randall pulled a stack of papers out of his briefcase. "As you know, everyone present this morning is included in Jack's will. He told me he went over his wishes with each one of you before he signed the will and you had each given your consent to have them carried out. If everyone is ready, I'll begin."

He picked up the top page. "Rose, I'll give each one of you a copy of these papers to look over and read before you sign, but to make it short this morning, I'll go over it briefly. Basically, what this legal document states is that Jack has bequeathed to Rose McClane this home and a sufficient allowance a month as long as she lives."

He glanced at Rose. "Any questions?"

"No. Not at this moment."

"Okay. The four of you, Shadow, Raven, Michael and John will each inherit one-fourth of McClane Construction Company. You will continue in your same positions with the company and will each receive your salary plus an allowance. Michael, as the eldest son you will have the final deciding vote on any major decisions concerning the business. Any questions?"

They each shook their heads. Jack had been clear on his requests before he was executed.

"All right. Other than a stated amount to be given out to the household help, I guess that covers everything."

Rose stood and smiled with fondness toward the lawyer. "Won't you join us for lunch? I'm sure Carol has something delicious cooked, as usual."

Randall clasped her hands and smiled down at her. "I would love to, but I have a previous lunch engagement. Can I take a rain check or maybe you'll allow me to take you to dinner some evening?"

Her smile dimmed. "I'm sorry, but it's too soon for me to be socializing."

"Of course. How insensitive of me. I was only concerned about getting you out of the house and relaxing for one evening, instead of what people would think. Please, forgive me." His charming manners brought warmth back into her eyes.

"Thank you, but I'll be fine, Randall. I appreciate everything you've done for us."

"My pleasure. Well,...," He looked around the room and included the other four. "If there's nothing else, I guess I'd better hurry or I'll be late."

"I'll walk you to your car," Raven offered. "There's a matter I'd like to discuss with you. It won't take but a moment."

"All right." After shaking hands with Michael and John and saying his goodbyes to Rose and Shadow, Randall followed Raven out to his car parked in front of the home. "What can I help you with, son?"

"I was wondering if you could give me a little information."

"Of course. If I can. What do you need to know?"

"I need the names of all of your suspects and leads in Jack's trial."

With an abrupt movement, Collins opened his car door and sat down closing the door behind him. Through the open window he looked up at Raven and spoke with a stern voice. "What I will give you, Raven is advice. Leave it alone. The trial is over and done with. Believe me, you'll only be making matters worse."

He turned the key and the motor sprang to life. With one push of his finger, the electric windows raised.

What in the hell...? Frowning, Raven watched as Collins drove away. He was still staring down the driveway when Michael and John joined him.

Standing shorter than his friend and brother, Michael's muscular build was similar to his active sibling. Even though he sat behind a drawing board ten hours or more a day, he still found time to work out.

Both brothers inherited their father's thick, dark black hair. Michael wore his brushed back from his forehead and cut collar-length, whereas his youngest brother's lay longer in the back and secured in a ponytail.

With one finger, Michael pushed his designer-framed sunglasses covering his dark brown eyes upward as he squinted after the departing car. He placed his hands into the pants pocket of his suit and looked back toward Raven. "What was that all about? Collins raced out of here like a jealous husband was after him," Michael commented.

Raven glanced back at the two standing behind him. A frown still marred his face. "Good question and one I intend to find out. He became very defensive and warned me to back off when I asked for names of the suspects he had on file."

John, dressed in his usual uniform of brown coveralls and work boots tossed his hard hat in the air. He glanced toward Raven and his normal good-natured grin appeared. "And, of course you took that as the ultimate challenge, didn't you?"

"Damn straight, I did. He was acting strange for even Collins." He turned his focus back on John and Michael. "You're not staying for lunch?"

John shook his head. "Nope. Got a shipment of ceramic tile coming in this afternoon that I have to check in. I'll be free after that if you need me for anything."

"I'll be at the drawing board, as usual. The new client you sent us wants his five billion dollar hotel built yesterday. I'll be close to the phone if you need either one of us. Don't try to take this job on by yourself, Raven. You know we want to help find the bastard as bad as you do," Michael told him.

"Don't worry. I'll need you both before this is over."

The sound of a car's engine speeding up the

driveway ended their conversation. They watched as Shadow's friend, Stacy Chandler screeched to a halt in her red convertible only feet from where they were standing.

Chuckling, Raven's attention was drawn to Michael's facial features captivated by the laughing woman emerging from the car.

Long, long, feminine shaped legs with a blue, silk skirt drawn up to her thighs appeared first followed by a curvy, well endowed upper body covered with a white silk blouse and matching baby blue jacket. Her facial features wouldn't be considered beautiful by model standards, but still attractive with her hazel laughing eyes, pouting lips and long, flowing blonde hair.

Standing eye to eye with the three men, she gave a sensual wink. "Been waiting for me long, boys?" Her velvety voice crooned.

"All of my life, doll face." John played along with a grin.

Michael sputtered. "What are you trying to do, kill us? You were driving like a maniac."

"Relax, sweetheart. I drive this car like I do everything else in my life that gives me a great satisfaction. Depending on my mood, it could be fast and furious or slowwwwww and lingering, but I'm always fulfilled in the end. Maybe you would like to take a ride with me some evening. I promise, I'm always a very, very good driver."

Her double entendre was not lost on Michael. His mouth opened and closed and his face turned red. Finally, he just grinned and shook his head. "Let's go, John. I'm always on the losing end of the battle with that woman."

Shadow's Justice

Raven watched the two leave before he turned back to Stacy. He laughed out loud. "You love tormenting Michael, don't you?"

"Absolutely." Her laughter rang out.

CHAPTER FOUR

Shadow greeted her friend with a warm hug. "Thanks for coming, Stacy. I know you're busy."

"I always have time for you, sweetheart. You sounded a little mysterious on the phone. Mind telling me what's going on?" She glanced from Shadow to Raven for answers.

"Carol has lunch ready. I'll tell you everything while we eat." Shadow led the way into the large, but intimate dining room where Rose was already seated. They waited until Stacy greeted Rose with a kiss on the cheek before taking their places at the large, oval dining table.

A warm rose pattern adorned the china placed for four around the table. Crystal glasses were filled with ice tea. A large salad bowl and a platter filled with sandwiches were placed in the center. They each filled their plates and began to eat.

"Okay, Shadow. Curiosity is killing me, here. What gives?" Stacy spoke between mouthfuls.

Shadow laid her fork beside her plate and looked up at her friend. "We need your help."

The seriousness in Shadow's tone had Stacy's smile disappearing. "You know I'll help you in anyway I can. What are best friends for? You're like a sister to me. You know that."

"Thank you." Shadow's voice caught with emotions.

"Ahhhhh, how sweet." Rose beamed at the girls.

All three women raised their faces toward Raven as he cleared his throat. Shadow ginned. She knew for a fact that emotional females made him want to flee toward a battleground full of men shooting real bullets at each other.

Raven changed the subject. "We were wondering if you might help us with a little investigation."

"Of course. That's what I get paid for. I…" Her sentence broke off. She sat straight in her chair. "Wait a minute. You're planning on digging further into Mr. McClane's murder trial, aren't you? And, I get the exclusive?"

"Yes and no. We're continuing with the investigation and you'll get an exclusive on the story if or when it breaks. But, not now. I need your promise you won't tell anyone outside this family what we're doing. That includes your boss," Raven told her.

Stacy fell back against her chair and looked at each one in turn while she made up her mind. "That's a big order, Raven. I could easily get fired for doing this over my bosses head."

Raven nodded. "I know."

"It's a big decision, Stacy. Why don't you go home and think about it. I want you to know that any decision you make won't have any influence on our friendship, at all," Shadow added.

"I don't have to think about it. I can tell you my answer now." She held both palms upward imitating a scale. She raised one higher. "Let me see. If I don't help you, I can spend the rest of my life reporting on who jaywalked or ran a red light in town." She lowered that hand and raised the other. "If I do help you, I can be the exclusive reporter on the biggest scandal in the history of McClane Ridge and possibly get a big promotion and raise." She looked at both of her palm scales. "Hmmmmm. Big decision. Not."

* * *

Randall Collins's fingers clenched around his cloth napkin. He'd consumed two martinis while waiting on his lunch companion and he was no calmer now than when he'd entered. "They've got to be stopped, dammit."

Judge Ben Adams took a slow sip of his bourbon and sat back, his wide girth pulling the buttons tight on his business suit. "Relax, Collins. They'll play sleuth detectives for awhile, find nothing and get on with their lives."

Randall glared at his childhood friend. Ben was getting way too pompous and careless to suit him. Money and prestige as the Honorable Judge Ben Adams had turned him into thinking he was a fat cat with a fancy feast, too high on the political fence to be knocked down. Randall knew better. He was smarter. He just had to make sure he didn't get pulled down with him. "What if you're wrong? What if they do find something? Dammit, Ben. I won't be there this time staying one step ahead of them destroying evidence like I did during the trial. I know Raven and Shadow. They won't stop until they clear Jack's name."

"Or, die trying." Ben added. Then, his heavy jowls widened into a grin looking like Satan himself. His gruesome meaning was clear.

* * *

"I'm going whether you like it or not. I can either go with you so you can keep an eye on me or I can dog your trail every step of the way. Your choice."

Shadow stood in place at midnight with hands on her hips blocking the front door and wearing the most ridiculous outfit Raven had ever seen. He didn't know which would be worse for him, wringing her neck or laughing until he hurt from her over-embellished Jane Bond costume.

She was dressed completely in black. Her hair was tucked beneath a black knit cap and she was wearing a black tee-shirt, black jeans, black tennis shoes, black gloves, but what topped it all off for Raven was the black Halloween type paint smeared all over her face. All he could see was her huge, heaven blue eyes glaring at him and a black leather Gucci handbag draped over one arm. He assumed she carried her newly, purchased gun inside.

Laughter won out. Chuckling, he threw his hands up in defeat. "Shady Lady, you win. You're the deadliest weapon a man could ever want. One look at you and the bad guy will kill over dead from laughter."

"You're just a regular frickin' comedian aren't you?" She unsnapped her purse and her hand reached inside.

Raven surged forward and put a grip lock on her hand as she pulled it out. Car keys dangled from her fingertips.

Shadow grinned and jerked her hand out of his grip. "I make you nervous, don't I, Raven?"

"You don't. It's that gun you're packing that scares the hell out of me. Are you sure you know how to shoot that thing?"

Shadow shrugged her shoulders. "Keep pissing me off and you'll find out. Now, let's go. It's past midnight and getting late."

Shadow slid in behind the wheel of her ten year old, blue Grand Am. Raven got in on the passenger side. After two tries the motor turned over and Shadow backed out of the carport.

Fifteen minutes later, she killed the lights and drove her car at a slow pace through the narrow alleyway and parked behind Collins's Law Office. Staying close to the building, they made their way to the back door without a sound.

Raven whispered to Shadow. "Keep a look out."

He glanced around the area and listened for any threatening noises. Hearing nothing, he slid his hand into the inside pocket of his jacket and withdrew a small penlight and shined the beam on the tarnished doorknob.

Holding the light between his teeth, he reached back into his jacket and pulled out a small case which he opened and withdrew a small, round pick. He inserted the tool inside the keyhole and turned it until he heard a distinctive click. The knob turned easy in his hand. The back door eased opened with one push and Raven entered first with Shadow close on his heels.

He shined the light over the main lobby. "Which is his office?"

"Second door on the left."

They walked to the door, opened it and entered Collins's office.

Shadow stumbled over a trashcan in the dark and knocked it over. The loud, clanging racket stopped them in their tracks.

"Shhhhhh. Why don't you wake the whole town, for Petes' sake," Raven whispered.

Shadow shot him a 'go to hell' look that he caught in his flashlight beam before she reached down to pick up the fallen trashcan.

Raven hid his grin and switched on the small desk lamp. He turned the shade downward so the light wouldn't shine toward the door and alert anyone who might drive by the building at this late hour.

He motioned toward the cabinets against the wall. "Check those filing cabinets over there and I'll go through these files on his desk."

He began fingering through the dozen or so documents inside. Finding nothing of interest there, he turned his attention to the desk drawers. The first two drawers held no more than his extra office supplies. The third drawer he pulled on was locked. He withdrew his case from his pocket, extracted his metal pick and unlocked the drawer.

"Are you finding anything?" he whispered without glancing up.

"Nothing. I can't find anything on Dad's case. Do you think he may have them archived somewhere else? The attic, maybe?"

"Possible. Keep looking. If we don't find anything in here we'll go up and look." Raven turned his flashlight toward the files in the open drawer and searched through the documents inside. He pulled one out and read the name on the cover. "Steven Tucker."

Brows drawn, he turned toward Shadow. "I wonder why Collin's would keep a thick file on Tucker's son locked up in a drawer."

"Beats me." She walked behind his chair and leaned over his shoulder to read.

"What in the world? Look at this." Raven handed her the top sheet.

She read it through and glanced sharply at Raven. "This doesn't make sense. Collins is having Steven followed by an investigator, which according to this report, he's paying out of his own pocket. Why would he do that? I could understand if Steven's wife was having him followed, but Collins? What is he hoping to find?"

"Damn good question. Here, hold my flashlight. I want to make copies of these." Raven handed her his flashlight and then withdrew a metal object the shape of a pen. He pushed a button and a small green light flickered as he began dragging the copier across each sheet of paper.

When he finished, Raven pocketed the pen and replaced the folder back in the cabinet. He relocked the drawer before standing and taking the light back from Shadow. "Let's go up to the attic and take a look."

* * *

Shadow followed behind Raven giving him directions to the door leading upstairs.

The door opened with a slight creak. They climbed up the short flight of stairs to the top. Raven glanced around the large room to see if there were any windows a light might show through to the outside. Seeing none, he flipped the light switch to illuminate the whole room.

Filing cabinets lined all four walls. Shadow groaned. "Please Lord, let it be filed under the "M's" or we'll never get through this many records."

She opened the drawer and began leafing through the files. Moments later, she whispered, "Bingo! I've found it."

Raven joined her. "Great. Grab it and let's get out of here."

"Suits me just fine. This place gives me the creeps." She handed the file to Raven and he slid it inside his jacket.

They made their way down the stairs and let themselves out the same way they had come in. As Raven locked the back door, Shadow unlocked the car door and slid inside.

With jittery fingers, Shadow turned the key and heard the usual click. She tried once again and the motor sprang to life.

Then, they heard a strange noise. Footsteps pounding the pavement sounded thunderous over the drone of the car's engine as they moved at a rapid pace away from them. No one should be around at this time of night.

"Shit!" Raven grabbed his gun from inside his coat and took off running toward the disappearing sound. "Wait here."

Like hell. They were being spied on and she wanted to know who and why. Shadow grabbed her purse with her gun inside and jumped out of the car sprinting after him.

Twenty seconds later, her car exploded.

The force from the blast propelled Shadow and Raven forward. They both hit the hard pavement face first and skidded to a stop.

The breath was knocked out of Shadow. She couldn't breathe or feel any pain other than the tight pressure in her lungs. The deep significance of what had just happened eluded her.

She lay there for long seconds too stunned to move. Then the breath gushed into her lungs and she felt the excruciating pain throughout her body as her memory of the blast returned.

Whimpering, Shadow raised her head scant inches from the pavement and let it fall back when the hurting became unbearable. The whole front of her body felt on fire from the scrapes and the hard hit she'd endured from hitting the pavement.

"Raven?" Her voice was weak. No answer. Moaning, she forced her head up. She had to find him. She saw him a few feet away lying on his stomach. He wasn't moving.

She pushed herself to her hands and knees and with short, painful movements, crawled to his side. She wiped away the tears and blood streaming down her face, the black paint smearing across her painful cheeks.

Shadow reached out and felt for his pulse. Then, she noticed the blood running down his face from a small gash on his cheek. A sob of relief escaped when her fingers found a strong pulse in his neck and then he moaned and opened his eyes.

"Shadow?" His faint voice was below a whisper.

"I'm right here, Raven." Her hand brushed gently against his brow.

"How bad are you hurt?" he asked.

"Not as bad as it feels, just a few scrapes. I'll live. My concern is you. Can you stand?"

He nodded. "I think so. Nothing feels broken."

"Good. Then let's get the hell out of here before the person decides to come back and finish us off."

Shadow made it to her feet and then she helped

Raven stand. Leaning on each other for support, they walked back to her car and stared in horror at the damage.

Flames shot into the air from the blackened shell that remained of her car. The door to the office building had been blown inward and broken roof shingles dangled perilously toward the ground.

Shadow's whole insides crumbled. Aftershock and uncontrollable fear coursed through her. Tears fell unheeded down her cheeks as the terrible realization hit her hard. If they hadn't come out of the building when they did, if they hadn't heard someone running, and if they hadn't followed in pursuit, they would be dead right now.

Shadow turned and threw herself in Raven's arms and into a safe haven. She cried long and hard, her body shaking from uncontrollable aftershock.

* * *

Raven's hands shook as he held her tight. He felt his throat restrict from his own dazed emotions. He rocked her back and forth whispering comforting words until dry, heaving sobs were all that was left in her.

He had been in so many dangerous situations and thought nothing would ever faze him again. Now, he knew how wrong he was. He had never before suffered the gut wrenching pain he'd felt when he'd believed Shadow had been killed in the explosion.

Now, he felt a need so powerful, so strong to make him feel alive, to assure himself she was alive. He leaned back and raised her face to his. With gentle hands, he wiped the tears from her cheeks. And, then he kissed her.

His kiss became urgent and demanding as he pulled

her tighter into his arms. He had no thoughts beyond the moment. All of his precautions concerning his battered heart flew away with the wind.

Shadow responded with a reckless abandon similar to a woman drowning and only his kiss could save her.

His lips parted hers, their tongues intertwined and their passion mounted.

Raven moaned in pleasure as he jerked her lower body even closer to his hardness. His hands roamed freely as his mouth ravished hers. Her giving response and small whimpers only fueled the fire burning deep in his lower region.

Shadow's fingernails raked over his back with desperation as she held on to sanity and lost her grip.

Then the loud sirens barreling down on them in the alleyway penetrated through their deep fog of passion.

Raven jerked his head back and brought Shadow's head against his shoulder. He fought to control his own harsh, shuddering breaths as he soothed her trembling body in his arms.

Seconds later, fire trucks arrived on the scene. Within moments the blaze was out, leaving smoldering smoke drifting into the sky.

A patrol car slid to a stop mere inches from where they stood. Intimidating blue lights flashed across the buildings and their faces.

A large man with the bright star of the law pinned to his uniform got out of the car. He stood with one arm draped on top of the roof as he looked over the damage. He glanced toward Raven and Shadow. Pushing his hat back from his forehead, he asked, "Would you two mind telling me what in the hell is going on here?" His Cajun drawl was pronounced.

Raven stepped away from Shadow. He gave her arm a warning squeeze and approached him. "It looks like attempted murder to me, Police Chief Walker."

Police Chief Edwin Dale Walker eyed him with a cold stare for a moment and then a sardonic grin appeared. "Are you confessing, Son?"

Raven crossed his arms across his chest and glared back. There had been an ongoing conflict between the Police Chief and the two Tolliver boys and Raven from their younger and wilder days of sowing their wild oats.

They had never attempted anything worse than partying a little too heavy on weekends with their friends and latest girlfriends, but each one of them in turn had been hauled into the local jail for drunk and disorderly conduct. That lasted until Jack McClane came into their lives and set them on a straight and narrow path.

The Police Chief and his local yokel attitude no longer intimidated Raven, no matter that the Police Chief was twice his size. "Are you going to do your job?"

Walker's jaw clenched before he turned back to the car and reached inside for the mike on his police radio. "Mary Ann, send backup to the alleyway behind the Collins Law Office. We have a possible attempted murder." The radio crackled and then he answered the dispatcher back, "Ten-four."

Walker moved away from his patrol car and closed the door. He walked at a slow pace to the simmering car and looked it over. "Whose car is this?"

"It's mine." Shadow volunteered.

The Police Chief nodded his head. "Taken out

anymore insurance on your car, lately, Miss McClane?"

Shadow's temper flared. She stomped up to an inch away and shoved her face close to his. She exploded. "Let me tell you something, Police Chief Walker. I came this close....," her thumb and forefinger measured a hair's width between each other. "...from getting my ass blown to smithereens tonight. I'm really not in the mood for your smartass attitude or drummed up charges on me. Now, you can either take our statement of what happened or you can stick that gun you so proudly wear up your...."

"Police Chief, take a look at this," A nightshift deputy hollered out. He was standing further down the alleyway staring down at an object on the sidewalk.

Police Chief Walker glared at Shadow for a moment before turning away from her and walking toward his deputy.

Shadow and Raven followed close on his heels.

Walker looked down to where his deputy was pointing. He reached into his pocket and pulled out a handkerchief. Using the cloth to protect any fingerprints, he reached down and picked up the object. He held it up to the light.

"What is it?" Shadow asked.

Raven pulled her into his arms and held her tight before answering. "That is a remote control device designed to detonate a bomb from a safe distance."

Shadow gasped. She looked up at him and her lips trembled. "He must have dropped it when you gave chase. Oh my God, Raven. We could have been killed."

Raven glanced back at the smoking car. He shook

his head. "I think this was just a warning. He waited until we were away from the car before pushing the button and then ditching the remote."

Shadow controlled a shudder. "A scare tactic? He wasn't trying to kill us?"

"No. Not this time."

CHAPTER FIVE

Police Chief Walker heard the approaching vehicles. He pocketed the remote in a clear plastic bag and turned back to Raven and Shadow, his voice quiet, almost apologetic. "I'm going to take you to the emergency room to let a doctor look at those cuts. After that, I need you two to come down to headquarters to answer a few questions."

When they nodded, he escorted them to his patrol car and waited until they slid inside the backseat before turning back to the crime lab arriving. He filled them in on the night's events and gave them further instructions on the investigation before climbing into his car. Then, he drove Shadow and Raven to the hospital.

* * *

An hour later with cuts cleaned and bandaged, Shadow and Raven left the hospital with Police Chief Walker. They pulled up in front of the police station a few minutes later.

Walker led them into the interrogation room and motioned for them to sit at the small round table in the center of the dingy, stark room. He stood facing them with one booted foot propped on the seat of a chair and his elbow resting on his knee.

He nodded to Raven. "You start. Tell me what happened."

Raven leaned back in his chair. He didn't plan on telling the police anymore than he had to. "Shadow got back into her car and started the motor while I walked around to the passenger side. That's when we heard footsteps running away. We decided to follow to see who fled into the alleyway at that time of the night. We'd gone maybe a few feet when the explosion knocked us to the ground. That's about all we know."

Walker listened to their statements and then he walked to the one-way glass window along one wall and gazed at them in deep thought. Finally, he turned back to the table. "Either one of you see who it was?"

They both shook their heads. The Police Chief nodded and walked back to the table placing both hands flat on the table. "Would either of you mind telling me why you two were in the alleyway in the middle of the night dressed like burglars?"

Shadow glanced at Raven, but retained a poker face. "I had to pee."

Raven choked on his laughter.

Police Chief Walker fumed. He glared at Shadow. "I ought to arrest you for indecent exposure."

Shadow shrugged one shoulder and glared back.

"Is there anything else you'd like to know, Police Chief?" Raven intervened.

"Yeah. You don't plan on leaving town anytime soon, do you?"

"Nope. We'll be right here."

Shadow's Justice

* * *

His whiskey-soaked mind ignored the distant sounds of the party behind him as they dragged the girl into the dark, infested swamp.
Her screams of terror ignited his virgin desires.
He was sixteen. Cocky as hell.
She was a pretty fifteen year old. Sweet and innocent.
So young.
Kiss her, B.J.. Kiss her. Make her hot for you.
He taunted, thrusting his hips forward with lewdness. He staggered against Bubba, both of them laughing.
And taunting.
B.J. laughed. He became more aggressive, pulling her to him. Kissing her.
Grabbing her breasts.
Hysterical, she cried and clawed, trying to get away from him.
She prayed.
The struggle only managed to anger and incite B.J..
B.J. backhanded her.
He watched with a primal excitement.
She landed on a bed of rotting leaves. Her party dress torn and dirty, her hair tangled.
Blood dripped from her split lip.
They held her down. Ripped her panties off.
B.J. brutally raped her.
When B.J was finished, He and Bubba took their turns.
He was last.
The musty smell of sex surrounded him. He plunged inside her.
She was conscious the whole time. Struggling for her life.
Whimpering.
Her warm, sweet breath mingled with the stench of the swamp.
He squeezed her breast, soft and plump. Bruised.
He yelled out into the night as He exploded inside her.
She screamed to high heaven.

Creatures scurried.
Reptiles slithered. Danger.
He felt the sharp pain from her fingernails raking down his face.
You bitch!
Anger and alcohol raged through him.
Her screams grew louder and louder, her cries for help unheard.
Stop screaming! He was yelling. Out of control.
She won't stop screaming.
His hand landed on a large rock beside her.
He raised it to the sky. Then back down. He struck her.
With each violent blow, He heard the distinctive crunch of her skull shattering.
He screamed louder and louder as warm, sticky blood splattered his face.
He tasted his sour vomit. He felt the sudden fear. He saw a black hole of rage.
Shut up! Shut up! Please, shut up.

The grown man sat straight up in the bed. He fought off the covers binding him to his predictable nightmare. Beads of cold sweat coated his body. Shaking hands covered his ears as tears streamed down his face. His heart pounded out of his chest, his erratic breathing out of control.

He screamed out into the darkness.

Over and over.

"Shut up! Shut up!"

Then he closed his eyes and whimpered and shook. He wrapped his arms around himself and rocked back and forth.

"She never stops screaming. Lord, please make her stop. Make her stop."

* * *

49

Shadow's Justice

"I refuse to leave my home or my family," Rose McClane stated Sunday morning, her voice firm. She sat at the breakfast table the next morning with tears drying on her face while Raven and Shadow warned her of the possible danger in staying.

Raven paced the floor while Shadow sat at the table holding her stepmother's hand. He stopped by Rose's chair and placed a hand on her shoulder. "Rose, you know you would be safer at your sister, Rita's."

"So would you, Son. Do you honestly think I would run away knowing my children were in danger? I've changed my mind. I want you to stop this investigation right now. I couldn't bare another murder in this family." Her voice rose close to hysteria.

Shadow squeezed her hand. "Rose, listen to me. This has gone way too far to quit now. We have to put an end to this nightmare. Whoever is behind this won't stop until he can feel safe and the only way he thinks he can do that is by eliminating the threat. We won't let him."

"She's right, Rose. Right now, he's playing mind games. He wanted us to know how easy it could be to kill one of us. Someone that demented wouldn't think twice about using you to get to us. If we left, the threat would still be here when we got back. I need to know you're safe at your sisters or I won't be able to stop the bastard." Raven didn't want to scare her, but he wanted her to know enough facts to be extremely cautious.

"Rose, I'm trained in this type of operation. It's what I do for a living." His voice softened.

Rose's gaze ricocheted between the two. A shudder

ran through her body as she gave in. Finally, she nodded. Sucking in a deep breath, she straightened her shoulders. "Okay. I know this is something you two are compelled to do. I'll leave as soon as I can pack. What about John and Michael?"

"I've already talked to them. They refuse to leave in case we need them, but promised to stay with a group of friends and workers at all times."

Rose stood and hugged Shadow and then Raven. Her hand cradled his cheek as tears ran down her own. "Please take care of Shadow and the boys. I love you."

* * *

A couple of hours later, Shadow stood at her bedroom window looking out. Her hip and shoulder rested against the frame while worried thoughts filtered through her mind. She was exhausted and felt battered all over. The warm, lingering bath she'd taken earlier that morning refused to calm her enough to sleep.

She pulled her silk wrapper tighter around her waist and sighed. She still couldn't believe her car had been bombed. She was lucky to be alive when someone was so adamantly determined to see her killed. Scared was a mild word for what she felt at this moment.

So, why did her mind go over and over the heart-stopping, mind-shattering kiss she and Raven shared afterwards? It started out as a placid kiss to comfort them both, but quickly changed to a searing blaze burning all the way to her soul. It could have, without a doubt, evolved into a clothes tearing, flesh-to-flesh, lay-me-down-in-the-bombed-out-debris, journey into unbelievable ecstasy if the Police Chief hadn't arrived when he did. By the very evident bulge in Raven's pants, she knew the desire wasn't one-sided.

Shadow shook her head in confusion. Where in the world had desire come from? All these years she'd thought she had gotten over her deep feelings for him and he had made it clear to her he had no desire for her. Maybe it was the adrenalin rush or after-shock from the near death experience that caused them to react so strong toward each other. Their lust for each other was a one-time deal and would be gone after a few hours sleep.

Yep. That was the answer. It would never happen again, so she would just put it out of her mind.

Shadow crawled into bed cursing beneath her breath. "Like hell I will."

* * *

Police Chief Edwin Dale Walker paced his office with the phone pressed to his ear. "Look here, Ben. I don't give a damn rat's ass that they said they saw no one. You saw me give the interrogation behind those mirrors and you know as well as I do they were lying through their teeth. I didn't believe for one minute they stopped to use the bathroom."

Police Chief Walker paced further as he listened to the other voice on the line. "Yes, I tell you. They were both searched when they were brought in even though no charges were being filed. There was nothing on them. Whatever they were looking for, they didn't find."

He listened again and then answered. "I'll take care of it."

Out of the corner of his eye, Walker saw his Deputy Police Chief, Paul LaCroix walking away from his office. His eyes narrowed and then he relaxed. He'd kept his conversation on the phone to the bare minimum. Nothing he'd said could be construed as suspicious.

* * *

Shadow didn't waken until 8:00 o'clock that Sunday evening. She took a quick shower, dressed in jeans and a tee shirt then went downstairs to find something to eat.

She hesitated for a moment at the door leading into the kitchen when she saw Raven sitting at the dining table. An empty plate had been shoved to the side and papers were strewn out in front of him. As she watched, he picked up one sheet of paper and began to read.

"Are you going to stand there all day staring at my body?" Raven teased without ever lifting his head to indicate he knew she was there.

Shadow's eyes narrowed and she humphed. Without a word, she walked to the refrigerator and opened its doors. She leaned way over and reached on the bottom shelf to give him a better view of her tight jeans from the backside. She heard his sharp indrawn breath and grinned.

She pulled out a casserole dish and took it to the microwave to zap. While it was warming, she leaned back against the counter. "When did you go back to the hospital and pick up those papers you hid?"

"About an hour ago."

"Anything interesting in them?"

Raven leaned back in his chair. He ran his hand over his short hair. "Nothing." He pushed the papers across the table. "Look through these files on your father and see if you can see anything I'm missing. I saw nothing in there that wasn't brought out during the trial."

Shadow's Justice

He leaned forward and rested his elbows on the table as he picked up the second file in front of him. "This file on Steven Tucker is a different matter." He tapped the papers in his hand with his forefinger. "According to this report, Collins has had Tucker followed for the past six months."

Shadow reached into the shelf above her head and pulled down a plate. She dished out a portion of the warmed food, fixed her a glass of tea and carried both to the table. "Does it say why?"

"No. The only things in the file are the investigator's report and receipts for five thousand dollars that Collins has paid him, so far."

Shadow whistled beneath her breath. "That's a lot of dough to pay out just to find out when someone is coming or going." Sitting down, she pulled the papers toward her and began to read as she ate.

Fifteen minutes later, Shadow pushed the plate and papers away from her. "This doesn't tell us diddly crap. Everything in Dad's files was brought out in court. I really hoped to find something new."

"Yeah, so was I." He slapped the papers down on the table.

With one manicured nail, Shadow tapped the file on Tucker. "I don't get it. Why would Randall spend that kind of money on tracking Steven's every move for months?"

She had known Steven and his family all of her life. Even though he was much older than her, he and his family had gone to the same social functions and the same church. She'd seen him often in the bank and even after his father had been murdered they had been cordial. He was the first person to say he didn't believe for a minute her father had murdered his.

That had meant a lot to her at the time, as it did now.

"It's not like he's a mobster or anything. He's just a stingy jerk." she added in annoyance.

Raven glanced over at Shadow. "Let's play 'what if'. What if Tucker is blackmailing Collins?'"

Shadow shook her head. "I wouldn't think so. Why would Randall pay an investigator? He would just pay Steven the five thousand dollars in payment for the blackmail and call it even. My turn. What if Steven has been threatened someway and Randall is providing him with protection by having the investigator watching him for twenty-four hours a day?"

Raven raised one eyebrow. "Get real. You can hire a bodyguard a lot cheaper than five grand and it would be difficult to protect someone while hiding behind the bushes with a camera and pencil as his only weapon."

Shadow scowled across the table. "Let's hear your next bright idea, Sherlock."

Raven shrugged his shoulder and stood. "What if...we quit wasting time and go ask Tucker himself?" He headed for the door. He turned back to her and grinned as he heard her chair scrape across the floor and the sound of her feet slapping against the ceramic tile.

"Dammit, wait on me."

He closed the door behind him.

* * *

Twenty minutes later, Raven drove his car at a slow crawl down the side street. A block away from Tucker's home, he pulled over to the curb and parked. He could go no further.

Blue lights flashed with an eeriness into the night

lighting up the whole block Tucker lived on. Neighbors were standing outside in their nightclothes looking toward the frenzied scene. They were whispering with unease amongst themselves and holding on tight to their loved ones.

With sickening feelings, Raven and Shadow climbed out of the car and began walking toward the lights.

As they neared his home they could see an ambulance backed up into the driveway leading to Tucker's home and two paramedics were carrying out a gurney. A white sheet draped with a tragic finale over the still body.

"Oh, my God, what has happened?" Shadow grasped Raven's hand and held on as they watched the gurney being lifted into the ambulance.

Raven wrapped an arm around her shoulders and pulled her to him. "I don't know. Let's see if we can get closer and find out."

They wound their way through a long line of patrol cars and officers and made it to the front steps where a young man in uniform stopped them. His freckled face turned even redder from embarrassment and his words rushed out. "I'm sorry, but you can't go in there, Miss McClane, Raven. This is an official police crime scene."

"That's okay, Todd. You're just doing your official duties. We only wanted to know what happened. Who did they just carry out?" Shadow spoke with soft words to the boy whom she had babysitted when he was a toddler.

The officer leaned down and whispered. "I'm not supposed to be giving out any information." He looked around and whispered again, "Oh heck, guess

I can tell the two of you. That was Steven Tucker."

"What happened?" Raven asked.

"He was shot point blank between the eyes. Just like his daddy."

Shadow's knees gave away. Raven caught her before they buckled and hit the pavement. He held on to her tight as cries of sorrow and then cries of relief escaped from her lips. This could be the proof they were looking for.

"What in the hell are the two of you doing here? Officer, get them out of here." Police Chief Walker bellowed out from behind them.

Officer Todd scrambled to escort them away.

Shadow pulled her elbow out of his grasp and wiped away her tears with the back of her hand. "Wait a minute. I know about Steven being shot and having the same M.O. as his father. You can't very well blame my father this time. Does this mean you'll be reopening the case?"

Police Chief Walker swung around and glared at Officer Todd knowing where Shadow had gained her information. "Get back to work. I'll deal with you later." He barked.

Then, he turned his head and glowered at Shadow and Raven. Ignoring Shadow's question, he raised one questioning brow. "What I want to know is what the two of you are doing here at this time of night? 10 o'clock is a little late for visiting, ain't it?"

He leaned closer. "Or, maybe you've already paid your visit. I think everyone knows that nine times out of ten the murderer always returns to the crime scene as an onlooker. Maybe I need to take the two of you back to headquarters for questioning, again."

"Maybe you need to search this crowd for the real

murderer and quit harassing us, Police Chief." Shadow spit out the words as she stared him down.

"Shadow, back down." Raven ordered in a stern voice. He heard her sharp intake of breath, but for once she obeyed and kept quiet. He glanced back at the Police Chief and with a nonchalant shrug he spoke. "We were driving through the neighborhood and saw the action. We thought we would stop and see what was going on. No crime in that, Police Chief."

"I'll decide what a crime is and what ain't in this town, young man." Police Chief's irate voice rose just above a whisper. His bullfrog face grew even redder as his forefinger jabbed hard into Raven's shoulder. "Let me tell you something, boy. Don't frickin' piss me off or I'll shove your face so far up your ass you'll never see daylight again. Now, get out of my sight. Both of you." Police Chief Walker straightened his vest, cocked his hat and walked off without another word.

Shadow pushed her hair back from her shoulder with a shaky hand. Reaching inside her purse, she withdrew a cigarette and lighter. Lighting one up, she inhaled deeply.

Glancing toward Raven, she watched the muscles in his jaw clench tight. She blew out the smoke from her lungs into the night air and then spoke with a considerable amount of smugness in her voice. "Well, you handled that quiet well. I couldn't have done better myself."

"Shut up, Shadow." Before she could react, Raven reached over and grabbed her cigarette and threw it to the ground, grinding it beneath his boot.

Shadow opened her mouth to tell him off and then

clamped it shut as his back disappeared into the crowd. Pushing the strap of her purse secure on her shoulder, she hurried after him, cursing every step of the way.

CHAPTER SIX

Monday morning, her phone rang. Groaning, Shadow rolled over and buried her head beneath the covers. On the eighth ring, Shadow cursed and reached for the phone and growled. "What?"

"Good morning to you, too." Stacy's cheerful voice gushed through the receiver.

Shadow moaned and sat up. She pushed her tangled hair back from her face and yawned. "What time is it?" she grumbled.

"It's early, only 7:00 o'clock, but you'll forgive me when you find out why I called."

Shadow sighed and rubbed a hand across her eyes. "Stacy, I had three hours of sleep last night and I'm exhausted. You have ten seconds to tell me why you called before I hang this phone up."

"Okay, okay, grouch." Stacy let the bomb fall. "Steven Tucker was murdered last night."

"I know." Shadow yawned and her head fell back to her pillow.

Silence. Then, deflated, "How...? Never mind. I don't want to know. I bet you don't know this, though. His home was torched an hour ago and is now blazing to high heaven."

Shadow's Justice

Shadow shot straight out of the bed. "What do you mean it was torched?" She began pacing the floor, her gown billowing out behind her.

"I mean, according to the evidence someone dipped rags in gasoline, set fire to them and threw the blazing torches in through the side windows that he knocked out. Whoever it was didn't bother covering up any of the evidence. Gas cans and soaked rags were tossed everywhere. It was like he wanted someone to know the fire was deliberate. The police are checking for fingerprints now."

"Oh my God. Janice and Brandon. Are they okay?"

"Yes. Janice's mother talked them into going home with her after the cops finished questioning her last night. I talked to her mother a few minutes ago. The doctor had sedated Janice and her and Brandon were sleeping."

Shadow ran a hand through her tousled hair and cursed under her breath. "Look Stacy, I really appreciate you calling me. I'm going to get a quick shower and wake up Raven. Can you meet us at Steven's home in about an hour?"

"Sure. I'm headed back there anyway to see what else has been uncovered. See you there. And Shadow...?"

"Yes?"

"Be careful." A snort of derisive humor sounded across the phone as Stacy hung up.

Shadow took a quick shower and dressed in a sleeveless pullover and a pair of white shorts. She slipped on a pair of sandals and hurried down the hall to Raven's bedroom.

She hesitated for a moment and then knocked with determination on the door. No answer. She knocked once more before the doorknob turned in her hand. She gave the door a small push. Shadow stuck her head around the door and almost collapsed to the floor with weak knees.

Her gaze zeroed in on the man sprawled flat on his stomach in a huge, king size bed. One corner of a bright red satin sheet was pulled across one leg. Other than that, Raven was bare-assed naked.

Never having a timid bone in her body, Shadow moved inside the room for a closer look. So, this is why all of those blondes with boobs bigger than their IQ's kept coming around throughout high school and college.

She stepped closer to the bed. Her probing gaze swept from the side of his face smoothed out in a deep, restful sleep to his dark, broad shoulders, down his muscular back, toward his rounded rear and finishing at his long, tanned, powerfully built legs. Her insides quivered and her teeth nibbled at her bottom lip. She took a deep, steadying breath and then allowed her gaze to begin ascending once again before coming to a final resting place.

"Nice butt," She observed with a raised voice.

Raven's head jerked straight up and his hand automatically reached for the gun tucked beneath his pillow. He turned his head and moaned as he saw Shadow standing beside his bed. He reached down and yanked the sheet up over his body and his head fell back to the pillow. His voice slurred from sleep still demanded an answer. "What in the hell are you doing in here, Shadow? I could've easily shot you."

Shadow grinned and sat down beside him on the bed and patted his rump. "I was admiring your bod until you covered it up. Do you always sleep in the nude?" She heard his growl and laughed. "Actually, I use to be very jealous of all those college girls I saw you with around the holidays. Just think, back then I was too young to want anything more than your undivided attention and kisses."

Shadow felt the bed shaking and turned to find he was laughing into his pillow. "What?"

Raven grinned and rolled over, sleep forgotten. "You never cease to amuse me."

"That's me, your endless source of entertainment."

Raven watched the sadness flash in her eyes. He wondered about it before she masked the emotion with her flippant answer. He shook his head, all humor fleeing along with his tiredness. "Are you always so outspoken? I remember you being very bashful and withdrawn when you were younger," he asked.

Shadow shrugged her shoulder. "I grew up and quickly learned life's harsh lessons. They have a way of knocking street smarts into you real fast. I learned the first lesson at sixteen."

Raven reached for her hand and squeezed. "I'm sorry," he said simply. The warmth in his eyes conveyed his sincerity.

Shadow felt herself withdrawing before she was drawn into that warmth. It would be so easy to give in and let Raven take care of everything for her, but she didn't.

Hiding her vulnerability had become second nature to Shadow. She'd learned a long time ago to never show her fears or her tears. Be strong. Act strong. It was the only way she could survive Raven's rejection and her father's imprisonment and death.

Angry with herself for being tempted for even a

second to lean on someone else's shoulders, Shadow stiffened her spine and reverted back to her mastered, tough lady persona. She use to want a lot of things from Raven, but pity wasn't one of them.

She pulled her hand from his grasp and stood. "Yeah, well, like I said. That's life." And she would handle her pain the best way she knew how. By herself and with her heart left intact.

Shadow glanced toward the door and took a step toward it. She hesitated and then with a calmer voice she spoke over her shoulder. "Look, the reason I came in here was to tell you that I got a phone call from Stacy this morning. Steven and Janice's home was torched early this morning." She heard his curse and then the rustle of sheets and she knew he had sat up on the side of his bed.

"What happened?"

Shadow turned back to him and noticed he had pulled the sheet over his lap. She told him everything she'd learned from Stacy and answered his questions with the little information she had. She finished up by adding, "I told her we would meet her there around 8 o'clock. I'll start the coffee while you're getting dressed."

Shadow walked out of his room, closed the door and fell against it. Both hands covered her face as her forced calmness evaporated and her body shook from released nerves. That red satin sheet hadn't hidden a damn thing.

* * *

Shadow and Raven found Stacy standing beside the Gazette's young photographer as he shot one frame after another in rapid fire.

Stacy looked up from her notes and greeted them.

"Hey, you two. Give me a minute to finish up here and I'll fill you in on what's been happening."

"Sure. Go right ahead. We want to get a closer look at the damage, anyway. We'll meet you by the front steps," Shadow told her.

Stacy nodded and turned back to the job on hand.

Shadow felt Raven's hand on her back as he led her toward the smoldering shell of a once beautiful two-story home. Intense, suffocating smoke still spiraled toward the sky. The stench of water hosed on to the blackened remains lingered heavy in the air.

They'd met the fire trucks leaving as they'd arrived. It looked like the Police Chief had done his usual thorough job. No one was on sight collecting evidence.

A yellow barrier tape with DO NOT CROSS was draped tightly across the front yard. Raven and Shadow walked under the tape and made their way closer.

Shadow felt the anger rising inside her at the total destruction before her. First Steven and now this. "Who in the hell would do something like this?"

Raven didn't answer. Instead, he moved in as close as he could and began walking around the perimeter. His gaze focused intensely on the fire ravaged remains and surroundings. Shadow followed close on his heels.

Raven knelt once to study a small, blackened object on the ground. Without a word, he stood and slipped the object into his pant's pocket.

"Finding any clues?" Stacy asked as she joined them.

"Nothing to speak of. Have you found out anything else?" Raven asked her.

"Not much." Stacy opened her notebook and her eyes scanned the pages. "Their neighbor to the right of them woke up when her dog started barking and wouldn't stop. She looked out her bedroom window where the security light was shining. She saw a large man, she was assuming it was a man by his heavy build, running across her front lawn. She said he was wearing a ski mask pulled down over his face, jeans and a dark T-shirt. That was when she spotted the fire coming from Tucker's home and called 9-1-1."

"Have the police uncovered anything?" Shadow asked her friend.

Stacy snorted. "Pu….lease. McClain's Police Department couldn't uncover their butt's to go to the bathroom. How do you expect them to solve this murder and arson?"

Raven grinned. "Another big fan of Police Chief Walkers, I see."

Shadow laughed. "You should see some of the wonderful caricatures she does of Walker for the paper. They're hilarious."

Stacy grinned and shrugged off the compliment. "He's an easy subject to ridicule. Listen, I've got to get back to work, but I'll let you know if I find out anything else."

"Okay. I'll call you later," Shadow told her.

"Thanks. We really appreciate your help." Raven said.

"Anytime." With a wave of her hand, she was gone like a whirlwind.

Shadow glanced toward Raven. "Now where?"

Raven stared at the remains of the house and then looked back at Shadow. Worry marred his brows. "I think it's time to pay Janice a visit to see what she might know about her husband's murder and then I need to make a few phone calls afterwards. Let's go for a drive."

"Okay. You think Steven might have said something to his wife about being followed?"

Raven shrugged. "He might have, but I doubt it. I don't think he would want his family right in the middle of whatever was going on, but his behavior and schedules for the past six months might give us some clue into the murder," he told her.

They reached the Corvette and within seconds they were driving south toward the countryside where Janice's mother lived.

Shadow rolled her window down and let the breeze wash over her. She used the time inside the car to think. Events were happening too fast, too horrible to comprehend. A man had died last night leaving behind a grieving wife and son. Both had lost their home and belongings. For what? Steven was shut up for a reason. Was it for revenge or a cover up?

Shadow rubbed her temples trying to ease the beginning of a tension headache. She leaned her head against the headrest.

Turning her head sideways, she studied Raven. He appeared unaffected by the past night's events, until she detected his white knuckles gripped like steel bands on the steering wheel.

She reached over with one hand and began kneading the tension in his neck.

"Mmmmmmm. That feels wonderful." His full-blown smile slid toward her and every one of her lust-filled sensations landed in her lower region. And probably showed in her eyes. Damn. She let her hand drop back to her lap and turned her head toward the window.

"Chicken." She heard the provocative, whispered dare, but decided to ignore it and him. Now was definitely the time to get back on course.

"What did you pick up off the ground back there?" She glanced back toward him and saw his grin still in place, but lucky for her he allowed her to change the subject.

"A gold cufflink."

"Recognize it?"

"Nope, but I bet there's another one around somewhere just like it. We just have to search for it."

Shadow laughed. "Damn, I would say you were good, if I didn't think the cufflink might belong to Steven Tucker."

"Nope, you're wrong. I bet you a massage it belongs to the one who torched the house." And, there was that grin again.

She glared at him and moved past that subject. She didn't need to be thinking about touching his bare skin at this moment when the memory of his naked body was still so vivid in her mind. "Who are you planning on calling?"

"Bob Green, my second-in-command. He'll be able to link up with the right people to find out what we need to know. There's not a whole lot we can do from here without the whole town knowing about it. I also want to express mail him these files Collins had on Steven. I don't trust sending them by email. I'll have him locate the private investigator Collins hired and see if he can get any more information out of him. There's got to be some connection between those files and Steven's murder," he told her.

Shadow took a deep breath and let it out slow.

"You think Collins, a close friend to the family murdered Steven, don't you?"

Raven glanced over at Shadow, his face grave. "Don't you?"

* * *

Three cars, one right behind the other pulled into the yard of a deserted cabin nestled along the banks of a swamp. No one ever came here anymore since old man Barnes met his maker a year back. No one except these three.

The men stepped out of their individual cars. One man nervously fingered his tie at the sounds of splashing from several alligators slithering from the bank into the lake looking for their morning prey. Hundreds of birds of different varieties screeched a loud cry into the stillness of the early hours as they dove toward the murky waters below in a wild, feeding frenzy.

And, the snakes. The man swallowed the lump of fear in his throat. With his head bent, he watched for the brown-colored water moccasins common to the wetland with every cautious step he took toward the other two men. He'd lived in Louisiana all of his life and if he lived to be one hundred, he'd never get use to the swamp and it's predators.

"Well?" Judge Adams asked with unhidden impatience as he watched his partner's slow approach.

Police Chief Walker leaned back against his car with his arms folded and waited.

Randall Collins stopped next to the two and looked out over the lake, once again. The knot in his throat moved up and down as he swallowed hard. Finally, he spoke. "It's missing."

He turned and looked into each of their eyes. "Raven and Shadow stole my file on Jack McClane when they broke into my office. The papers on Tucker were messed with, too. They probably made copies. They won't be able to question Tucker, though, unless they do a séance."

"Shit!" The expletive flew from the Police Chief's mouth

and his fist slammed into the hood of his car.

The sounds of hundreds of frightened birds taking off in flight boomed across the waters as Judge Adam's voice rose. "You fool. Steal the damn things back."

Collins's hair stood on end as the Judge's voice lowered to a menacing whisper. "I want those two dead."

CHAPTER SEVEN

Raven drove his car down the long, winding lane bordered by towering, century old magnolia trees. The lane led up to the white plantation style home belonging to Janice's family. He pulled up in front of the drive and killed the motor.

Walking up to the wide, double doors, Shadow stood to the side while Raven pulled back on the large brass ring knocker and rapped twice on the door. A moment later the door was thrown open by the maid and she inquired, "Yes? May I help you?"

Raven smiled a greeting. "Yes, we're here to see Mrs. Tucker."

"May I ask who's calling?"

"Tell her Raven Deveroux and Shadow McClane is here to see her."

The maid ushered them into the hallway to wait. Within moments she returned and led them into a large sitting room.

Janice Tucker rose from an elegant covered rosewood divan and greeted them. "Shadow, Raven. I'm glad you stopped by. Please, have a seat. Can I get either of you any refreshments?" Her thin voice quivered even as she portrayed the perfect hostess.

"Nothing for me. Thanks." Shadow answered.

Shadow's Justice

Not a hair was out of place on Janice's head, Shadow noticed. Her makeup had been applied from a long time expertise and the black, sleeveless dress she wore looked casual, but Shadow guessed it carried a designer label sewn in the back.

The only outward signs of being distraught over her husband's murder and her home torched were her reddened eyes and the torn tissue in her hand.

Shadow walked up to her and put her arms around her. She felt her own heart breaking. "Janice, I'm so sorry."

A sob caught in Janice's throat, but emotionally drained, her eyes remained dry. "Thank you," she whispered as she stepped back.

Janice allowed Raven to lead her back to the divan. Sitting beside her, he held her hand as Shadow sat across from them.

Even though Shadow was younger than Janice and Steven they still ran in the same social circles and met up and mingled at many functions. Raven often joined them when he was home.

Janice patted Raven's hand. "I really appreciate you stopping by, but I know this is more than just a social call to see how I'm doing. I've been expecting you. You both know as well as I do that Steven's murder and his father's is somehow connected. You also know the police force in this town is nothing but a big joke."

She took a deep breath and continued. She stared straight into Raven's eyes. "I've heard you're specially trained in these matters and the two of you are pursuing Father Tucker's murder case. I need your help in catching whoever killed Steven for Brandon's sake. I believe both murders are related. The Police

Chief was here earlier. I have no faith at all in him finding the killer. I want our son to know when he gets older his father's murder was avenged. I'll help you in anyway I can."

Raven didn't bother asking how she knew about his secret missions. She had only heard what he had allowed to be known to the public. "Thank you, Janice. I know this is hard on you, but I do have questions with no answers. Anything you could tell us would help."

Raven sat back and organized his thoughts. "Do you have any idea who might have done this? Did Steven have any enemies that you were aware of?"

Janice shook her head and sighed. "No. None that I know about. I've been racking my brain this morning trying to come up with a reason for all of this. He's been under a lot of stress at work lately. He's mentioned a few disgruntled customers at the bank, a couple of disclosures, a few turned down for a loan, those kinds of things."

She shrugged a shoulder. "Unless one of them just lost sight of reality, I can't see any one of them murdering Steven. I can get their names for you if you want to check into it further."

"I do. Thanks. We want to check into all possible leads. I need to ask you one more question, if you don't mind. Were you aware someone had hired a private investigator to follow Steven?"

Janice sucked in a shocked breath and shook her head as the startling information filtered into her mind. "No. Why would someone have him followed? He went to the bank in the morning and came home in the evening at the same time everyday. He liked his life organized and on schedule. But, that might

Shadow's Justice

explain...," Janice paused and looked down at her hands holding the shredded tissue.

"Explain what?" Raven's soft voice was assuring.

Janice raised her head to look at Raven and took a deep, determined breath. "It explains why he'd been acting so strange for the last few months. He was short-tempered with Brandon and myself, which was unordinary for him. Some evenings, instead of spending time with Brandon, he would go straight into his office after dinner and shut the door behind him. On a couple of occasions I've walked by the door and heard him on the phone talking to someone. He sounded agitated both times and maybe a little frightened."

"Do you know who he was talking to?"

"No. When I asked him about it he only grew angrier and told me to stop eavesdropping. I even accused him of having an affair. He was sarcastic and wanted to know when I thought he had the time to be with another woman."

"Could he have been in trouble financially?"

A mere whisper. "I don't know."

Raven glanced over at Shadow, his thoughts grim. Turning back to Janice, he squeezed her hands. "Do you know if the police have taken Steven's files out of the bank, yet?"

"Yes. His secretary called me this morning and told me they were hauling away boxes full of papers from his filing cabinets as evidence."

Raven swore. He rubbed his tired eyes in frustration. He wanted to look at those files and now they were in the hands of the McClane Ridge's version of the Keystone Cops. He reminded himself to find out where the police department stored their evidence.

He stood preparing to leave. "Janice, thank you for your help. If you think of anything else, please call us."

They said their goodbyes and let themselves out. Back in the car, Raven drove toward town.

"Now what?" Shadow asked.

Raven began dialing his cell phone. "Right now, I'm going to put a call into Green while we're headed to the Post Office to mail this envelope. Then…"

Raven stopped in mid-sentence and spoke into the phone when the other line picked up. He stressed his needs in quick and precise terms without revealing any names over the phone other than Steven's and the private investigator who had followed Tucker. "I need this information as quickly as possible. You should be getting the package by tomorrow."

"I'll get right on it. Do I need to bring this information down personally?" Raven knew what his friend was asking. Green would be there in a New York second if he thought his commander was in trouble.

"No. Things are fine for now. I'll call you if I need you."

"All right. I'll get right on this, then."

"Thanks. Call my cell phone when you have the information."

"You bet."

Raven hung up as he heard the line go dead. If things went as planned, Green would be calling him by tomorrow night and he could proceed from there.

He had a gut feeling there was more to the private investigators report than what he found. Janice was right. According to the report, Steven went straight to the bank and then straight home in the evening. Collins could have figured that out on his own and saved himself five thousand dollars. But then again, there was something in the report that made the lawyer very nervous or Steven would still be alive.

Entering the town's city limits, Raven drove his car at a slow pace down main street and pulled up in front of the Post Office. He glanced toward Shadow who seemed to be in deep thought while she stared out the side window. "I'll be right back."

"Okay." Shadow answered. She continued staring out the window.

Five minutes later, Raven returned. He climbed behind the wheel and glanced over at Shadow. "How about some lunch?"

Shadow nodded and smiled up at him. "Sounds good. I'm starved. Pete's Grill makes a mean, jumbo steak sandwich. The steak hangs about two inches outside this enormous bun and the taste is out of this world."

Raven shook his head and laughed. Shadow had just gone from brooding to bubbly in two point five seconds at the mention of food. A man would never get bored with this woman. He backed the car out of the parking lot and headed across town to Pete's Grill.

Arriving, they walked up to the window and Raven ordered their sandwiches and drinks. When their order was ready, he paid and they moved to a table and chairs sitting outside under a shady oak tree. A family with two young children sat at a table nearby. Lively chatter and laughter filled the silence.

Raven and Shadow ate, each in deep thought, yet enjoying the good food and fresh spring air.

Shadow's Justice

Shadow bit into a fry and chewed, her mind back on the investigation. She picked up another fry and pointed it toward Raven. Her thoughts spilled out in questions. She leaned forward and lowered her voice. "What I don't understand is the motive."

Raven grinned. Keeping up with her erratic train of thoughts was an ongoing challenge. "Revenge?"

Shadow seemed to considered that, then shook her head. "No. I don't think so. Steven's profile is too family-oriented to be a threat to anyone. The only thing he might have done was turn down someone needing a loan or foreclosed on someone's property. That's a possibility easily checked into. I can't see him blackmailing anyone, either. Nor, is there anything in the investigative reports that indicates he might've been susceptible to blackmail."

"Then, the only thing left would be greed." Finished with his meal, he wiped his hands with the napkin and placed the trash into the paper bag. "I think the first thing we need to do is find out who he owed and who owed him."

Shadow nodded. "Money is a strong motive." She wadded up her trash and added it to the bag. "But, I don't think so."

Raven raised one brow in question. "You don't?"

"Nope. It's as Janice originally said. Steven's murder somehow ties in with his father's. Revenge, blackmail or greed may be the reason Mr. Tucker was killed, but I'd bet you next weeks pay that Steven found out the 'who' and the 'why's' and was permanently shut up by the same person who killed his father."

"That's pretty far-fetched. But, say you're right."

"I'm right."

Raven grimaced and rolled his eyes. "Why didn't Steven take what he knew to the authorities?"

Shadow shrugged one shoulder. "Maybe to protect his family? Who knows?"

"That's a possibility. From what Janice said, she may have overheard him being threatened over the phone." Raven stood with abruptness and began walking to the car. "Let's go."

Shadow scrambled to her feet. "Where are we going?"

"To call another friend of mine who has access to phone records. I want a full list of every call Steven made and of all calls made to him." Raven called over his shoulder.

His gut feeling was pointing him toward Collins, but what if he was wrong? They needed to check out every avenue.

Ten minutes later, Raven ended the phone call and turned toward Shadow. "He's going to email me with an attachment of all of Steven's incoming and outgoing calls for the past month."

"How long will it take him to get the listing? Did he say?"

"We should have something by this evening." Raven watched Shadow nibble her bottom lip. Reaching out, he cupped the side of her face with a tender hand. "Hey, quit worrying. We're going to catch this guy. Trust me," he told her.

Raven became lost gazing into her big, soulful, blue eyes. He lowered his head and brushed his lips against hers. His calm kiss of comfort soon changed to a tidal wave of need. With a low growl deep in his throat, he deepened the kiss with a growing hunger.

Shadow trembled and leaned in closer to drink

from his lips. Her hand reached behind his head to draw him closer. She felt her breast brush against his chest and moaned when they immediately ached for his touch.

Raven heard her soft moan and stilled. With every ounce of decency he'd ever displayed in his thirty-two years, he slowly broke off the kiss. With a whispered curse, he leaned back in his seat with his eyes closed willing his erratic breath to calm.

"Raven."

He heard the unspoken question in her quivering voice. He turned toward her and saw her red swelling lips from his kisses.

Groaning aloud, he let his head fall back against the headrest before he could do something stupid like grabbing her again and pulling her into his lap, unzipping his pants and ravishing her right there in a public parking lot with children around. He was acting like a randy teenager who'd seen his first glimpse of boob heaven.

"Look. I'm sorry. That should've never happened."

He missed her sharp, piqued glance and only heard her soft spoken words. "You're right. It shouldn't have."

He glanced her way and she continued. "Next time you kiss me to a boiling point like that, you'd better damn well be prepared to finish what you start." She turned her face away and stared out her window without uttering another word.

Raven couldn't help it. A grin emerged threatening to split his face. Boiling point, huh? It was very tempting to find out what point she would get to with a second kiss.

Sitting up, Raven started the car. He glanced in his

rearview mirror and his grin vanished.

Several feet behind them Police Chief Walker was leaning against his patrol car staring toward them with an air of hostility.

Raven put the car into gear. He drove away, but kept a watch in his rearview mirror.

* * *

Shadow's thick skin was peeling away one layer at a time and it was really beginning to piss her off.

She furiously paced her bedroom floor while undressing. Jerking her t-shirt over her head, she flung it across the room where it landed in an untidy heap on the floor. Her bra soon followed, the crème silk billowing on top of the bed behind her.

"Trust me, he says," she mimicked. Since when had she ever put her complete trust in anyone other than her father?

"Never. All I can trust Raven to do is to break my heart, again. I would deserve it for letting him," she muttered through clenched teeth.

Hopping on one foot, she pulled one sneaker off and threw it over her shoulder. It hit the wall with a resounding thud. Hopping on the other foot, she was attempting to do the same with the other shoe when her bedroom door flew open and Raven stood in the doorway.

"What in the hell is going on in here...Damn!" Raven's mouth dropped open His breath sounded erratic. "Damn!"

Shadow's mouth went dry.

His smoldering eyes held her captive for many seconds before she came to her senses long enough to lower her foot and stand before him.

She didn't bother to cover her breasts. His bold

gaze told her he thought they were beautiful. She didn't back away from him. His questing hands were beckoning her forward.

His head fell back on his shoulders. With his eyes closed, a frustrated sigh erupted through his lips. His hands dropped to his side. "Please, tell me to leave, Shadow." His words were a mere whisper and a prayer.

Raising his head he looked into her sensual eyes as she took a step toward him. He raised one hand and shook his head. "Don't. I've discovered that no matter what my mind tells me, I have no control over the way my body reacts to you when you come near me."

"Then tell your mind to shut up and let your body take complete control." Her sultry voice was his undoing.

Raven grabbed for her and pulled her into his arms. His mouth clamped down on hers, hard...grinding, drinking in her unique, sweet taste and texture.

Shadow whimpered and pressed herself closer, both hands pulling his head down to meet her own, not giving him a chance to pull away until her breath gave completely out.

His lips left hers and began a sensual trail down her neck and lower. Reaching down, he raised one of her legs to rest on his hip and he pressed intimately against her heat with his hardness. "Feel how you affect me."

"Oh God...." One erotic shiver after another weakened her and her head fell back from a stronger desire than she'd ever experienced in her life.

She collapsed against him with a whimper. She was

swept into his arms and placed gently on to her bed.

Raven discarded his clothes and joined her. His fingers, with promptness mastered the button to her shorts.

She raised her hips to help him as he pulled her shorts, panties and one shoe off in one final swoop leaving her completely naked.

He sat back and looked his fill. He shook his head in wonder. "You are so beautiful, Shadow and I want you so much. I don't think I can wait any longer."

Shadow smiled a siren smile. "Then don't. I want you, now. We can play later."

CHAPTER EIGHT

What happens, happens. Shadow turned the bacon sizzling in the pan. The way things were going, she could be murdered in her sleep by the same person who had killed Steven and his father. She was relentlessly and publicly pursuing the killer and knew she was making someone very nervous.

A slow grin appeared out of nowhere. But, damn if she wouldn't die a happy and a very sexually, satisfied woman.

"You're grinning, again."

Shadow yelped in surprise and turned toward the doorway to find Raven leaning against the door jam with his arms crossed. Freshly showered, his hair was still damp and finger combed. He had donned a shirt, but it was left open exposing his chest and rock-hard stomach. His denim jeans clung tight to his body with the top button undone. Even his bare feet were sexy.

Raven straightened and walked toward her with purpose. When he neared, he pulled her into his arms. The searing kiss he dealt to her lips had her standing on tiptoes as her arms wrapped around his neck. He pulled away to nibble sensually against her lips. "Good morning."

"Mmmm, morning."

"Bacon's burning."

Shadow's Justice

Shadow screeched and turned back to the stove. Using the spatula, she removed the charred bacon and added fresh before turning back to Raven who was still laughing. She waved the spatula under his nose. "Don't you dare laugh. This is your fault for distracting me. Besides, you're the one who told Carol to take a vacation to get her away from danger. So, eat my cooking or do without."

"Who? Me? I would never laugh at you. Nor would I ever refuse your cooking. I'm hungry enough to eat anything."

Shadow's eyebrow rose in affront.

Still grinning, Raven leaned around the spatula and gave her a quick kiss on her pouting lips. "Is that fresh coffee I smell?"

"Yes." She turned back toward the stove before doing something stupid like throwing him down on the table and having him for breakfast. Even though, that wasn't a bad idea.

"Rose called earlier."

Raven took a sip of coffee and sat down. "What did she have to say?"

Shadow laid a plate filled with eggs, bacon and toast in front of Raven. "The same as usual. She wants to come home."

Raven sighed. "She knows she can't. I'll give her a call a little later."

"She'll like that. She misses everyone."

Silence filled the room as they ate their breakfast. Afterwards, Shadow stood to clear the table. "Have you had a chance to check your emails, yet?"

"No. I've been distracted." Raven's sensual grin almost knocked her to her knees.

Shadow turned away to hide the rising flush and

pleased smile on her face. This rush of pure happiness was new to her and only happened when he was near. She didn't know how to handle this new emotion, this new Raven. She needed time to think. "Why don't you go check them while I clean up the kitchen?"

She heard his quiet chuckle as he left the room and knew he was aware of her newfound shyness. Well, so much for showing off her worldliness and experience in the love arena. Zeeze!

* * *

Raven turned on his computer and waited until it booted up before checking his emails. He grinned. "Let's see what my boys have dug up." He started printing.

Ten minutes later, he had a month long list of calls made from and to the Tucker's home telephone sitting on the kitchen table before him.

He handed a stack to Shadow who he had joined moments before and began looking through the ones left in front of him.

Ten minutes later, he flung the papers back on the table and swore. "Nothing. There is not one suspicious phone call in this whole stack. Have you found anything?"

Shadow shook her head. "No." She shuffled the papers around. "All I have is calls from his secretary, a few people who head up charity functions and some from family and friends, but that's it."

Raven stood and poured more coffee into their cups before sitting back down. "That's all I'm finding, too. There's a couple from Judge Adams. They were made right after your dad died. He might have wanted to let Steven know that the ordeal was over. Who knows?"

Shadow's Justice

Shadow's sigh held regret and a little angry frustration. "So, we're back to square one."

"I guess so and I'll be damned if I know where to go from here."

Raven stood with his coffee and walked over to the window overlooking Rose's flower garden and stared out. He was missing something. Some small clue and it was frustrating the hell out of him. His gut instinct was telling him Collins was involved up to his neck, but he hadn't found one shred of evidence to back up his theory.

His hand plunged into his pocket, his fingers playing with the loose change in his pocket as his thoughts ran rapid. His fingers stilled as they lay on the foreign object he'd placed into his pocket the day before. Pulling it out, he studied the smoke-damaged cufflink he'd picked up off of Tucker's lawn after the fire. He had forgotten all about finding it.

Walking over to the sink, he rinsed it off until it gleamed and held it up to the light.

"What time does Collins go into his office?" He asked without turning around.

Shadow glance up from the papers she was reading. "Probably around 9:00, I would think. Why?"

Raven glanced down at his watch. 9:15. He walked to the table and turned off his laptop and placed the computer into his case. Grabbing the case in his hand, he turned to Shadow. "Let's go pay a visit to his home."

Shadow was getting use to this craziness. Without questioning his reasoning, she went to get her purse and joined him in the corridor a few minutes later.

* * *

Shadow's Justice

Raven pulled up beside a curb two blocks away from Collin's home. Killing the motor, they got out of the car and began walking.

A few minutes later, Raven and Shadow stood at the beginning of the long circular drive. They stared up at Collins's modern three story home nestled in the midst of huge oaks and magnolia trees planted over a hundred years before.

Shadow glanced over at Raven. "Now what?"

"We go to the front door and ring the bell."

"Smartass," she muttered under her breath. She followed him to the door and waited beside him while he rang the doorbell.

When no one came to the door, he rang again and they waited. Satisfied no one was at home, he turned to Shadow. "Let's go around to the servant's entrance and see if anyone is at home."

When they arrived at the back entrance, Raven knocked and waited. No one answered.

"Now what?" Shadow asked, again.

"I don't guess you know what time the housekeeper gets here, do you?"

"Nope."

"That's what I was afraid of." Raven pulled his trade tools out of his pocket. Inserting a metal pick, he unlocked the door and slowly pushed it open.

"Anyone home?" he hollered out, listened for a moment and shrugged. "Guess not," he said and walked into the kitchen.

Shadow followed on tiptoes, muttering sarcastically to herself. "Why would we want to break in under the cover of darkness when breaking in during broad daylight is so much more fun."

"Shhhhhhh. Show me Collins's study."

Shadow's Justice

With a murderous glare, she walked past him and down the hallway until she came to a closed door. She stepped back as Raven reached around her to turn the knob and enter the office. He walked over to the desk and turned on the lamp.

Shadow quietly walked up behind him and looked over his shoulder. "What are we looking for?"

Raven glanced back at her. "We're looking for anything that will nail Collins's butt to the proverbial board."

"Sounds like a plan to me." Shadow said as she pulled open the top drawer of a filing cabinet.

When Shadow closed the bottom drawer, she stood and faced Raven. "I didn't have any luck. How about you?"

Raven shut the desk drawer he was looking in and stood. "Not much. I don't guess you would know which room upstairs is his bedroom, would you?" he teased.

Shadow's glare and unflattering name calling told him the answer he already knew. Laughing, he wrapped an arm around her shoulder. "In that case, we'll look until we come across it."

They found his bedroom on the third try and entered.

Shadow turned a complete circle in the middle of the room and grinned. "Wow. Would you look at this? I would've never thought ol' Collins had it in him," she said as she glanced around the room in astonishment.

Gold-trimmed mirrors lined the ceiling of the enormous room. Deep red, plush carpet that her feet sank down into covered the entire floor. An extra-sized king bed with a red silk spread and pillow shams was pushed up against one wall. One mirrored-lined wall was partially opened to reveal a huge walk-in closet. Expensive paintings of nude couples hung on another wall.

Raven whistled. "Looks like this stodgy lawyer isn't so stodgy after all. I wonder what other secrets lover boy may be hiding."

Shadow shrugged. "Let's look and find out." She went to the bedside table and began looking for anything that might help in their case.

Raven went straight to the large dresser against one wall and studied the locked jewelry box lying on top. Pulling his pick back out, he unlocked the box and lifted the lid. Peering inside, he found what he was looking for.

Careful to not move anything out of place, he lifted a single cufflink from its resting place and shoved it into his pants pocket. He locked the jewelry case back at the same moment he heard a car door slam outside. He turned toward Shadow.

"Let's get out of here."

Shadow heard the same noise and was already moving toward the door. "I'm ahead of you."

They hurried to make their way downstairs to Collins's study. Opening the French doors leading to the outside, they left the house a lot quieter than when they'd arrived.

Ten minutes later, Raven pulled up in front of their home. Getting out, he strode around to the passenger side and opened the door for Shadow.

Climbing out, Shadow glance up at Raven. "Are you going to share your finds from Collins's bedroom with me?"

"I'll think about it." He grunted and doubled over

Shadow's Justice

as her elbow connected with his ribs.

Grinning, Shadow walked toward the front door. Reaching out to insert her key into the lock she felt her arm jerked back and she was pulled back into Raven's arm. Still grinning, she moved to twist into his arms and was stopped in mid-turn. His hand covered her mouth. Her eyes widened.

"Shhhhh. Don't make a sound." His whispered voice frightened her into obedience.

Reaching around her, he pointed toward the damaged lock on the door. He pushed easy on the door and it swung open. "Stay here while I check it out," he whispered before pulling his pistol out of its shoulder holster and entering the foyer. Two steps later he felt her hand on his back.

Swinging around to berate her, he decided he would be wasting his time and just shook his head. "Stay close," he whispered instead. He waited for her nod before walking into the sitting room. He stopped in mid-stride and looked around in dismay. He heard Shadow's shocked gasp behind him.

The room was in a complete shamble. Every piece of furniture was turned over. Cabinet drawers were opened and the contents were strewn across the floor.

They made their way from room to room to find the same disorder in them as they had in the last. Who ever ransacked her home had come and gone. White-lipped, Shadow stood trembling against the door facing as she took in the shambles inside the kitchen.

"Well, at least we know of one thing the bastards were after," Raven said as he put the pistol back into its holster.

Shadow glance up at him in question and he

pointed toward the cleared top of the kitchen table. The telephone records from earlier were missing.

"Damn! What was on the phone records that we missed?" Shadow cried out in frustration.

Raven smiled. "I don't know, but as soon as I get my computer out of the car, I'll print off another copy and we'll take another look."

Shadow's mouth turned up into shocked grin. "My God. That's right. You took your computer with you this morning." She grabbed his face between both hands and kissed him. "You're my man."

"And, don't you forget it," Raven laughed to ease the tension. With one arm wrapped around her, he turned back to survey the room. He pulled her close as if to protect her. "We're still missing something. They would've seen the printouts first thing when they started searching downstairs. So, what were they still looking for upstairs?"

Shadow shrugged. "I'm sure by now it's well known that we have the files from the private investigator. They might have been looking for those."

"And, didn't find them. You may be right."

Shadow sighed. "At least you had the foresight to mail those pages to Green. Have you heard anymore from him on his investigation?"

"No. Not yet. I'll check my computer again a little later."

"Okay." Shadow glanced up at him with a sudden thought. "You're not going to call the cops about this break in, are you?"

Raven's laugh was ironic. "What good would it do? They couldn't find their rear from a hole in the ground much less find out who broke into our home."

"You've got that right. In that case, let's clear this mess up. Right now, I can't make heads or tails of anything else they might have stolen." Shadow said as she pushed away from the door.

"I've got a quick phone call to make and then I'll help you," Raven said.

Shadow nodded and with a determined stride she began tackling the kitchen.

* * *

Collins cursed to blue heaven, his red face livid. A vein throbbed strongly in his neck. "What do you mean you didn't find the papers? What in the hell am I paying you for?" he yelled into the phone. He listened for a moment longer before slamming the phone back into its cradle.

How could he have been so stupid to hang on to those files? He had been so careful until now. He was screwed.

A shaky hand reached inside the bottom drawer and pulled out a bottle of his finest Irish whiskey. Pushing aside his shot glass Collins popped the cork and took a long swig straight from the bottle. He wiped the moisture from his mouth with the back of his hand before bringing the bottle back up to his lips for another long drink.

Replacing the whiskey back into its hideaway he leaned back in his chair with his eyes closed willing his volatile nerves to calm.

Damn. He had to be in court in two hours in the next town to defend a client on theft charges. He needed a sharp mind to get him off.

It was going to be a tough case without Ben residing as judge, Collins thought. Hell, he knew the guy was guilty. He was the one who had hired him to break into a home and plant some damaging evidence while making it look like a theft.

If he didn't need the guy for further jobs he'd send him down the river for being stupid enough to get caught. But, he did need him and the guy wouldn't think twice about squealing like a pig to the authorities with the name of who had hired him if he went to the pen.

A whiskeyed grin appeared. Two more jobs, three at the most and the guy would be a feast for those hungry alligators in the swamp and no longer a threat.

One thing at a time, he thought as his nerves calmed enough to rationalize. First, he had to get his client off scot-free and then hire him to find the missing investigator reports since the last guy was an incompetent fool.

Collins leaned forward and found his clients file on his desk. He began reading through his notes. He couldn't afford to lose this one.

* * *

Shadow pushed a strand of hair from her face. With hands on her hips she looked around her father's office she had just finished putting back in order. She was weary to the bone. She'd waited to the last to tackle the worst room destroyed from the break in.

Going through and organizing her father's papers scattered across the floor, seeing his familiar handwriting on his business forms had been heartbreaking. So much had happened in less than a week since her father's funeral and yet, it seemed like a lifetime since she'd been mourning his death.

She rubbed the aching muscles in her neck. She was tired and dirty, but finally finished with every room. Her stomach growled making her realize she'd missed lunch.

Reaching out, she flipped the light switch off and left the room to find Raven. She had left him upstairs a couple of hours before attacking the damage to the bedrooms.

Shadow's steps slowed as she began thinking about the man upstairs and the new stage of their relationship. What do you do, she wondered, about a man who is in your every thought? One whom you crave beyond belief to be near? One whom you trust with your life? One who brings you to unlimited heights mentally and physically? A man you've known for most of your life? One who you can laugh with, fight with, cry with? Love....?

Shadow came to a standstill and she fell back against the door. Her knees weakened and her heart raced. Her fingers covered her trembling lips. Damn! Damn! Damn! This wasn't supposed to have happened. No man. No misery. Especially, no Raven. Remember?

Maybe it was just the good...No...great sex last night that she loved about him. Maybe her heart wasn't involved at all. Yeah. Right. Shadow sighed. She could lie to herself all day long, but the truth would remain the same. She had fallen completely in love with Raven. Again.

She could no longer pass her emotions off as a young girl's long infatuation with an older man. His first touch, first kiss had pushed it way passed that. His sweet thoughtfulness, courage and family loyalty, his smile and wit and breathtaking good looks had weaved themselves straight into her adult heart.

So, now what? She was in love with a man who would never know how she feels about him. She would never allow her love to tie him down to McClane Ridge. His business took him all over the world into dangerous situations. He loved the thrill of adventure his own business gave him. Raven would

Shadow's Justice

never be happy with the 9:00 to 5:00 mundane job at the family's construction sight on an every day basis. Nor, would he ever allow her to accompany him on his dangerous missions.

So, that would leave her at home worrying and waiting for his safe return. And furthermore, she wasn't about to sit at home and wait on any man, especially a husband she would be tied down to till death us do part. She had her own life to live and she was used to living it the way she wanted. She didn't need any macho man trying to run her life for her.

Shadow took several deep breaths and blew them out. A wide grin split her face. Here she stood with her temper rising high enough to have a stroke over a marriage that would never happen. For all she knew, Raven would hightail it out of town if he ever suspected she was in love with him. She ought to know from experience the only emotion Raven would ever feel for her was lust. So there.

Shadow's grin faded. But damn, the dream of 'happy ever after' was good while it lasted for that one precious moment.

CHAPTER NINE

Shadow and Raven sat in the living room that night pouring over the telephone records when the doorbell rang.

Shadow glanced with a nervous look at the door. The robbery had spooked her more than she had realized. "Who could that be at this time of night?"

Raven stood and reached out his hand for the pistol lying on the table beside him. "I'll go see." His hand held the gun steady to his side as he opened the front door.

Shadow saw a derelict standing in the doorway. She stood and started toward Raven. The man's clothes were filthy and torn. His dark, oily hair with gray streaks hung flat to his head. A long, dirt-brown, tangled beard covered the bottom half of his face. The man could have been twenty years old or ninety. She couldn't tell. This was the first homeless person she had seen up close and in person and he was standing at her front door.

Shadow watched as Raven pulled the man inside and shut the door behind him. Her uneasiness changed to disbelief as he pulled the stranger into his arms with a heavy-duty, backslapping greeting.

"You made a quick trip. I didn't look for you until

in the morning," Raven told the man.

The man grinned. "Didn't take me long to get dressed and the traffic was light from the airport."

Raven laughed and turned toward Shadow. "Shadow, I want you to meet my good friend and right-hand man, Bob Green. Bob, this is Shadow."

"It's nice to finally meet you, Shadow. Raven has talked a lot about you." Bob took a step forward to shake her hand.

Still at a loss, Shadow returned the greeting with a half smile. "It's nice to meet you, too. I'm sorry if I seem a little flabbergasted, but I wasn't expecting anyone."

Raven laughed. "What she is trying to say is she wasn't expecting a bum to show up at her door."

Raven turned to Shadow. "This is one of Bob's many covers. He's an expert in disguising himself. I called him this morning after we got back and found our home had been demolished. I clued him in on everything that's been going on for the last couple of days and asked him to come as quick as he could. We're going to need some outside help. I thought he would be able to move around a lot more freely than we can and no one knows him here."

"People tend to ignore homeless people and may say or do something that will be useful to our case," Bob added.

"Well, I for one will be thankful for your help," Shadow told him. "There's only one problem that I can see."

"What's that?" Bob asked.

"There has never been a homeless person in McClane Ridge that I know of. Won't people notice you even more because you are an oddity in town?

This isn't the big city, boys."

"That's true. But they'll only see the bum for a couple of days, a drifter passing through. Then there will be the salesman stopping for lunch. A service man heading home, a motorcycle rider renting a motel room for the night..."

"Okay. I get the picture." Shadow threw up her hands and laughed. "Have you eaten?"

"No. I didn't take the time to stop."

"You're probably starving then. I'll go to the kitchen and warm up the leftovers from dinner while you two talk. Raven can show you to your room."

"I don't want to be any trouble."

Shadow waved away his concern. "It's no trouble. I'll be back shortly."

"Thank you." Bob watched her as she left the room. "Mmmmm. Nice. Is your friend available?"

"You know damn well she's not just a friend. She is Michael's stepsister and no...she's not available." Raven growled and glared at his friend.

Bob's laughter reverberated throughout the room. "So, that's the way the wind blows. I thought so. I'd already figured that out by the sexual electricity running between the two of you. I was getting a sexual charge just by watching you."

A sheepish grin emerged. "That obvious, huh?"

"Oh, yeah!"

Raven laughed. "Well, since we're getting so personal here, you can clue me in on your love life while I show you to your room."

Bob's teasing grin faded. "That will take about two seconds. My love life at this moment is to my unfortunate fate, nil...nada...nonexistent."

Raven opened the door to the spare bedroom and

glanced at his friend in concern. "What happened to Maria? I thought you two were planning a big wedding?"

Bob entered and threw his bag on the floor. He pulled the wig off his head and rubbed his hand over his brown, military style haircut before turning back to Raven. With a dry tone, he answered. "Maria is history. After dating for two years, planning a big wedding, she decides three weeks before the big day that she's going to elope with the manager of a department store she works for. She said she needed a husband who would be at home every night. She wanted a stable life that she would never have with me and the job I have."

"Man, I'm sorry. I know you cared for her. Why didn't you call me? You didn't need to be going through something like that by yourself."

Bob shrugged. "I'm okay. I had a rough couple of days, but I bounced back. Besides, you've got enough problems going on without having to deal with mine, too. I know you tried to warn me about Maria's clinging ways and I wouldn't listen. I wish to hell I had."

"In your case, I was hoping my assessment of her was dead wrong. You know I will always have the time to help friends out. You've been there for me before, man."

"I know. I just needed time to think. After a couple of days, I realized she'd actually done me a favor. I still don't know if I really loved Maria or if she'd just become a habit in my hectic life. I do know I wasn't willing to give up my job to stay home behind a white picket fence and work at a dead end job for the rest of my life."

Shadow's Justice

"She didn't know you or love you well enough to ever suggest you would. Me and you, we're a special breed. It will take very special women to understand our need for excitement and adventure. We make damn good money at what we do and most of the time we're doing a good deed in the process. The best we will ever be able to do is give our women our love and support when we're home and expect them to love and support us while we're away on a mission. I would never expect to control my wife and I wouldn't tolerate her trying to control me by insisting I close down my company and stay home."

Raven heard a gasp behind him. Turning he saw Shadow standing in the doorway, her face a pale. He took a step toward her. "Shadow, what's wrong?"

Shadow shook her head and took an unsteady step back. She forced a weak smile to her face. "Nothing's wrong. I just came to tell Bob his dinner is ready whenever he is."

Bob smiled toward Shadow. "Thanks. I'll be right there."

With only a nod, Shadow turned and left. Her heart brimmed with hope that Raven would never know how much his last words to his friend had wounded her soul.

* * *

John Tolliver pushed his hardhat back on his head and studied the thirty acres of overgrown field situated on the outskirts of McClane Ridge he stood on. The high ground appeared solid and dry. Old man Fletcher's land would make a prime location for the new owners.

An old, tumbling down shack sat right smack dab in the middle of the thirty acres that would have to be removed. A lot of bulldozing would need to be done, but the spot wouldn't need much dirt hauled in to fill, he thought. They should be able to wipe the job out in a few days and then they could begin on the construction.

He turned to the five men standing beside him and smiled. "Well, gentlemen. You've bought yourself some top-quality land for your new hotel. I'll bring in the heavy equipment tomorrow and we can start clearing. Before you know it, we'll be staring up at a five star hotel brimming with guests."

* * *

Shadow could feel Ravens piercing gaze directed toward her from across the kitchen table. She refused to look up from her breakfast plate to give him the satisfaction of seeing her puffy eyes that makeup failed to hide.

Instead, she brought the fork to her mouth. She chewed and swallowed without interest. The bite of eggs could have been cardboard for all she cared.

Bob's silence told her he was very aware of the tension in the room. Shadow expected him to bolt at anytime, leaving her alone with Raven.

She figured she had only minutes to spare before she would be forced to explain to Raven her bizarre actions. Telling him why she had turned him away from her bedroom last night and then her unusual silence this morning would be difficult. Even though her heart was breaking, he deserved an honest answer and she would give him one. She had no doubt he would be in total agreement when he heard her explanation.

Shadow heard Bob's chair scrape across the floor. Her head jerked toward him and she forced a smile.

Shadow's Justice

"Shadow, thanks for breakfast. I don't get home-cooked meals very often. It was delicious."

"You're welcome. Are you leaving?"

"Yeah. I've got to go upstairs and get into my working clothes. It won't be long before people will start stirring. If I wait much longer someone might see me." He turned toward Raven. "Give me ten minutes and I'll meet you in the garage."

Raven nodded and Bob left to get ready. Raven clued Bob in last night on everything that happened so far. They decided the tavern would be the perfect location to start his snooping.

Their plan required Raven to hide Bob inside the car and drive him to the opposite side of town. Bob would get out and make his way back on foot into town. He would be living on the streets for the next couple of days observing McClane Ridge's dirty, little secrets.

Raven pushed back from the table and stood. Placing both hands flat on the table he leaned over until he towered over Shadow. His piercing green eyes told her more than his words. "We will have a talk when I get back," Raven warned before pivoting on his heels and walking out of the room.

A reprieve. Shadow's hand shook. She tucked a strand of hair behind her ear and sighed. She stood and began clearing away the breakfast dishes. Stacking the dishwasher with plates, Shadow let her mind wage a war between her heart and common sense.

She loved Raven. Plain and simple. She didn't need time to think if what she felt for him was true. She knew. Loving him was as natural as breathing and equally crucial to exist. She would go through life knowing another man could never replace him in her heart. She also knew what she had felt for him at sixteen would never compare to this.

Did love always happen like this, she wondered? Creeping up on your heart while you least expect it? Shadow shook her head. Hell, it didn't creep up on her. It had body slammed her.

Shadow had so many questions about love and no answers. She needed another woman's input and wished Rose was there to advise her on love and relationships. She would give her a call later and have a long chat, she decided.

There was one thing she did know. From the conversation she'd heard the night before, marriage was completely out of the question. Hearing Raven confirm what she already knew had still hit her hard as a freight train. It took her breath away. Her hope away.

She knew by his sensual gazes and his constant touching that he desired her. She could always remain his lover, accepting him in her bed the two or three times he came home a year or flying out to meet him on occasions. He would still be a huge part of her life outside of marriage.

That is until he fell in love and married a woman who could be everything to him. A woman who was willing to be patient and sit home with their children day after day waiting on her man to return home from dangerous missions. Then Shadow would fade from his life.

It seems to be her unfortunate fate to always lose the men she loved.

* * *

Police Chief Edwin Walker fidgeted with the badge pinned to his jacket. His quick gaze shifted back and forth from one viewpoint to another as the bulldozers were unloaded from the trailers on the edge of town. Their motors roared loud into the stillness of the country.

The Police Chief dug into his pocket and pulled out his handkerchief, mopping the beaded sweat from his brow. "Lord have mercy, because all hell is about to break loose," he muttered.

He turned and took two steps toward his squad car before a sharp pain near the region of his heart had him frantic and clutching at his chest. He fell to his knees fighting for breath and then he knew nothing.

* * *

Raven unlocked the front door and started looking for Shadow. He walked into the kitchen and found her wiping the counters down. Her hand moved the rag in circles over and over in the same spot.

"Shadow?"

Startled, Shadow's head jerked toward the door. "Oh, you're back." Her head lowered and she attacked the countertop, once again.

Raven walked to where she was standing and with gentle hands took the dishrag away from her. "We have to talk." He led her to the table and pulled the chair out for her to sit. He sat down across from her and leaned forward, resting his arms on top of the table.

"Do you want to tell me what's going on, because for the life of me, I can't figure out what I've done to upset you."

Shadow blew out a sigh and leaned back in her chair. Her time had run out. Pushing her wayward hair back from her face, she glanced up at him ready to confront the problem head on. "You've done nothing."

"Then, why are you upset?"

"I'm upset, because I've finally figured out that a relationship between the two of us is impossible."

Raven leaned closer. His words became ominously quiet. "And how, pray tell, did you come to this conclusion?"

Shadow's bravery diminished for just a second before she rallied back. Hiding her hurt behind angry, quiet words, she leaned forward, almost nose to nose with Raven. "If you had the sense God gave a goose, you would come to the same conclusion. I won't be a man's whore. And I damn sure won't marry a man and sit at home month after month waiting on him to come home to me for a short visit before he's off and running again.

I'd already figured that one out before I overheard you overshooting your mouth to Bob about how you would never give up your business for any woman. So, get this into you thick head. This woman won't be asking you to give up you business."

Raven leaned back in his chair. He felt like he'd been stomach punched by her words. He ran his hand over his short hair while he tried to figure out how in the heck she'd come up with her off-the-wall reasoning.

Evidently, she'd overheard his consoling, conversation with Bob last night and had come up with her own brilliant conclusions.

Raven pinched his bottom lip as he eyed her with wariness. She was in a humdinger of a fighting mood.

Good. He grinned. "I don't recall asking you to."

She began sputtering, her eyes flashing fire. Oh, he was going to enjoy this.

"So, are you saying I'm nothing more than a one

night stand to you?" she asked through clenched teeth.

"Oh baby, I'll want more than just one night with you."

She smirked. "Dream on, Raven lunatic. Hell will freeze over before that happens."

He leaned forward and winked. "I don't think so, my Shady Lady. Admit it. You want me right now."

Despondent, Shadow stood to leave before the tears began to fall. "When you're ready to take this conversation seriously, let me know." She swept past Raven and was brought up short by his hand reaching out and grabbing her arm. With one jerk, she landed in his lap.

Raven held her still. All playfulness fled. "Stop fighting, Shadow. You've had your say and now you're going to listen to me."

With a gentleness Shadow had come to expect, Raven turned her face until he was staring into the liquid pools of her eyes. "What you overheard me saying to Bob about relationships was my way of consoling him. The woman he was involved with was a loser and a leach. She admitted being after his money and didn't give a damn how she went about getting it or who she hurt in the bargain. The only thing that pissed her off was that he wasn't around to take her to all of the 'social events' of the season. She wanted to be seen, to fit into the rich and famous 'elite' circle.

So, she looked around and found another man with money and one who was always there to take her out and pant after her like a dog in heat. When she found him, she dropped Bob like a hot potato.

If I had given Bob one notion I believed she would

go back to him if he quit his job, I'm afraid he would have. Bob is the brightest man I know, except when it comes to this woman. He was that crazy about her and too blind to see how she was using him. So..."

Shadow finished his sentence. "So, you poured it on thick about how you wouldn't allow any woman to dictate to you about closing down your business and staying at home. And this was to keep Bob from leaving his job?"

Raven nodded. "Exactly."

"That's the stupidest thing I've ever heard."

Raven grinned and shrugged. "It worked, didn't it?"

Shadow laughed and Raven's heart clenched. His tender hand cupped her cheek. "Forgive me?"

Elated and past caring about them not having a future together, Shadow nodded and with a feline grace, she leaned her face further into his hand. "Kiss me." Her tongue brushed along his palm.

With a shiver and a smile packed with sin and sensuality, he answered. "Believe me, sweetheart. It will be my pleasure and I plan to turn it into yours, as well," he whispered as his mouth lowered to hers.

With a bone-melting, passionate kiss only Raven could master, he proved his statement over and over, again as they climbed the stairs and entered her bedroom.

CHAPTER TEN

Screeching to the curb in her car like a bat out of hell, Stacy Chandler threw on her brakes and skidded to a stop. Killing the motor, she threw open the door and stepped out of her red convertible.

"Dammit!" Stacy cursed under her breath, glancing down at her watch. She was twenty minutes late for her meeting inside the tavern. If her informant had given up on her and left before she could talk to him, she might wring his neck. It had taken her days to set up this meeting.

Stacy took a hurried step toward the tavern's door and went flying when she tripped over a large object lying unnoticed in front of her feet.

With flaying arms and fancy leg movements she fell in an undignified heap, landing full length on top of something unyielding and warm. And yelling out obscenities toward her.

"Dammit, lady. What are you trying to do, kill me?"

Stunned, but unhurt, Stacy raised one hand and raked back her long, blonde hair that had fallen forward and now covered her face.

She was almost nose to nose with the stranger while she stared down into the most incredible pair of electric, blue eyes that she'd ever seen on any man. Blue eyes that stared right back at her with the same growing interest.

Her gaze drifted down further and landed on a set of full, wickedly sexy, kissable lips. Without thinking, her tongue glided across her own lips in anticipation.

She heard him moan. "Lady, as much as I'm enjoying this, you might want to get off of me before I end up embarrassing both of us." His hips rose in demonstration.

Mortified into anger at her own crazy behavior, Stacy scrambled to her feet, her hands busy straightening her designer clothes. "What in the hell do you think you're doing by lying on the sidewalk with your legs sprawled out like that? I could have been seriously hurt. Are you drunk or just plain crazy, mister?"

That's when she glanced up and for the first time with clear eyes, she saw the man who stood up during her tirade.

A long, dirty beard covered the bottom half of his face. His second-hand clothes covering his tall physique and broad shoulders were filthy and torn. Dark, oily hair hung flat to his head. His wide grin showed off his pearly white teeth and he really smelled good.

He bowed low at the waist. "Let me introduce myself. My name is Bob. I believe we know each other well enough now to be on first name basis, don't you?"

Stacy's hand flew to her mouth and her loud screech filled the air.

* * *

Judge Adams savored the last bite of pecan pie he

was eating for lunch. Laying his fork on his plate, he reached for his napkin and dabbed at the crumbs on his mouth. Looking up, he frowned, his heavy jowls lowering into a grimace as his new housekeeper entered the dining room.

"You have a phone call, Judge. It's Mr. Collins." She handed him the phone.

"I thought I told you I didn't want to be disturbed," he growled.

"I'm sorry, sir. He said it was important."

"What I say is always more important. Don't ever forget that, Susan. You can leave now." His puffy eyes gazed lustily over her young, firm body dressed in the tight uniform he insisted she wore. He laughed when she made a hasty retreat from the room.

He looked forward to the day when she would be in his bed as he pounded hot and hard inside her while living out his lustful fantasies. It didn't really make him a shit whether she came to him willingly or by force like the last one before her.

They were all alike. Too damn scared of his power in the town to open their mouths and tell anyone what went on under his roof or to quit his employment until he was finished with them. A few mild threats went a long way.

Grinning in anticipation, he brought the phone to his ear and spoke. "Yeah. What do you want?"

"Walker's had a heart attack. He's at the McClane Medical Center," Collins reported without preamble.

Judge Adams leaned forward, clutching the phone to his ear. "How bad is he?"

"I don't know. The doctors are still with him. But that's not our immediate worry."

"What else has happened?" Judge Adam's asked,

edgily. Damn, but he didn't have time for this crap.

"Walker's deputy called. He said that he'd gone looking for Walker when he couldn't get him on the radio. He found him right outside of town on the edge of old man Fletcher's land sprawled out on the ground beside his car and called 911."

Collins hesitated as if readying himself for the explosion. A slight tremor could be heard in his voice. "He said a construction crew was there with several bulldozers and other heavy equipment pushing up dirt and leveling the ground."

Judge Adams swore.

* * *

Under the cover of night, Bob sat in the shadows with his back against the tavern's front wall. One leg was raised, his arm dangling off his knee.

The town was quiet, even for a weekday. Only a handful of men had entered the rustic bar during the past hour. None had left. Only a couple glanced his way. Inside the tavern he could hear the shouts and cheers from the patrons as a television announcer broadcasted another touchdown for their favorite football team.

Nothing suspicious going on tonight. Two more hours and it would be midnight and the tavern would shut down. And, only then would he sneak off into the night.

But, until then the quiet solitude gave his mind time to wander. He still didn't know the name of the sensuous blonde tornado who literally fell into his arms.

For the first time in years, his interest had been awakened, stirring up his senses, one by one. For only a few seconds while gazing into her eyes, he'd forgotten what he had become, what he'd always wanted to be. He bragged on being a fighting machine with a mission and no emotional garbage hanging around his neck to weigh him down.

For those mere seconds, he'd reacted as a man who felt his frozen heart begin to crack. And for once in his life, he'd actually considered letting his mystery lady thaw his heart out completely.

* * *

Chances are life won't get any better than this, Shadow thought as one sexual climax after another rocked her world. Her body continued moving on top of Raven's in an age old rhythm until she heard his answering moan and felt his explosion inside of her.

Shadow's head fell forward, her hair flowing sensually across Raven's chest, her lips trembling against his wet skin. She felt his hand moving soothingly up and down her back as he held her tight against him.

Long moments passed as they lay as one. No unnecessary words were spoken, only whispered endearments. Words she wanted...no, needed for Raven to hear and to hear from him.

A deep imbedded fear of losing him resurfaced. Shadow felt uneasy all through the night as they made love or just lay in each other's arms. She'd pushed her fears from her mind, but her anxiety still lingered.

She wanted to cling to him and hold him close, but instead, she rolled to face his side with one knee lying across his midsection. She watched as his eyelids drifted down in sleep. The morning light played soft across his face showing a boyish innocence that hardened as he turned into a man.

Shadow knew Raven would laugh and tease her if

she expressed her fears out loud. But, call it a woman's intuition. Something was about to happen.

* * *

Stacy turned off her computer and sat back in her chair in deep, troubled thoughts. What she had just read didn't make sense. She'd read the article over and over because she couldn't believe it and even printed off the report to reread. She shook her head. It had to be a mistake even though it was right there in black and white.

Stacy reached for the phone and dialed. Two minutes later, she hung the phone back up. She had her confirmation. It was un'damn'believeably true.

She reached for her purse and car keys, grabbed the printed sheets of paper and a letter off her desk and rushed from the office.

Twenty minutes later, she stood on the doorsteps of Shadow's and Raven's home ringing the doorbell.

Without a hello, she swept through the door and past Shadow as she held the door open.

"Where's Raven? We've got to talk."

Shadow raised a brow, but only replied, "He's in the kitchen. We were eating breakfast. Care to join us?"

Stacy never glanced back at her friend as she walked into the kitchen. "Only, if you're serving stiff drinks."

Sitting down across the table from Raven, Stacy looked up in time to see an amused glance pass between the two. Their expression quickly disappeared when her fire-spitting glare singed them both.

"Oh, oh. What's got your panties in a wad?" Raven asked as he continued eating.

"This." Stacy shoved the opened letter to the center of the table.

Raven laid his fork down. Reaching for the sheet of paper, he began reading. He felt Shadow's hand on his shoulder while she stood behind him leaning over to read it, as well.

"Son of a ...!" The quiet expletive flew from Raven's lips as he finished reading.

"How accurate is this?" Shadow asked, rounding the table. She had to sit down.

"One hundred percent accurate. I triple checked." Stacy pushed back her hair with trembling fingers before reaching across the table to pick up the handwritten letter.

Stacy began reading out loud. "Miss Chandler. You don't know me, but my father passed away 6 months ago. I have only recently found this following letter that he wrote and addressed to you. He died before he was able to mail it to you. I think that you should have this. I sincerely hope this doesn't get to you too late."

"This person's father wrote," Stacy read on.

"How does this sound for your Front Page headline? "JACK McCLANE IS INNOCENT OF MURDER!"

"I have proof, girlie. I saw a murder with my own eyes. I may be an old man, but I'm not stupid. I've lived this long by keeping my mouth shut and by moving the way hell out of town. But, I'm dying, anyway. Can't beat this damn worn out heart of mine. Yet, I can't go to my grave knowing what I know without trying to clear Jack's name."

"But, please understand that I can not put the rest of my family in jeopardy. That's why I can't give you my name or full details. I can tell you this. To solve the banker's murder in McClane Ridge you will have to look to the past. You work at the newspaper office, girlie. Should be easy for you.

I remember the date and the headline just like it was yesterday. August 6th, 1950. "GIRL VISITING GRANDPARENTS GOES MISSING!"

"Look to the Brotherhood, girlie."

Stacy laid the letter on the table. "There was no return address." She leaned her face into her hands and vigorously rubbed before throwing her hands back to the table in frustration and helplessness. "Not that it matters. It arrived too damn late to help your father. I'm so sorry, Shadow. Are you okay?" She glanced up in concern.

Shadow swallowed a sob. Tears glistened on the surface, but none fell. Raven's hand pulled her head to his shoulder and she leaned on him feeling his love so strong that it made her raging emotions calm.

Taking a deep breath, she nodded. "I'll be fine. I'm pissed as hell at our crappy fate on one hand and on the other hand very grateful to the old man who tried to help. It's just our bad luck he died too soon. At least the son was kind enough to forward the letter on to you."

"You said you checked out the information. What did you find?" Raven asked Stacy.

Stacy pulled a sheet of paper from her purse and handed it to Raven. "This. I made a copy of the newspaper article. I found it on the third page of the newspaper. It was such a small article that I almost didn't see it. Basically, it's just saying a young fifteen year old girl visiting her grandparents for the summer came up missing. The local law enforcement was investigating."

Shadow stood and poured coffee for the three. "Do you know if they found her?"

Stacy shook her head. "No. I haven't had a chance to look. I came straight over here when I got the letter and printed off the article."

Raven pushed back from the table and stood. "Looks like we've got some investigating to do. You girls with me?"

Stacy stood and grabbed her purse. "You bet."

"Hey. Where's everybody going?"

Stacy stopped in her tracks. She felt her knees weaken. That voice. She would know it anywhere. She raised her head and glanced at the newcomer standing in the doorway.

If she hadn't recognized the voice, she would have known the electric blue eyes and wickedly sexy mouth, anywhere. Even without the grungy clothes and matted beard. Her eyes widened. She pointed a finger toward the man. "You!"

Bob glanced away from Raven and saw the blonde bombshell for the first time since walking into the kitchen. He sucked in an astonished breath and almost choked. "You!"

Raven glanced at Shadow and she shrugged.

"Do you two know each other?" Shadow asked.

"He tripped me on main street." Stacy accused.

"She had her nose so high in the air that she didn't see me and fell over my feet."

"You tripped me."

"You fell on top of me."

Stacy turned to glare at Shadow. "What is he doing here?"

"What is she doing here?" Bob asked Raven.

Shadow's Justice

Shadow threw one hand out. "That's enough, you two. Stacy, this is a friend of Raven's, Bob Green. Bob, this is a close friend of mine, Stacy Chandler. I hope...." Shadow's words turned into a scream.

Earth shattering explosions rocked the town.

CHAPTER ELEVEN

Sirens wailed in the distance. Red balls of flames shot straight up to the sky toward the west of town. People stood on their sidewalks holding on to their loved ones and whispering and wondering amongst themselves. A terrible dread settled over them all.

Raven took in their faces showing shock and despair as the four of them flew out of the front door and rush to his car. He threw his car into reverse, backing out into the street before changing gears and floorboarding it toward the edge of town, speeding toward their new construction sight.

* * *

All Raven could think about was John. He knew John was always the first to arrive at the sights and the last to leave. He could hear Shadow on her cell phone talking to Michael and knew he was on his way, as well.

A few minutes later they pulled up to the sight. Chaos was running rampant. Two ambulances were already there, setting up at a safe location with their medical teams working on the injured.

Firefighters were busy hosing down out-of-control flames erupting from four destroyed bulldozers. Firewalls were being cut as quick as humanly possible.

Shadow's Justice

As they looked on, another fuel tank from a fifth dozer exploded. Fire began to spread through the overgrown grass in the field adjoining the sight and became the next backbreaking task for the firefighters.

Raven and his companions threw open their car doors and started running toward the bedlam. Stacy grabbed her camera from around her neck and with rapid clicks began recording the scene to film while the other three began searching for John.

The closer they got to the scene the more the moans from the injured and the emergency in the crew's voices could be heard.

Raven ran up to one medical team and asked. "Has anyone seen John?" They glanced up for a second and shook their heads no before returning their attention to their patient. Raven ran to the next and then to the next getting the same response from each.

"Raven. Over here." Raven looked up as he heard Shadow call his name. She stood beside another group waving her arms to get his attention.

Raven ran toward her. "Did you find him?"

Shadow glanced up, unable to hide her fear. "They've already rushed him to the hospital." Her voice caught. "They said it was bad."

Raven's expression darkened. "Let's go."

They turned to leave and saw Bob rushing toward them. "Did you find him?"

"Yes. He's at the hospital. Michael should be here at any minute. Will you stay and let him know where we're going?" Raven asked.

Bob clamped a reassuring hand on Raven's shoulder. "You bet. I'll stick around here and see what I can find out and get a ride with Stacy and her photographer. I'll check in with you later at the hospital."

"Thanks, man." Raven reached for Shadow's hand. They ran to the car.

A few minutes later they pulled up at the hospital.

Hurrying into the crowded Emergency Room, Raven asked the nurse at the front desk about John.

The nurse looking haggard checked her records. "Here it is." She looked up at Raven. "I'm sorry, but Mr. Tolliver is in surgery now. If you will have a seat in the waiting room, Dr. Roberts will be with you as soon as possible to let you know how he is doing."

Raven wanted to curse. He wanted to slam his fist into something or someone and to demand some answers from the nurse concerning John's injuries. He felt Shadow's calming touch on his elbow and resisted doing any of those things. With a somber thank you to the nurse, Raven led Shadow into the waiting room.

Several worried families of the victims from the explosions sat around talking in hushed tones amongst themselves. They looked up and saw Raven and Shadow enter. One of the fathers stood and approached them. "What in the hell happened out there, Raven?"

Raven shook his head. "I honestly don't know, Joe." His gaze scanned the rest of the families. His voice rose to be heard. "But, I promise everyone in here I will find out. I also want to promise you that our company will take care of all the financial burdens involved that your insurance doesn't cover. You will have enough worries for awhile."

Shadow stepped forward and hugged Joe. "Has the doctor came out and told you anything about your

Shadow's Justice

son, yet?"

Joe nodded. "Yes, he came out a few minutes ago and said they were putting Jason into a room and they would come out and let us know when we can go in to see him. He has second degree burns on his hands, legs and face."

"Thank God. Those injuries are bad enough, but they could have been so much worse," Shadow said.

Joe nodded. "It could've been a lot worse. How's John?"

"He's in surgery. We don't know anymore than that." Shadow's voice broke and then she gathered herself together and put on a brave front. As one of the owners of the company, she knew she had to stay strong for the other families.

Turning to the rest of the people, she checked on the reports of their injured ones and was thankful once again that most were minor injuries.

The door to the waiting room opened and Michael rushed through. With anxious strides he hurried toward Raven and Shadow's side. "How is he?"

"We don't know. He's still in surgery. We're waiting for the doctor to come out and tell us something," Raven answered giving his friend a quick hug.

"Damn. I don't understand. How did this happen?" Michael asked.

"We don't know. Yet." Raven said. "Come on. Let's all sit down over there for awhile. I don't know about you two, but I could use some caffeine. Can I get either one of you anything?"

"I'll take a cup." Shadow answered.

"None for me, thanks." Michael said. He sat down beside Shadow and pulled her close. "How are you holding up, kid?"

"Oh, other than being scared and pissed, I'm okay." Shadow gave him a watery smile. "How about you?"

"The same. I would feel a lot better if the doctor would come out and let us know something."

"Hopefully it won't take long," Raven said as he returned with their coffee. Handing one to Shadow, he sat down on the other side of her giving her a reassuring smile. He would've liked nothing more than to pull her into his arms and holding on tight to comfort her, but he resisted the need. They had yet to tell the family of their new relationship and now wasn't the right time.

Shadow glanced from Michael to Raven and sighed. "I hope you know that we can't keep something like this from Rose. She's will want to come home."

Raven groaned. "Damn. This is all we need. But, you're right. We need to call her."

"I'll call her," Shadow said and stood to leave the waiting room for privacy.

Raven waited until she left the room before turning to Michael and spoke. Coiled anger was no longer suppressed. "You do realize this wasn't an accident?"

Michael nodded. "I know. Bob said to tell you he would report back to you later today and let you know what he digs up."

"Until we know what in the hell is going on, you need to take extra cautions when you go back out to the site." Raven warned.

"I will and I'll have a talk with our workers this evening. They need to stay on their toes, as well."

"Tolliver family?"

Raven and Michael stood and hurried toward the doctor standing in the waiting room doorway. Shadow quickly hung up the phone and joined them.

How is John?" Raven asked, worry evident in his voice. He shook hands with the elderly doctor.

The doctor smiled with reassurance. "John will be fine. He's a very lucky man. He has a mild concussion and a couple of places on his arms with second degree burns. With time, he will recover easily with those problems. But, what has me concerned is the deep gash down his leg. I had to clean a lot of metal out of the wound before sewing him back up. I would like to keep him in the hospital for a couple of days under observation to make sure that no infection sets up with the gash or the burns."

Shadow released the breath she was holding in relief. The injuries were bad, but not life threatening. "Can we see him?"

The doctor nodded. "Yes, but only for about 5 minutes. He is sedated and won't be very responsive right now. You can visit longer tomorrow after he's had some rest. The nurse will show you his room."

"Thank you, doctor." Raven shook the doctor's hand. The three of them followed the nurse to John's room.

They entered the hospital room where John lay in his bed looking like hell warmed over. His head was wrapped in gauze and ugly bruises were starting to appear on his face. The red, puckered burns splattered across the top of his arms were left bare of any covering other than the medication creams. His left leg was wrapped in gauze and pulled up in a sling to dangle in the air. He looked like he'd met his match in a fight and had lost.

Shadow's Justice

"John?" Shadow's voice shook as she moved to his side.

John's heavy eyes lifted. "Shadow?" His tongue ran across his dry lips. He saw Raven and Michael approaching the bed. "What happened?"

Shadow lifted the water pitcher from the stand beside the bed and poured some water into a glass. She dipped a napkin into the water and pressed it to his lips and let him moisten his mouth. "There was an explosion at the sight. The doctor said you will be fine, but he wants to keep you for a couple of days for observation."

John's eyes started drooping closed, his words slurring. "Too dangerous...promise me that every one of you will be careful." He was asleep before he heard their words of assurances.

* * *

Raven and Shadow stood by their car outside the hospital. They watched Michael drive off, heading back to his office.

Raven looked down at Shadow and crooked his finger at her. "Come here."

Shadow walked into his safe and comforting arms and sighed as he held on tight. "How did you know I desperately needed to be in your arms, right now?"

"Because, I needed it, as well," Raven whispered, his chin resting on the top of her head.

"Oh, Raven. What are we going to do? I think we need to give up the investigation. It's not worth someone else getting killed over. John and the others almost died today." Her voice quivered.

Raven shook his head. "I think it's gone too far for us to back off, now. The killer is getting desperate and scared. He would always believe that at one point we might find out the truth and tell the authorities."

"So, what do we do?"

Raven's lips brushed across her hair. "Are you up to driving back out to the sight?"

"Yeah." Her head nodded against his chest. "I'm anxious to see what Bob and Stacey found out."

"Me, too. Let's go." Raven stepped back and opened the car door for Shadow. They drove toward the sight.

* * *

"Don't tell me how to do my job." Stacy stood with her hands on her hips glaring at Bob. That man just irritated the crap out of her.

"Stacy, my love, I'm not trying to tell you how to do your job. I was just suggesting that you might want a picture taken of those pieces of explosives scattered across the ground." Looking through her telescopic lens on her camera he'd borrowed to get a close up view of the debris, Bob's voice was calm as if he was talking to a rebellious teen.

Which made her angry enough to slap the composed look right off of his face. She pointed a finger in his face.

"First of all, don't call me your love and second of all…stay out of my way, Green." Stacy threatened through clenched teeth.

Turning back to her photographer, she spat out an order, "Get some shots of those." She turned and stomped away, missing the amused grin shared by the two men.

"Smooth move, Green."

Bob turned around and saw Raven and Shadow approaching. His only response to Raven's teasing was a shrug of his shoulder and a sheepish grin. "I didn't know you guys were back."

"We drove up just in time to watch the comedy played out in front of us." Raven told him.

"Very funny, Deveroux."

Shadow grinned, glad to get a reprieve from the gloom of the morning. "Leave him alone, Raven. Can't you see he's in loooove?"

Bob grinned. "It's more like lust at this moment, but who knows? With time, it might turn into love. Now, would you two like to talk about your love life or about what I've been able to find out here?"

Raven and Shadow spoke at the same time. "What you found."

"That's what I thought you'd say." Bob's features turned serious. "This has the earmark of a professional. Those explosives were handmade with hard to find materials. Not any Tom, Dick or Harry would know where to get the ingredients or how to assemble them. I would say it was someone who has been in the service trained in explosives or someone who has been in prison learning his trade from his street smart inmates. They knew exactly what they were doing."

Bob rubbed his chin in thought. "I would say that this was more of a scare tactic than anything. If it was anything else, there wouldn't be any witnesses to tell the tale."

Shadow paled.

Raven swore. "What else have you found?"

"Not much. The Fire Department pretty much took care of any foot or hand prints with their fire hoses. It doesn't really matter, though when you have hundreds of people stomping around the area taking care of any evidence that might've been there. Fine police department you have in this town. I didn't see one officer trying to quarantine the area for evidence. The fire inspectors came out about forty five minutes later and roped off the area and did their own investigation. Stacey asked them what they found and all she got was a "No Comment."

"That sounds about right. It's like watching a slapstick comedy when the police are around. They did show up, didn't they?" Raven asked.

"Yeah, the deputy Police Chief was walking around. He was the only one with any sense. I saw him questioning some of the witnesses. He wrote everything down in his book and left. I haven't seen him back out here," he reported.

Bob glanced down at Shadow. "I haven't had a chance to ask about John? Will he be alright?"

Shadow nodded. "Yes. The doctor said he will be fine. He has a few burns on his arms and a deep gash on his leg that will take time to heal, but he was lucky it wasn't any worse. All the other injured men will be okay, as well."

"Thank God, for that." Bob turned back to Raven. "If you don't need me out here anymore I'll catch a ride back to your place with Stacy. It's time for George, the salesman to wander around town and visit the tavern for awhile. Not much telling what he might hear if he listens hard enough."

"Go ahead. I'm going to look around while I'm here."

Saluting, Bob left to catch up with Stacy and her photographer.

Raven glanced around the area. He didn't know what he hoped to find, but he wasn't leaving until he was confident no crucial evidence was being left unnoticed. He touched Shadow's arm. "Let's start over there by that old shed and go from there." Stepping over the yellow tape, they made their way to the crumbling building.

An hour later, Raven gave up. They walked the entire construction site and found nothing helpful to the investigation.

"Damn." He swore beneath his breath. Why were the McClane's and the Tuckers being targeted? What common link connects the two families? Raven's thoughts were interrupted by the sound of a car approaching.

"Well, well, look who finally shows up. The big, bad Police Chief, himself," Shadow muttered.

"No. That looks like Paul getting out of the Police Chief's car. I guess Walker is too busy to bother with a small crime scene like this one." Raven watched as Deputy Police Chief, Paul LaCroix walked toward them.

"Paul, good to see you, man. I'd heard you'd moved up in the world." Raven told him as they shook hands. He hadn't seen his good friend from high school since he'd gotten back to town.

Paul laughed. "I guess if you can call more work and very little more pay as a Deputy Police Chief, moving up in the world, then I guess I have. But it's enough to keep my family fed. Speaking of which, Angie wants to know why you haven't come by to have dinner with us one night."

"Tell her I will, soon. It's been kind of hectic lately."

"Just make it soon or Angie will give us both hell." Paul grinned before turning to Shadow and giving her a hug. "Hey, kiddo. How are you holding up?"

Shadow shrugged. "As good as can be expected, I guess. This has been a total nightmare, Paul. Have you learned anything new?"

"No. I'm afraid not. I just came from the hospital where I interviewed the injured men. No one saw or heard anything before the explosions. I'm back to square one."

"Did you see John?" Shadow asked.

"No. The doctor said he was finally sleeping peacefully and he didn't want me to disturb him. He told me to come back tomorrow."

"He was sleeping when we left, so we decided to ride out here and look around. I figured Police Chief Walker would be out here stomping around messing up all the evidence."

Paul glanced down at her. "You haven't heard?"

"Heard what?"

"Police Chief Walker was out here yesterday and had a heart attack. I couldn't get him on the radio, so I drove out here and found him lying on the ground beside his car. He's in the emergency room in critical condition."

"Are you serious? That's horrible. Does the doctor think he will recover?"

"He's saying that he has a small chance to survive. They're still running tests to see if they can operate. He's too weak right now to have any type of surgery, but they're hoping they can keep him stabilized enough for later on this week."

"What was he doing out here yesterday, anyway?" Raven asked.

Paul shrugged. "I don't know. Curiosity, maybe? He came on the radio saying he was exiting the car at this location. That's the only way I knew where to look for him."

"No. I don't buy the curiosity bit. Walker doesn't do anything without a reason."

"Surely, you don't think he planted the bombs, do you?" Shadow asked.

Raven knew what she was asking. Walker was a big, bad Bubba, but one brick shy of a full load. He didn't have the intelligence to make a bomb and with a Police Chief's pay, he doubted he had the money to pay the street value of a ready-made bomb.

Raven shrugged. "Maybe not. I would still like to know what he was doing out here."

"Unless he gets strong enough to have surgery, we may never know." Paul threw in.

Before he could respond, Raven's cell phone rang. He answered and listened for a long moment before speaking. "I want two men out here all night guarding this place. Who's your best men?"

He was quiet while the man on the other end spoke. "Good. Tell them to stay on alert. We can't let another disaster like this happen, again."

He listened, again. "Keep me informed." Raven ended the conversation.

Turning to Shadow and Paul, he clued them in on the phone call. "That was Michael. He's planning on sending the crew back out here in the morning."

"Good. We're on a tight schedule and I want the bastard who planted those bombs know we don't scare easily." Shadow told him.

Paul laughed. "You're one tough lady."

"And don't you ever forget it." Shadow teased.

"Not in this life time." Paul bantered. He turned back to Raven. "Tell your men on duty tonight that I'll be sending a patrol car around ever little bit in case they need help."

"I appreciate it, man."

"Anytime. I want to catch these guys as bad as you do. I'll see you two later. I've got to head back to the office."

Raven and Shadow waved him off before heading to their own car. It was time to shake things up.

CHAPTER TWELVE

George, the Bible salesman targeted the old timers. There was something about the letter Stacy received at the newspaper office that kept tickling his mind.

When Stacy let him read a copy of the letter on the way to town he'd passed the ominous words off as those coming from an old senile man. But, there were too many truths throughout his letter to totally ignore.

The old man had said to look to the past and to the Brotherhood to solve the McClane Ridge murders.

So, he was.

George, in his Sunday suit and tie wandered the streets going from store to store with his briefcase in his hand. Every place he went in who was owned by an elderly person, he'd casually mention reading in the paper about the latest murder.

Every one of the owners became very talkative, until he brought up the events from fifty years ago and then they clammed up tighter than a virgin. When he mentioned the one word, 'Brotherhood", they all became visibly upset and each one ran him from their store with a dire warning to leave the past where it belonged.

Which made him want to dig even deeper into the

dirty history of McClane Ridge.

It was now time for George, the salesman to leave town.

* * *

Shadow leaned her head against the headrest and closed her eyes as their car ate up the miles heading home. The evening sun had descended an hour before and she was mentally and physically exhausted. She smothered a yawn with the back of her hand and settled more comfortable into the seat.

The only bright moment of the day was when they stopped back by the hospital and found John awake and sitting up eating his dinner off a tray.

They'd visited for a few minutes before John grew weary. Shadow had removed the tray and lowered the head section of the bed so he could sleep. They left him to rest.

Now, all she could think about was a long, relaxing bath, a quick bite to eat and then lying in bed wrapped in Raven's arms as they make exquisite love until sleep claimed them both.

Shadow turned her head and stared at Raven's hand clutched to the steering wheel and vividly remembered how his hands felt on her body. They were workman's hands that sensitized every erotic nerve in her body.

Her gaze traveled upwards to his mouth. She shivered thinking of the different ways he used his lips and wet, abrasive tongue to work her into a screaming, steaming, wild woman and loving it.

All of a sudden, she was no longer tired.

Raising one hand, Shadow wrapped it around the back of his neck and began a sensual massage. She felt him tense and then relax as her fingers whispered soft across his skin.

As the headlights of an oncoming car illuminated his face, she saw his broad smile. She grew bolder. Her hand slid around to his mouth and her finger glided across his lips.

She gasped in surprise as his mouth opened and sucked in her finger. His tongue teased and tortured her mind. She almost told him to stop the car right then and there, and pull over to the side of the road, but she wanted to get home quick. Very quick.

She pulled her finger out of his mouth and trailed her hand down to his chest until it rested on one nipple. His chest rose and fell as she rolled the sensitive nub between her thumb and forefinger.

Her hand began to descend down his hard rock stomach just as he drove into the driveway and braked.

Raven threw the car into park and killed the motor a second before he turned and pulled Shadow into his arms and kissed her hard and relentless.

With his breathing close to out of control, Raven released her. He fumbled with the handle until the door opened. Within seconds he was around the car, had her door open and helping her out. He allowed himself one more passionate kiss before grabbing her hand and almost dragging her to the front door.

Raven dropped the house key, cursed and released her hand long enough to reach down and retrieve the key. At last, he unlocked the door and they both came close to tumbling into the foyer.

"Raven? Shadow? Is that you?"

Shadow stopped dead in her tracks. Raven plowed into her.

"Rose?" Shadow's voice squeaked.

"Rose?" Raven pulled Shadow in front of him and cursed his luck.

"There the two of you are. I was getting worried." Rose said walking toward them. She gave Shadow a warm hug.

Raven reached down and gave Rose a kiss on the cheek. "When did you get in?"

"About twenty minutes, ago. I was just fixing a sandwich. Come join me. I'm anxious to hear news on John. I was hoping to make it home in time to see him tonight before visiting hours was over with, but I got tied up in traffic. I called and checked on him with the nurse, though." Rose chattered as she led the way to the kitchen.

Shadow glanced back at Raven, her expression showing frustration before turning back to follow Rose. She heard Raven's deep sigh. A grin emerged when she realized his disappointment would be a lot harder to hide than hers.

Entering the kitchen, Shadow poured the three of them glasses of tea before sitting across the table from Raven. She glanced over at Rose. "We just left the hospital. John was a lot better this evening. He was able to sit up for a few minutes and eat before he drifted off to sleep, again."

Shadow saw some of the worry leave Rose's face. "Thank goodness. I've been so worried. I talked to the doctor on the phone before I left, but I needed to see for myself how John is doing. I'll go first thing in the morning."

"Then you'll head back to your sister's?" Raven asked.

Rose laid her sandwich on her plate. She dabbed her mouth with her napkin before answering. "Now,

Shadow's Justice

Raven. I know you're worried about me being here, but I'm not leaving. I'm going to insist that John stays here after he's released from the hospital. He will need me to care for him while he's recuperating."

Recognizing her steel tone, Shadow spoke. "Raven, that's her son in the hospital. John is in no shape to travel to Aunt Rita's. He will have to come here. We can't expect Rose to do any less than to stay here and take care of him. We'll just have to do everything we can to keep them safe."

Raven opened his mouth to argue, but clamped it back shut, again. Damn!

The conversation around the table turned general. Even though they had talked almost daily on the phone, certain things had been left out of the conversation.

Raven and Shadow caught Rose up on all the news they hadn't deemed necessary to worry her with since she'd left six days before. She was home now and needed to be made aware of the dangers.

They told her more details on Steven's murder and his home being torched. They told her about the letter Shadow received from the man whose father had written before he died, claiming he knew Jack was innocent and they told her about Bob and his role in the investigation.

Knowing Rose would become upset, Raven waited until the last minute to tell her about the break-in into her home. Raven was only half right. Not only did Rose become upset, she became very angry.

"Why wasn't I told about this sooner?"

"We didn't want to worry you."

"That's no excuse, Raven. In case you haven't realized it, this is my home and my family. I have every right to know when either one is being threatened. I've had to hold this family together for too long, to now be put in the role of a weak female."

"You're right. We shouldn't have kept this from you." Raven said.

"We're sorry, Rose." Shadow's tone brought a smile back to Rose's face. Shadow always brought forth the meekness when she was being reprimanded. She was angel when caught in the act of being a little devil.

Rose patted her hand. "Just remember that I'm the mother around here. I'm supposed to be protecting you. Now, back to the letter you received. Have you never thought that I might know this person who sent it? I've lived here all my life."

Shadow and Raven looked at each other. Shadow glanced back at Rose. "No. I'm surprised I didn't."

"The guy didn't leave a name. We don't know who sent it." Raven added.

"It had a postmark on the letter, didn't it?"

"Yes, it did. With the explosions at the sight this morning, I haven't thought anymore about it." Shadow got up from the table and dug the letter from her purse where she had stuffed it that morning. "Here it is. It was mailed from Baton Rouge, Louisiana."

"Pete Sanders."

Shadow looked up at Rose. "Who?"

"Pete Sanders. He moved to Baton Rouge years, ago. He knew your father well. He has a son. Let me think…yes, I remember now. The son's name was James Sanders. He's probably in his 40's about now. I'd heard Pete's wife died a few years after they moved there."

Raven and Shadow looked at each other and grinned.

Raven turned back to Rose. He stood and walked to her side. Leaning down, he gave her a big hug. "Thanks, Rose. You're wonderful. I'll track down James Sanders first thing in the morning. Maybe he can shed more light on his father's letter."

"You're welcome, son. Now, that you two know I'm not weak or senile, I think I'll head on to bed. See you in the morning." When Rose walked outside the kitchen door, she started laughing. Their wide-eyed, open mouth expression was hysterical.

* * *

Stacy yawned and then brought the coffee cup to her lips and blew on the hot beverage before taking a sip. Sitting the cup on her desk, she rubbed her tired eyes. She'd been up most of the night digging up information from old newspaper articles and locating the whereabouts of the missing girl's relatives. With a few hours sleep she was back at her desk that morning anxious to make some phone calls.

Stacy waved to her boss as he walked by her office and then picked up the phone and went to work.

An hour and a pot of coffee later, Stacy hung up the phone on her last call. She had tracked down one relative who remembered a few details of her cousin, Karen's disappearance.

The sixty five year old woman only knew what she had heard from Karen's grandmother when it happened and informed Stacy over the phone of the facts as she remembered them.

That summer at her grandmother's, Karen had been invited to a party her friends were throwing one Saturday evening. Karen's grandfather had driven her to town around seven o'clock that evening and when he dropped her off at the party he had made arrangements to pick her up at 10:00 that night.

When her grandfather arrived back at the appointed time her friends had told him that Karen had left on foot by herself around 8:00.

Fifteen year old Karen Jacobs was never seen or heard from again. No clues or witnesses were ever brought forward and after a short while the case was dropped.

Which is no help, whatsoever, Stacy thought as she hung up the phone. Stacy massaged her aching temples. Feeling like her head was about to explode, she reached into her desk and pulled out a bottle of aspirins. Popping two out into her hand, she swallowed them down with cold coffee.

"Are we having a stressful morning?"

Stacy's head jerked toward the door and her eyes narrowed. "What are you doing here, Green?"

Bob shrugged his shoulder and moved further into her office. "I thought I would check in to see if you'd found out anymore about the missing girl."

"Nothing, Nada. Not a damn thing." Stacy's voice stayed lowered even though she felt like shouting out for him to leave her alone. She wasn't up to a sparring match this morning and her throbbing head refused to take the noise.

Instead, knowing he was as obligated and cared as much for Raven and Shadow as she did, Stacy filled Bob in on her earlier phone conversation with the cousin. With his connections world wide, she knew he might be able to take the information and run with it and hopefully coming up with a better lead than she ever would.

When she told him everything she'd learned that morning, she sat back in her chair with a sigh. Her hands moved once again to her temples and her eyes closed in pain.

Stacy heard a slight noise seconds before she felt his hands on the back of her neck. She jumped and attempted to rise. "What do you think you're doing?" She felt a gentle pressure pushing her back into her chair.

"Shhhhhhhh. Hold still and let me massage that headache away." He whispered into her ear.

His words seduced her and his skillful fingers made her feel as if her body was turning to a hot, passionate molten liquid. She moaned and leaned back into his hands as his magical fingers massaged every sore pressure point in her neck and shoulders until she felt the headache completely disappear.

Stacy opened her eyes and took in her surroundings. Her mind cleared from a deep, sensual fog and she realized to her astonishment that the back of her head was lying comfortably against his hard, rock stomach as if it was in its rightful place.

And, it scared the hell out of her.

She stood and walked several feet away from him. Looking over one shoulder, she froze him with a glare. "I guess I should thank you. My headache is gone." Her surly tone belied her actual thoughts.

Bob's growing grin widened even further. "It was my pleasure."

It was her unfortune to be hers, too.

* * *

A man in a white lab coat entered the Police Chief's hospital room in ICU. He glanced down at his watch to note that visiting hours was ten minutes away. Taking his time, he looked around the sterile room before walking toward the side of the bed.

He stood in silence staring down at the shell of a man lying there unconscious with several tubes hooked into his I.V. An oxygen mask rested smug on top of his nose and mouth.

Expressionless, the man pulled a syringe from the lab coat. He leaned over the bed and inserted the needle filled with the right amount of heroin into the I.V.. He watched calmly as the drug began taking effect.

The monitor's alarm sounded and he heard footsteps running toward the room, but still, he waited seconds longer until the patient took his last, harsh breath and then he walked with composure out into the corridor where he disappeared among the growing crowd of nurses and doctors.

* * *

The hour and a half drive to Baton Rouge that morning gave Raven a long time to think. He needed this time away from Shadow. Frankly, when she's around, it's not his intellect that was doing the thinking, he decided.

Raven reached over and turned the volume way up on the radio. The light jazz station released his tension and he began to unwind enough to enjoy the drive.

The traffic was light and the interstate scenery went unnoticed as he thought of his upcoming visit with James Sanders. With the information Rose had given him, he was able to locate Sanders exact business address off the internet. His retail gift store was located close to the center of the business district and would be easy to find.

Shadow's Justice

He just hoped this wasn't a wasted trip. He needed some leads and fast. Every bit of information they came across had come to a dead end. His gut feeling told him things were about to come to a head and he didn't know how to stop it. Yet.

He had left Michael with Rose, Shadow and John for extra protection. Bob would show up later to stand watch, but he still worried about leaving them. Everyone he loved in this whole world was in that one house and was an easy target for a maniac killer.

Raven thought back to the conversation he had with Bob last night after Rose and Shadow had gone to bed. Everything that had happened to him or the McClane family this past week had been a forewarning. He even felt Tucker's death and his home burning to the ground was a warning in itself.

Someone was running scared and paying a lot of money to hired killers out of desperation. And as Bob mentioned the night before, the warnings would eventually stop.

Arriving in Baton Rouge, Raven drove slowly down the Central business district. He spotted Sanders Unique Gifts and pulled into a nearby parking garage.

Stepping onto the sidewalk, he looked around the district. The historical old south beauty always took his breath away. Various cultures from Creole, African American, and Caribbean to French/Cajun influenced the architecture with the large balconies and many doors, as well as the superb cuisine and even down to the different types of music from the Blues to Cajun zydeco that could be heard throughout the town.

Raven crossed the busy street and walked back a

block to the shop and entered. A bell on the door chimed and a middle-aged, Tom Hanks look-alike, busy stocking a shelf looked up.

"Good Morning. How may I help you?"

Raven walked toward the man. "I'm looking for a man named James Sanders."

The man smiled and walked toward Raven with an outstretched hand. "That would be me. What can I do for you?"

Raven shook Sanders hand and answered. "I'm Raven Deveroux from McClane Ridge. Your father wrote a letter to a friend of mine, concerning Jack McClane before he died. I wanted to talk to you about the letter."

The man's smile faded. "I don't know what letter you're talking about. If you don't mind, I'm a very busy man." He turned away from Raven and continued restocking.

"I think you do." Raven moved in closer. "I don't think you're the type of man who could keep his mouth shut and allow someone else to be killed. You might have some information that could stop that from happening."

The bell jingled on the door. Both men turned toward an elderly lady walking in. Raven received a glaring look from Sanders before he moved to greet his customer.

Raven wandered around the store looking at the various gift items for thirty minutes before the store became empty of customers. His patience was running thin. "Are you ready to talk, now?"

With a resigned look, Sanders nodded. "What do you want to know?"

"I'm sure you read your father's letter. How much

did he tell you about the things that happened fifty years, ago?"

"He never did really tell me anything at one time. Over the years, small bits of information would slip out in his conversations. I know he both hated and feared certain people from McClane Ridge."

"Did he say who?"

"Not by name. Father always referred to them as the 'Brotherhood'. He said their crimes reached above the arms of the law and that their sins would never be uncovered."

"That's where your father may be wrong. I plan to dig up all the dirt I can on these killers. He also mentioned he witnessed a murder. Did he say anything to you?"

"No, but I've been thinking about it for the last few days. Almost in the same breath, he brought up the murder and the missing girl. I believe in my heart he saw the girl murdered, which means he saw the killer or killers."

"He didn't go to the police with what he saw." Raven's quiet words were more a statement than a question. The newspapers back then would have swooped on an eye witness account. In fact, they had stated that none had come forth.

"Why would your father have kept silent?"

Sanders shrugged a shoulder. "Basic rich man against poor man storyline, maybe. My grandfather was a sharecropper with a wife and seven kids to feed. They lived in a run down shack and only ate what they were able to grow on a pitiful plot of land. They wore hand-me-downs and clothes donated from the church.

Father told me that he had a run in with the law

when he was about fourteen. He stole a chicken out of a neighbor's pen because the family was starving and he was caught red-handed. Who would believe a chicken thief over a rich, powerful family? I'm sure he thought no one would. So, he kept silent all these years."

Raven pondered Sander's words. Their was still something he didn't understand. "Why would your father wait ten years before he moved away? I had the feeling from his letter that he moved out of fear for his family. I would think he would feel safer after that many years had passed."

"I think I may have an answer for you." Sanders reached into his back pocket and pulled out his wallet. He retrieved an old newspaper clipping and unfolded the yellowed paper. "I was going through Father's papers and found this yesterday." He passed the clipping to Raven.

Raven read, "Jake Fletcher was found shot to death in his bed early Thursday morning. His neighbor, Mrs. Wilson became worried when he didn't answer her knock. She entered his home and found him lying in a puddle of blood. She called the police and an investigation is underway." Raven glanced toward Sanders. "You think this has something to do with the girl's possible murder and your parents leaving McClane Ridge?"

Sanders nodded. "Look at the date at the top of the newspaper."

Raven read, "March 4th, 1960."

Sanders words were grim. "I was too young to remember, but I searched and found papers showing that we moved to Baton Rouge, March 6th, 1960. I don't believe in coincidences and I know my father didn't murder Mr. Fletcher, so the only other possible explanation is that he was running scared."

Raven's nerves started tingling. A cold excitement began to build. "I don't believe in coincidences, either." Raven told Sanders.

He laughed. He felt like dancing the jig. Instead, Raven thanked Sanders for his help, told him he would be in touch and left the store.

Raven remembered why Fletcher's name sounded so familiar. His name was signed on the deed for the land at the new construction site. The same land where only yesterday, bulldozers were blown up and employees and John were injured from the explosions. Coincidences, be damned.

CHAPTER THIRTEEN

Randall Collins replaced the receiver. He sat back in his office chair and rubbed his face with both hands. Years of misery were taking its toll. He was getting to be an old man. Maybe it was time to retire and take a long vacation. Mexico would be a nice place to visit or maybe even to live.

With a deep sigh, he reached for the phone and dialed Ben Adam's number. When the Judge answered, he simply said, "Walker is dead." He hung up the phone.

* * *

Shadow stared out of the bedroom window. The sunlight glimmered off the crystal clear water in the pool below her. The temperature of the water was still a little cool for her, but she'd stood at her bedroom window earlier this morning and watched Raven swim with vigorous strokes several laps down the length of the pool.

Shadow wondered if it was to keep up his athletic build or to work off frustration. Either way, it seemed to be working. Or it did until he sauntered into her bedroom and stole a kiss that left them breathless and wanting before he left for Baton Rouge that morning. She smiled at the memory.

"You look deep in thought."

Startled, Shadow twirled around and saw John

watching her. She stepped closer to the bed and smiled. "I thought you were asleep. How are you feeling?"

"Like I was run over by a bulldozer or blown off of one. Wait a minute, I was." He was able to grin. His lips were about the only thing that wasn't cut or bruised on his whole body. Even his eyes looked like someone had sucker punched him.

Shadow laughed while situating his pillow higher so that he could sit up in the bed. She handed him a glass of water with a straw and watched him take the straw out and take several large drinks. She shook her head and took the glass from him when he was through. "At least you haven't lost your sense of humor or enormous appetite."

"Hey, I've got to keep my strength up, you know. Speaking of which, when is lunch?"

"Carol is getting your lunch ready now, pig."

John laughed.

Shadow saw him wince. "If you weren't so stubborn, you would take something for that pain."

"I'm okay. I don't like the way the pain pills keeps me knocked out. I want a clear head." John hesitated for a second before stating. "I need you to do me a favor, Shadow. I need you to go out to my Jeep and bring my pistol to me."

Shadow stared at him for a long moment before nodding her head. She wasn't about to argue with him. John may not be able to run from danger right now, but he sure as hell can shoot it. "Rose will be here shortly to visit with you. I'll get your gun then."

John merely nodded. "Thanks, Shadow."

A knock sounded on the door and Carol entered with his lunch and bless her heart, it wasn't soup.

John grinned and helped her situate the tray on his lap. "I love you, Carol," he told her as he dug in on a three-tiered roast beef sandwich loaded with cheese and lettuce.

Carol laughed. "Save room for that large Ribeye steak I'm grilling you for dinner tonight."

John's mouth was full, so he nodded with vigor and a smile.

Shadow grinned as Carol left. Carol had half-raised John, herself and Michael and if John ever needed a little pampering, now was the time. Shadow couldn't resist teasing. "You're spoilt rotten."

John nodded. "I know. Women love spoiling me for some reason." He grinned and took another bite.

"Son, you're not too big that I can't turn you over my knee and spank some humility back into you," Rose said with a smile as she entered the bedroom. She leaned down and kissed him on the top of his head.

"Hi, Mom."

"Hi, yourself." Rose turned to Shadow. "Honey, go get something to eat and some rest. I'll stay with John."

Shadow nodded. "Okay, but only for a short while. I don't want you to wear yourself out."

"I'm fine. Take your time. It won't be long before Romeo here will be fast asleep. I'll go to my room and lie down while he's sleeping."

"Okay. I'll be downstairs if you need me." Shadow waved her goodbye and left the room to freshen up before going downstairs to eat lunch and walk out to John's jeep to retrieve his gun. She hoped to find time to call Stacy to see if she had learned anything new about the missing girl. Hopefully by that time Raven will be back from Baton Rouge with new information.

* * *

The clamor of the bulldozer's thunderous commotion was deafening, but the drivers were use to it. Since early dawn, man and machine had cleared and leveled a small section of the ten acres at the construction sight. So far, nothing catastrophic had happened. The area had been patrolled all night by McClane's own men and by the local cops and would continue to be watched until the job was finished. They couldn't take the chance of anyone else getting hurt or any major delays.

Michael had left the sight later to pick up John from the hospital and to take him home where their mother could watch over him. He left the Foreman in charge with an order to call him if they ran into any kind of trouble.

Michael pulled the hotel's blueprints out of his satchel and rolled it out across his stepfather's desk. He could work here just as well as he could at his office and still keep an eye on the family.

They were on a tight schedule and yesterday had thrown them behind by one day. They had to bring in a couple of independent heavy equipment operators to take the injured men's place on the crew, but they were men they had used before and they could do the job.

If the weather played fair, they should finish the groundwork in a few days and then they would pour the concrete. After that, the construction of the fifteen story hotel and casino would begin.

* * *

Raven stopped by the newspaper office on the way back from Baton Rouge. He was anxious to get home, but he was hunting for information on one more thing. He needed Stacy to check out any articles in the paper written after March 4th, 1960 concerning Fletcher's murder.

He found Stacy in her office talking on the phone. He waited until she was off before crossing the threshold into her office. "Knock, Knock. Are you busy?"

Stacy glanced up and smiled. "Hey, Raven. No, I'm glad you stopped by. Grab you a chair." She motioned to an expensive, cushioned chair across from her desk. Stacy was too busy to decorate her office in a 'womanly' way, but she believed in being comfortable and her boss approved her elegant taste.

Raven sat down and asked, "Were you able to find out anything on the missing girl?"

Stacy picked up her notes off her desk. "Actually, I did. I located a relative who remembered her mother talking about the girl when she came up missing. According to her, fifteen year old Karen Jacobs was dropped off by her grandfather at her friend's house for a party she was attending."

Stacy checked her notes. "Grandfather arrived at appointed time of 10:00 to pick her up and found out that Karen had left on foot around 8:00. No one has seen her since. Cops investigated for a couple of months and then the case file was pushed back into the unsolved file drawer and forgotten."

"Do you know if we can get our hands on those files?"

Stacy shrugged. "I can give it a shot."

"Good. Let me know. One other thing, can I get you to check into any articles you can find on a man named Fletcher who was murdered March 4th, 1960?"

Shadow's Justice

Stacy raised a brow as she made notes. "You bet. Mind telling me what's going on?"

Raven clued her in on his conversation with Sanders.

Stacy's eyes shined with excitement. She could smell an award out of this. "I'll get right on it."

Raven pushed himself up out of the chair and walked to the door. "Thanks for your help."

"Anytime. Uh...Raven. How much do you know about your friend, Bob?"

Raven grinned and winked. "Everything and he likes you, too." Raven turned and walked out the door.

Flustered, Stacy sat back in her chair chewing on her pencil. "Well, I'll be damned," she muttered. Then, a huge, jubilant smile appeared.

* * *

Shadow strolled in the flower garden soaking up the sunshine. How long had it been, she wondered, since she had been able to enjoy the garden with a carefree, peace of mind? Forever and a day, she thought.

Her fingers idly caressed the tips of a red rose and then she leaned down to inhale the sweet fragrance. She smiled in contentment for a brief moment before she continued to walk and mull over her immediate and future problems.

It was bad enough worrying about her father and all the murders and accidents happening, but now on top of everything else, she had to worry about falling in love with a man who could only be in her life part time.

Raven had hinted before that he could put his traveling behind him and settle down behind a white picket fence with the right woman. But would he, really? Could he replace traveling to exotic places with changing diapers? Or trading danger and adventure with construction work? Maybe for awhile, but Shadow knew him well enough to know he would soon grow bored and want more.

She also knew she loved him enough to allow him to follow his heart even if it destroyed her own. Which made her a complete fool. If she could reach it, she would kick her own butt.

Well, hell. Her mood was completely trashed, now. So much for a peaceful walk, she decided. Shadow kicked at a clump of dirt and sent it flying. It was a good thing her old boyfriends couldn't see her now. Instead of calling her a hard-boiled, kick-ass bitch, they would call her a sappy, "Yes, dear, I will see you in six months and we can have great sex", wimp. It was all Raven's fault. He just had to kiss her that first time and throw a monkey wrench into her whole thought process. Life sucks.

Stressed out to the point of pulling her hair out, Shadow groaned and sat down on a bench in a shade beneath a maple tree. That's where Raven found her moments later.

"Hey, Shady Lady. What's up?" Raven leaned against the tree trunk and smiled down at her.

Raven's deep, sexy voice grated on her nerves and yet, she'd been longing for the sound all morning. She raised her gaze skyward, rolled her eyes and scowled. "Don't call me that."

Raven grinned. "Okay. How about Sexy Lady?"

A smile was forced out even though she tried to maintain her scowl. "I think I like the name Sexy Lady, Stud Muffin."

Raven groaned at the name she dubbed him. "Pleeease, don't call me that outside the bedroom."

Shadow laughed out loud. Within two seconds, he had turned her mood around. She stood and wrapped her arms around his neck and kissed him slow and sensual. At that moment, she needed his kiss and arms holding her tight too much to care who saw them.

Raven pulled away after the kiss ended. Using his forefinger, he raised her chin so that he could look into her eyes. "Why the anger and hint of sadness when I walked up?" he whispered.

Shadow pulled back and then with a sigh, she leaned her head against his chest. A shoulder lifted. "I guess I was letting my thoughts turn ugly. I do better when I don't have time to think."

"Well, I can think of a better way to take your mind off things, but until we have more privacy, I'll tell you what I found out, instead."

Stacy sat back down, pulled Raven down beside her and grinned. "I'll hold you to the first part and settle for the second, for now. Did you meet with Sanders?"

"Yes. I also stopped and talked to Stacy on the way home." Raven told Shadow everything he had learned that morning from Sanders and Stacy.

The information troubled Shadow. She turned everything he'd told her over and over in her mind. "This is too frickin' unbelievable. You're telling me you think the girl's disappearance fifty years ago, old man Fletcher's murder forty years ago, Tucker's murder and my father's imprisonment six years ago and now these recent murders and accidents are all connected?"

Raven nodded. "Yep, that's what I'm telling you."

Shadow's Justice

"How?"

"I haven't a clue. What I do know is that someone is trying very hard to make sure we don't find out."

"Well, sorry Charlie, but I'm determined we will."

* * *

Bob was being followed. He slowed his pace and then stopped in front of a shop's display window. His reflection glared back at him. Dressed in a Hawaiian print shirt, cargo shorts and sandals, a camera hanging around his neck and his wig that portrayed baldness on top protected his identity. Or, it should have.

Out of the corner of his eye, he saw a glimpse of the man dressed in a business suit who had tailed him for three blocks. Bob had played the game of Simons Says many times before in his business. It was time to compete again.

He had detected the man right after he left Stacy. He had gone in dressed as himself and came out of the newspaper office's bathroom dressed as a tourist. He stepped down on the sidewalk and that's when he first saw the man across the street staring across at him.

He was 100 percent positive he hadn't been tailed before he entered the office. His U.S. Special Forces and mercenary training was too extensive for him not to have noticed being trailed. He had too many enemies in his line of work. His daily survival depended on his close observations.

Bob stopped often and looked into a window to see what the man would do. Glancing to his side, he'd noticed the man would stop each time, never getting any closer than a block away. The man gazed into a window, but would start walking again as soon as he did.

Shadow's Justice

Why was he being followed? If he thought it was a basic robbery, he would have taken the character out two blocks back. He knew by the way the man dressed he didn't need to rob anyone, especially a poorly dressed tourist. He also knew from experience the man was a professional.

Someone had to have tipped off the suited man. How else would he have known where to find him? Who knew he was there besides Stacy? No one. The receptionist had been away from her desk when he'd arrived and when he'd left. He hadn't seen anyone else even though he had heard several voices in the loud printing room in the back. He would deal with Stacy later. And then deal with his disappointment.

Bob's hand rubbed across his stomach and lay across the handle of his gun hidden beneath the loose shirt. He turned and began walking again.

Horns blared and he heard a crash. Looking toward the street he witnessed two cars involved in a fender bender. He saw his chance and acted while his follower was distracted.

Bob ducked into an alleyway and waited. Mere seconds later he heard footsteps running down the block and past the alley entrance where he was hidden.

Bob eased back onto the sidewalk and began following his tracker. He picked up his pace until he was a few feet behind him.

The man stopped and glanced around in agitation trying to locate his prey. Bob walked up behind him, pushed his hidden gun into his back and with quiet, ominous words said, "I have a gun pointed at your back and unless you want your blood splattered all over these nice people around us, you will start walking."

The man at first stiffened and then began walking, as ordered. They walked only a block further before Bob shoved the man into another dark alleyway. He gave him one hard push sending him flying and landing face first in the dirt. Bob reached down and jerked him onto his back and landed down hard with one knee into the man's midsection. He pulled the gun out from beneath his shirt and put the barrel against the man's forehead. With his other hand, he searched him for weapons. Finding one pistol inside his jacket, Bob pulled it out and threw it further into the alley.

"Why are you following me?"

"Fuck off."

Bob's face twisted in anger. He cocked the hammer back and his forefinger landed on the trigger. His knee pressed down harder.

The man grunted and seemed to gage his options, deciding they were not in his favor. "Okay. Okay. I'll talk."

Bob eased back on the hammer and shifted his weight back. "I'm listening."

"I was hired to follow you, because you're gonna be a dead son of a bitch, no matter what and I might as well be the one who gets paid the ten grand being offered to knock you off."

Bob's fist landed on the man's lips. The man's head rolled to the side. Blood poured out of his mouth where a tooth had cut through one lip.

"Who hired you?"

The man spit out blood and turned to glare at Bob. "I don't know." Seeing Bob's fist pulled back, the man raised his hands to cover his face and quickly said, "I really don't know. He called me, told me you were asking too many questions and he wanted you silenced. He told me where he would leave half the money now and the other half after I finished you off. I picked up my money, so I didn't give a shit who had put it there. In my line of business, I don't ask too many questions."

"Sounds like you need a new line of business." Bob's fist came down hard, once again. The blow knocked the man unconscious. He had gotten all the information he was going to get out of the goon. Bob stood and wiped the dirt off his clothes. He hid his gun beneath the waistband of his shorts and turned to walk out of the alleyway.

That's when he heard the unmistakable sound of a hammer being cocked back. Twirling around, he pointed his gun from beneath his shorts and fired off one fatal shot to his assailant's head. The man fell backwards and the gun he had earlier thrown further into the alley now lay still in the dead man's hand.

CHAPTER FOURTEEN

Daunting blue lights bounced off the walls on each side of the darkened alleyway. Blaring sirens from moments before were now silent as a tomb. Numerous voices droned on and on around the area from the different authorized officials on site.

The Coroner examined the body where it laid, making his ruling into a small microphone. The police roped off the crime scene and kept curious bystanders away. Gathering evidence took them all of two minutes. The bullet was dug out of the dirt where it had gone after passing through the dead man's skull. The weapon was handed over to the police by the one who had shot it.

Raven and Shadow stood next to Bob as he told Deputy Police Chief Paul LaCroix what had occurred right before he had called 911 from his cell phone to report the shooting. Bob had then called Raven.

Raven brought his attention from the surroundings to the conversation beside him. "Do you know who he is?"

Paul shook his head. "No. I've never seen him around here before. I'll get on this as soon as I get back to my office."

"That won't be necessary." Raven turned to Bob.

Shadow's Justice

"I have your laptop in the car. See what you can find out, okay?"

Bob nodded and walked to Raven's car. Climbing in, he turned on his computer and went to work.

Raven turned back to the deputy Police Chief. "Bob has all the resources to find out everything we need to know on this jerk."

Shadow spoke up for the first time since arriving. "I'm more interested in the jerk who hired him."

"You and me both. That will be harder to do, but not impossible," Raven told her.

"While Bob's checking that out, I'm going to see if I can find the guy's car. I imagine it was rented, but it might have some type of identification in it," Paul said.

Raven shook his head. "You can look, but I guarantee you his car will be as clean as his pockets. The only thing they found on him was a cell phone he probably stole. That hired gun is a professional and wouldn't leave anything behind to incriminate him. I'm sure the name he gave to the rental company was fake."

"I don't doubt that. Bob said he'd first noticed him standing across from the Newspaper office. I'll have someone start searching there first," Paul told Raven. He left them to find a deputy to send out on a hunt for the car.

Raven glanced around the scene once more before turning to Shadow. "Let's see if Bob is having any luck."

Throwing an arm around her shoulder, Raven and Shadow approached the car. "What have you found out?"

Bob continued pounding the keys and staring at

the screen as one image after another came into view and then disappearing. "Give me two seconds." Distracted, Bob typed in one more name off the list he'd found. In an instant, a clear picture of the man who had just tried to kill him came into view on the screen. "Bingo."

Bob typed in a few more commands and the killer's profile popped up beside his image. He hit the Print key and sat back in the seat and waited until the printed page emerged. Grinning, he glanced up at Raven and Shadow and held the paper out the window. "Damn, I'm good."

Raven snatched the paper out of Bob's hand and grinned. "If you weren't, I'd fire you for your arrogance." He bent his head and began reading, missing the amused glance pass between Bob and Shadow.

"Jonathon Matthews. Age 39. No permanent residence or any known relatives. Known hired killer. Wanted in ten states for questioning on suspicion of murder. $100,000 Reward offered for capture or information leading up to his arrest. Matthews is considered armed and dangerous."

"No, I would now consider him dead and harmless." Bob interjected.

"And I would consider you $100,000 richer." Shadow added.

Raven heard their chatter, but his mind was on the dead man and his FBI profile. He'd heard of Matthews. He was big time gang member turned small time hired killer. His cruelness overshadowed his lack of talent with a gun and it showed on his victims. His cowardly M.O. was always the same. Multiple gun shot wounds to the back was fired until the victim fell to his face and then with gloved hands he would turn the body over and complete his deed with one shell shot point blank between the eyes.

Raven shivered and looked toward his friend. Matthews had met his match. Thank God.

Raven's attention was drawn back to Paul's return.

"We found the car. The cocky bastard parked it across from the Police Station. The team is checking for evidence and dusting for fingerprints, now." Paul leaned against Raven's car and crossed his arms. "Did you guys have any luck?"

"Yeah. This is your man." Raven handed the profile over to Paul.

Paul read it and his breath hissed through his teeth. He looked toward Bob. "I would say they wanted you dead."

Bob grunted. "No kidding. I just hate they spent all that money for nothing." He grinned.

Paul laughed and straightened. "I've gotta run. I was summoned to the office, but I wanted to stop by and let you know about the car before I left. I'll let you know if we find out anything."

"We'll do the same," Raven told him.

"Good. I'll talk to you guys, later." Paul saluted his goodbye and his long legs carried him to his patrol car.

Raven watched his friend walk away and marveled at the changes in the police force since Paul had taken over after Walker's death. Paul was determined and professional when it came to his job. He'd been the same way in school when he'd helped carry the high school football team to the playoffs and winning two years running. Raven felt for certain that Paul would win in the election for the Police Chief's position, now open.

"Hey, you guys. I just heard what happened." Raven glanced up as Stacy ran up to the car. Worry was etched on her face.

Stacy leaned down to look in the car window. "Bob, are you okay?"

Bob glanced up. Stacy took a step back as she took in the anger flashing in his eyes.

Bob opened the door and stepped out. He faced Stacy, slammed the door behind him and eyed her coldly. "Why did you do it?" His voice was controlled and intimidating.

Stacy shook her head. "I don't know what you're talking about. I've just arrived. What was I supposed to have done?"

Bob took a bullying step forward. "How much money did you get out of this or was it ambition that almost got me killed?"

"I don't know what you're talking about, but you had better start explaining." Bob wasn't taken back by her defiance or her crossed arms.

Raven stepped forward. "Bob, what's going on here?"

Bob jerked a thumb toward Stacy. "Ask her. My trail was never picked up until I left the Newspaper office. The only person who knew I was there is Stacy. No one else saw me in the building and even I didn't know I was going there until the last minute. They certainly didn't know I would be coming out of the building dressed as a tourist, looking nothing like I did when I entered. It doesn't take a genius to figure out who sold me out."

"No, but it takes an idiot to jump to conclusions," Stacy shot back.

"Bob, there's got to be another explanation." Shadow added. "I've known Stacy all my life and she would never do anything like that."

"Have you heard her deny it?" Bob questioned, furious that Raven and Shadow defended her.

All three turned to look at Stacy.

Stacy took turns looking each one in the eye. "Go to hell." She turned and stormed off.

Bob watched as Shadow took off running to catch up with her friend. He turned back to Raven, his shoulders sagging. In his mind he had begged for Stacy to deny his charges, but she hadn't. And he wasn't really surprised. She'd only proved what he already knew. No woman was to be trusted.

How many more times of having his heart trampled on would it take before it finally hardened enough to never get involved with a woman, again? It looks like he would've learned his lesson from his money hungry, social climbing ex-fiancé. Even then his heart hadn't taken a beating the way it was, now.

He'd known Stacy for only a few days, but somehow she had become twisted into his mind and soul. She would be hard to forget, but he was determined that he would. He would immerse himself so deep into this case that he wouldn't have time to have dreams and wishes concerning one Stacy Chandler.

Bob glanced over at Raven. Raven's brow rose, but he waited in silence. "You think I'm wrong about Stacy, don't you?" Bob asked him.

Raven shrugged and glanced over at the two women still talking before looking back at Bob. "I've known her a long time, Bob. I don't want to believe she is involved in anyway, but I also trust your instincts." Raven sighed and then making a decision, he slapped Bob on the shoulder. "Check it out and get back to me."

Bob nodded and watched as Raven walked away to join the women. Bob turned and walked down Main street.

* * *

A nerve pill or a very stiff drink would be good about right now, Shadow thought as she watched Raven approach. Her nerves were stretched to the limit. She had heard every curse word possible coming out of Stacy's innocent looking mouth and every one of them was aimed like darts toward Bob. To put it in blunt words, Stacy was pissed. Shadow hadn't been able to get a word in edge ways and had given up trying five minutes before.

By the time Raven drew to their side, Shadow was like a pistol, cocked and ready to fire. The first bullet directed at Raven shot out of her mouth. "Your friend is a freakin' lunatic. I can't believe you stood there and allowed him to fling those horrible accusations at Stacy. What in the world were you thinking?"

That shut Stacy up and Shadow was forever grateful.

Raven took his time answering until Shadow's frayed nerves were ready to snap. He sighed and glanced at her and then at Stacy. He spoke. "Actually, I was thinking Bob could possibly be right."

"What?" Stacy's screech could be heard a block away. Before Stacy could start in ranting again, Shadow spoke up. "Well, I think you are both wrong."

"Prove it."

Shadow lost it. Her forefinger landed in the middle of his chest with several hard punches. Her voice rose, her anger evident. "No. You prove it, Buster." She gave one more poke for emphases before adding, "And don't expect me or Stacy to be around when you come back to grovel after you are proven wrong." She turned and marched off before he had a chance to speak.

Stacy caught up with Shadow a block away. She walked by her side for a moment before speaking. "I really appreciate you taking up for me back there, but you know I can take care of myself. I don't want to be the cause of you and Raven having a falling out."

"Yeah, well, I figured it was going to happen sooner or later, anyway."

"Wanna talk about it?"

"No."

Stacy nodded and walked in silence beside her friend for a moment. She nodded again. "Well, that confirmed it."

Shadow glanced over at Stacy in exasperation and took in her smug grin. "Confirms what?"

"It confirms that you and Raven have become lovers. I think it's wonderful." With that, Stacy wiggled her fingers to say goodbye and turned to enter the Newspaper office in front of them.

Shadow stood alone on the street's sidewalk contemplating Hari Kari. She didn't know which one she wanted to murder first, Raven or Stacy. At this moment, they were both high on her crap list. Bob came in third.

Shadow had to admit that if she was in Bob's shoes and didn't know Stacy as well as she did, she might assume Stacy had alerted the hit man to Bob's whereabouts.

The evidence was damning. Bob's disguises were precise and professional. He was good at what he did. Even if the hit man had, by good fortune, seen Bob enter, he would have never recognized him coming out. Unless someone from inside had tipped him off, the hit man would've still been standing there right this minute waiting on Bob to come out of the Newspaper office.

But there were also flaws in Bob's theory. Stacy hadn't known Bob was going to show up for a surprise visit at her office that morning. He was with her for at least a half an hour. She wouldn't have had a chance to contact anyone.

Granted, there had to be a second person involved who was there. Someone could have seen Bob enter the building. He could have followed him inside and waited around until he spotted him leaving Stacy's office carrying a bag. Following him down the hall and into the bathroom, he would have waited and watched in a concealed spot as Bob left wearing his disguise.

A quick phone call when Bob entered the building would have alerted the hit man giving him time to drive to the Police Station and park. Another phone call would have let him know about Bob's new disguise when he left.

That was one theory. The second could be that the hit man just made one heck of a good guess and followed his professional instinct.

Shadow looked toward the Newspaper office one more time. She felt a foreboding shiver run down her spine. Maybe, she thought, time will tell the truth and maybe, Stacy will actually deny Bob's accusations.

* * *

Arms crossed, Raven leaned back against his car and watched Shadow approach. He knew she would show up sooner or later when she realized she needed a ride home.

He pushed himself away from the car and opened the door for her. Without a word, she slid into the seat. He shut her door and rounded the car to the driver's side. Sitting behind the wheel, he turned the key and the motor roared to life.

The ride home was oppressive with silence. Both had chosen their sides and neither wavered. Shadow had never seen or lived the cold, hard life that he had. She had never had the misfortune to see first hand how greed could destroy a person's life. He had.

This murder case was nothing compared to the atrocities he had witnessed in the third world countries. Bodies blown away over a kilo of cocaine, big businesses hiring bomb experts to eliminate their competition and brothers turning against brothers to take over the mob family were only a few of the horrifying bloodsheds he had witnessed. All because of greed.

Money or a career recognition from a big story would be a powerful motive to entice Stacy into making one phone call to let someone know Bob was there.

Her innocence would be hard to prove or disapprove. Bob could get the phone records from every phone in the Newspaper office. The time consuming part would be tracking down the employees personal cell phones. The hard part would be proving an employee or a stranger off the street hadn't walked into an empty office and made the call from another person's phone.

Even though Raven didn't think the phone records would turn up anything, he still wanted Bob to check them out. At this point, he didn't want any stone left unturned.

Raven glanced at the clock on the dash. He would give Bob time to grab a bite of lunch and then he would give him a call.

Raven drove his car into the garage and killed the motor. He turned in his seat and faced Shadow. His expression was grave and his voice a whispered steel. "I want you to know, I don't like investigating Stacy anymore than you do. But don't ever think that I wouldn't dare to take her down if I thought she was a danger to the ones I love."

With that said, Raven opened his door and stepped out. He walked inside the house, leaving Shadow still sitting inside the car pondering or fuming over what he'd said. He would wait inside for the battle to begin.

CHAPTER FIFTEEN

Randall Collins paced his office floor. He'd turned off all the lights earlier and let the full moon's glow lead his steps back and forth across the room.

His hand carried a full glass of whiskey straight. The bottle on his desk was near empty and his mind still hadn't reached to the point of numbness he sought.

He had never felt so alone as he felt tonight. He worked late on a client's file that could have waited until morning to delay leaving the office. He couldn't bring himself to go home to an empty house.

Walker's death scared the living hell out of him. It could have been him instead of Walker who suffered a massive heart attack. Walker, himself and the Judge were all born within the same year. Sixty-seven, in this day and age was not considered old. He felt young at heart even though his movements had slowed some in the last few years.

He still on occasion turned the women's eyes toward him and he enjoyed a good romp in the sack every now and then. He still had a lot of living left to do and the realization that he was fallible hit him like a ton of bricks.

Randall brought his whiskey glass to his lips and

took a lengthy drink. And then another. He walked to his desk and poured the brown liquid down his throat straight from the bottle until it was empty.

With a wavering stagger he raised his glass in a toast to his missing partners. "May you finally rest in peace, Walker." Randall hesitated before adding. "It's just you and me, now, Judge." With a feeling of helplessness, he set both his empty glass and the bottle on his desk.

He still wasn't numb enough to forget his lifelong friend and member of their "Brotherhood" had been murdered. Or that he would have to stand next to the Judge and before the Lord tomorrow as Walker's family laid him in his final resting place.

Randall staggered out of his office and drove to the nearest liquor store to buy more courage.

* * *

Shadow stood in her shower beneath the soothing flow of warm water cascading over her tired body. She had gone to bed early the night before to escape another confrontation with Raven, but her troubled mind caused her to toss and turn most of the night. She woke up exhausted and no closer to solving her dilemma.

Shadow lathered shampoo into her hair and as her fingers massaged her scalp, her thoughts returned to their senseless argument the day before. She could understand Raven wanting to protect the people he loved. She whole-heartedly felt the same way, but he was wandering off the beaten path.

Shadow leaned back and allowed the water to rinse the shampoo from her hair and the cobwebs from her mind.

She rose from her bed this morning clear-headed

about one thing. Raven was wrong to accuse Stacy without anymore proof than Bob's say so. He would end up spending precious time investigating a dead end and possibly letting the real accomplice get away scot-free.

Well, let him, she thought. It would keep him out of her hair while she did her own investigation.

With a plan in mind, Shadow finished her shower and dressed in jeans and a pullover top for the day. She stopped in for a moment to check on John and Rose and to borrow Rose's car. Finding them both okay, she left to retrieve her purse from her room and the key to Rose's SUV.

Leaving the house, Shadow sped off toward the construction sight, relieved that she had managed to miss running into Raven this morning. She didn't have the time or the patience for anymore arguments with him.

Shadow arrived a few minutes later and maneuvered the SUV next to Michael's car. Climbing out, she walked toward the construction trailer. Sauntering up the steps, she entered the open door without knocking.

She noticed Michael bent over the table, staring at the drawings he'd laid out. He glanced up and smiled when she entered.

"Hey, I thought you might use an extra hand since John is out of commission."

Michael grinned. "I'll take all the help I can get. First thing I need for you to do, since you're over payroll is give John a raise. We don't pay him near enough."

Shadow laughed. "I'll send out a memo to my secretary in big, bold letters. INCREASE JOHN'S

PAY! How's that?"

"Wonderful. Now, you can tell me what you're really doing out here and without Raven. You know it's not safe."

Shadow made a face at him. It never did her any good to try to lie to him. Michael always read her like a book. She crossed her arms and leaned against the counter. "Look. Here's the deal..." Shadow filled him in on everything that happened the day before. She finished. "...so, I'm pissed at Raven right now. If he wants to waste his time on checking out Stacy, let him. I plan on spending my time with more efficiency."

Michael whistled his surprise. "He actually believes Stacy is involved?"

"Yep."

"Wow!" Michael focused on Shadow, his concern obvious. "He may be right, you know."

"Dammit. Not you, too." Shadow turned toward the door to leave. She felt Michael's hand on her shoulder and stopped.

His voice was quiet as he spoke behind her. "Raven's a good man, Shadow. He would never hurt anyone he cares for. If he's investigating Stacy, it's for a good reason. I'm not saying he's right. I'm only saying he has a reason. Okay?"

Shadow nodded and turned back to Michael. She leaned over and kissed him on the cheek. Michael had a point. She couldn't dispute the reasoning behind Raven's concern about Stacy. He felt he had to follow every lead brought to him even if he thought it would dead end with the proof of her innocence. He had more or less said the same thing the night before. She only had one problem with that. The real culprit was getting away.

"Mind if I look around outside for awhile before I head to the office?"

"I don't know what you hope to find, but go for it. Grab you a hard hat off the counter. And Shadow, be careful."

Shadow grinned and slapped him on the shoulder. "I'm always careful."

"Yeah, right."

Shadow laughed, grabbed a hard hat, waved and left the trailer. Standing at the bottom of the steps, she placed the hat on her head before looking around the area.

The bulldozers were clearing out the spot for the hotel's parking lot. Other workers were busy preparing for the hotel's massive foundation to be poured. Within a week, the actual structure would begin to arise.

Shadow glanced around the perimeter and shuddered. Her father would turn over in his grave to see armed men standing guard over his construction crew and equipment. But then, he probably did a back flip when his dozers were blown up and his stepson and men were hurt from the explosions. She took comfort in knowing her father would have taken the same measures they did to ensure his men's safety.

Shadow pushed back a wave of sadness and longing for her father and set off at a brisk pace toward old man Fletcher's rundown shack. It was due to be pushed down and cleared that morning to become part of the parking lot. She wanted to look around inside once more before it was destroyed.

The rusty hinges creaked as she pulled the door wide open. Reaching into her back pocket, she pulled out a small flashlight she had brought from home and turned it on. The light shining from the one small dirty window in the front of the shack wouldn't be enough to allow her to see the whole room.

Shadow stepped inside and yelped as she became enveloped in spider webs. Her arms swiped at the air with vigorous jabs until they were knocked down and in the process she managed to drop her flashlight. She heard it hit the ground and roll.

Shadow groaned and vigorously rubbed her hands over her face, arms and clothes trying to get the worst off of her. Luckily, most of her hair was covered with the hard hat. "This is just frickin great," she sputtered and spit away the web clinging to her lips. Running her fingers over her face one more time, she looked around the room and saw the dim beam from her flashlight. It had rolled only a couple of feet away.

She took quick, hopping steps until she got close enough to grab it into her hand and shine the light on the ground at her feet. Spider webs she could handle, but she had a real problem with varmints like snakes and rats. A breath of anxiety was released when she saw neither.

With a steadier hand, Shadow moved the lights beam across the small, empty living area. Raven's and her own footprints from two days before still showed on the dirty wooden floor. She walked from one corner to the last, sidestepping a couple of rotten boards without seeing anything that would help with the case.

She walked to the doorway of the kitchen. Before entering, she shined the light above her head and on the floor at her feet. Not seeing any varmints, she ducked her head beneath a large spider web and walked in. Other than the one large sink and an old fashioned pump spigot, the kitchen was as empty as the living room.

Leaving there, she walked to the only bedroom in the house. She followed the same procedure as she did in the kitchen before walking into the bedroom.

She stopped dead still.

"Holy crap." Shadow shined the light from one side of the room to the next. She shook her head in disbelief. Every board of the floor had been removed to reveal the dirt ground below. Several deep holes had been dug fresh into the dirt between the floors supporting beams. The holes were deep enough that if she stood inside of one, her head would be below the top surface.

She started backing up, turned and ran out of the house hollering Michael's name at the top of her lungs. Even with the roar of the bulldozer's engines, Michael heard her and came running out of the trailer. They met up in the middle of the field.

Shadow bent over and placed both hands on her knees trying to control her breath. Her eyes were wide from her find. Spider webs clung to her clothes and dirt streaks were smeared across her face and arms.

Michael grabbed her by the arms and forced her to stand straight. "Shadow, my God, what's wrong?"

Shadow took a deep, calming breath. Her voice shook as she answered. "Michael, you've got to come see this." She grabbed him by the arm and started pulling him toward the shack.

"Whoa. Hold up. I'm coming." Michael pulled back his arm from her tight grip and ran to keep up with her.

Shadow led the way into the house and went

straight to the bedroom door. She turned the beam of the flashlight to shine on the floor. "Take a look at that."

"Daaaaamn!" Michael stared at the destruction below him. He turned toward Shadow. She heard the worry in his voice. "This was dug recently."

Shadow nodded. "It wasn't like this two days ago when Raven and I came in here."

"Which means, someone has been sneaking past our guards at night to come in here and dig for who knows what." Michael said. He took Shadow's hand and began leading her out of the house. "We need to report this to the police."

Shadow argued. "No we don't. They will keep it tied up for days while they investigate. You know as well as I do that we're on a tight schedule. That building needs to come down as soon as possible."

Michael stopped outside the shack and stared down at Shadow as if she'd grown two heads. "Are you crazy?" He shook his head back and forth. "Uh uh. I'm not listening to any of your hair-brained ideas. I'm calling the police." He pulled his cell phone out of its case and began dialing.

Shadow grabbed his arm. "Michael, listen to me. If you call the police in now we won't have a snowball's chance in hell in catching them tonight when they come back."

Michael disconnected the call. He threw his hands up in the air and then glared down at her. "Have you ever thought that they may not be back? That maybe they found what they were looking for and are long gone?"

"We don't know that. Look Michael, I'll make you a deal. If they don't show up tonight, we'll call the police first thing in the morning. How's that?" She stared up at him with a pleading look. "Please."

"Oh hell. Okay. All right. You win. I won't call the police." When she laughed and moved to hug him, he stopped her with a finger pointed at her face and a scowl. "On one condition."

Shadow stepped back and a brow rose. "What condition?"

"I call in Raven and Bob to be here with us tonight."

"Oh hell no. Uh uh. There's no way I'm calling those bast...."

"Shadow ...?" Michael interrupted with a warning. "It's either them or the police. Take your pick."

Shadow glared at him and then relented. She could tell by Michael's stance he wasn't backing down. "Oh, alright. Call the backstabbers if you have to. I'm going home and taking another shower. You can find me at the office later." Shadow turned and stormed off toward the SUV.

Michael grinned. He was very glad he couldn't hear the words flowing out of her mouth as she marched off. They couldn't be good.

* * *

Raven turned off his computer just as his phone rang. He answered with a distracted hello.

"Hey. This is Michael. I thought I should warn you Shadow is on her way home and she's not a happy woman."

Raven grinned, his mood restored. "Thanks for the warning, but I'm up for the challenge. I take it she told you what happened yesterday?"

"Oh yeah. In vivid, Technicolor language."

"And?"

"And I told her to trust you."

"And?"

"She agreed your reasoning is sound, but she still doesn't think Stacy is involved. I have a hard time believing it myself."

"Michael, you know I still have to check it out." Raven reminded himself of a broken record. He began pacing the floor.

"I know and I'll be more than happy to help you in anyway. But, that's not why I called. We've got a problem." Michael began telling Raven about Shadow's discovery that morning and her crazy plan to catch the diggers in the act.

Raven stopped in his tracks. "I'll be right there," he barked into the phone and disconnected. He dialed Bob's number. "Meet me at the construction sight. Now."

Fifteen minutes later, Raven drove up to the construction sight and parked. Getting out, he stood beside his car and watched Bob pull up beside him.

They headed toward the trailer and met Michael walking toward them with two hard hats in his hands. Greeting each other, Michael handed a hard hat to each man and all three headed toward the old shack and entered. Michael led them to the bedroom.

Raven and Bob stood in the doorway staring in disbelief at the ground and the dug holes where a bedroom floor should stand. They both began analyzing the destruction and asking questions.

Raven's gaze covered every inch of the room. He shook his head in contemplation. "Maybe old man Fletcher buried his life savings and someone found out about it."

"From the way this old shack looks, I would say

Shadow's Justice

that was almost possible. He sure didn't spend any money on simple comforts to make his life any easier. But, I don't think anyone would bother burying money six feet or deeper. Especially, when it's hidden by a bedroom floor," Bob said.

"What I want to know is how they got in here to dig. They would've been spotted in an instant if they had come through the front. There's no back door and that old window over there looks like it's been nailed shut for years." Michael looked at the four walls still standing and then at the window.

"Good question." Bob walked across the beam until he came to the back wall. He took one hand and pushed against a wide plank. When it held steady, he moved across the beams from one plank to the next until he came to one that gave outward as he pushed. The next one was the same way. He turned and began walking back to Raven and Michael. "We have one mystery solved, anyway."

"Well, at least now we know where we need to set up our stake-out tonight," Raven told them as he beamed the light across the floor.

"Do you want me to see if I can find out how long it's been since they last dug? I can get some samples from the overturned soil," Bob said.

"No, we know that it's been within forty-eight hours and you'd have to disturb the dirt to get samples. I don't want them to see anything suspicious if they return tonight and then take off before we can grab them."

"If they return," Michael added.

"Let's hope they do or we'll be in for a long night," Raven answered. He looked down at his watch. It was almost noon. "Let's get out of here. I need to stop in at the Police station when I get to town. Today might be a good day to buy Paul's lunch. We might need his help tonight."

Michael glanced over at Raven as they walked toward the front door and grinned. "Shadow wouldn't let me call the police, earlier. She thought they would swarm the place during their investigation and tip off the bad guys before tonight."

"Yeah? Well, this part is out of her hands. Paul needs to be kept informed of what's going on if we expect any kind of help from him. He won't need to investigate anything if we catch them red-handed tonight."

"Oh, I agree with you one hundred percent as long as you're the one who tells Shadow."

Raven laughed. "Chicken shit."

Michael grinned and slapped Raven on the back. "You bet. That woman scares me when she's pissed. I'll see you guys later. I've got to get back to work. Let me know what time we're meeting up tonight."

"I'll call you. Keep your eyes and ears open, my friend," Raven told him in warning.

They walked outside into the fresh air. With a wave of a hand, Michael headed back to the site. Raven and Bob walked to their cars.

* * *

A stranger slowly released the hammer down on his pistol as he watched from his hidden vantage point the three men leave the shack.

CHAPTER SIXTEEN

Shadow patted the pistol holstered at her side. On one hand she felt pretty darn safe carrying a firearm tonight, but on the other hand, the loaded gun made her nervous. Knowing herself, she'd go off half-cocked and shoot her own foot off, she thought.

She glanced over at Raven, Bob, Michael and Paul standing together talking in muted voices. Not wanting their vehicles to be seen at the site, Raven had Paul's deputy to drop the five of them off at the trailer at seven o'clock to ready themselves before nightfall.

They applied their dark camouflage, loaded and checked their weapons and packed their supplies. Now, it was time to move to their chosen hiding place.

"It's getting late, boys. Are we ready?" Shadow asked without letting her gaze stray toward Raven. So far, she had been able to ignore him by simply staying out of his way. She knew the confrontation between them was soon in coming, but not tonight. Right now, they had more important matters than their faltering relationship to concentrate on.

"Ready as we'll ever be," Michael answered.

Shadow grabbed up her pack and led the other four men out of the trailer. The spot they picked for the stake-out was perfect for their purpose. Fifty yards or so from the back of the shack was an area not yet cleared by the bulldozers.

Tall brush surrounded a small lean-to shed that was ready to topple from age. Earlier, they had cleared out a spot to hide inside and thinned the brush enough to be able to see the back of the house. Shadow had made them check every inch of the shed for snakes and spiders before they left.

Walking inside the shed, they began setting up there equipment and supplies. Raven had brought each of them night vision goggles. He handed those out as well as flashlights.

Shadow packed water and sandwiches in case it turned into an all-nighter and was teased without mercy by the men wanting to know if she thought this was going to be a picnic. Let 'em starve, she fumed, knowing they would be the first to grab a sandwich.

She set up her stool in one corner, placed her supplies close at hand and prepared to wait. She watched the others do the same. Dismayed, she watched Raven set up beside her. She gave him a dirty look and he only grinned before sitting down and placing his rifle across his lap.

Raven had warned them earlier that all conversation and unnecessary movement would stop as soon as darkness fell. They were close enough to the shack that any noise could be heard by anyone approaching.

Shadow squirmed until she was comfortable in her seat. Long minutes later, she watched the sun set until complete blackness engulfed them. The quarter moon's dim light only made the night seem more eerie.

She heard Raven's even breath and wondered if he felt he was in his element. She realized this was a small part of his dangerous job when he was off on one of his missions. She would see for the first time, the real mercenary inside the man she had fallen in love with.

The dangerous side of him excited her.

She wanted to know this man, the mercenary. She wanted to compare the man who was a friend and a lover to the one who easily faced hazards with unknown foes and harsh elements to complete his operation.

She knew from the few conversations she'd had with Bob that his men would follow him into hell and back if he asked them to. Raven commanded their respect and earned their trust with his strong leadership. He was a loyal friend and a master of intelligence operations. What Bob was saying was Raven maneuvered his men in and out safely with mission accomplished.

Maybe, just maybe, she should put as much trust into Raven as his men did, Shadow thought. Especially, since she herself had considered and then rejected the thought of calling Stacy to let her know about the stakeout. She knew in her heart Stacy wasn't involved in anything, but the 'what if?" stopped her from picking up the phone.

Shadow closed her eyes for a moment and settled in her chair. Her butt was going numb and her neck was stiff from sitting still for so long.

Shadow glanced down at the illuminated hands on her watch and was surprised that two hours had already passed. She was bored stiff and fighting sleep.

Shadow's Justice

It's just not natural for a woman to sit still and not talk for this many hours, she grumbled to herself and stifled a yawn.

Shadow kept her gaze focused on the shack. No action, there. The silence was only broken by the crickets and other creatures of the night. She felt her eyes grow heavy and they drifted shut.

* * *

Two hours later, Raven knelt beside Shadow and shook her awake. He placed his hand over her mouth to keep her from making any noise when she woke. He whispered in her ear. "They're here."

Raven waited until Shadow reached for her night vision goggles and put them on before he stood and joined the other men. Shadow moved with quiet steps to his side.

With a wave of a hand, Raven sent Michael to one end of the house and with the wave of the other, Paul and Bob took off on silent feet to the other side. He motioned for Shadow to stay behind. Grabbing his rifle, he turned and blended into the darkness.

Raven slid in beside Michael, his back pressed hard against the outside wall. He glanced up in time to see Shadow running toward him. He reached out and grabbed her arm pulling her against the wall.

He cursed under his breath. When this was over with, he was going to wring her neck for deliberately disobeying his orders. When the action began, he only hoped he could keep her safe.

Raven pushed himself along the wall until he came to the edge. He peeked around the corner and saw Bob doing the same on the other side. A dim glow from a lantern could be seen through the cracks of the wall. He listened for a long moment to get his bearing on the location of the diggers inside. He glanced back at Bob and gave the nod.

Rushing to the back, the four men kicked in the wall and with guns raised, they stormed the shack.

The three men inside dropped their shovels and raised their hands into the air.

"Bob. Search them," Raven ordered.

Each man in turn was searched and found carrying a pistol. Bob tossed each one to the ground in front of Michael.

Michael retrieved the guns and threw them into a bag slung across his back. Raven kept his rifle trained on the men.

"Mind telling me what you guys are doing here?" Raven noticed two of the younger men glancing toward the one he labeled, 'Bulldog' because of his flat nose and wide, massive shoulders. Raven figured him to be the leader.

"Just digging for worms. Goin' fishing tomorrow." Bulldog answered with a smirk.

Raven turned his rifle until the barrel was pointed toward the man's heart and cocked it. "You're trespassing and destroying private property and what's worse, you've caused me to lose sleep and now you're pissing me off. I'll ask you one more time. What are you doing here?"

"Raven, watch out behind you," Shadow screamed.

A smoke bomb went off in the room causing visibility to be nil. Numerous rounds of gunshots were fired. Moans and shouts blended into the darkness. The sound of running feet disappeared into the distance. Then, there was silence.

* * *

Several moments later, the thick smoke began

Shadow's Justice

dissipating. Shadow lay on her stomach, her face pressed into the dirt. The total silence around her gave her enough courage to lift her head and look around. She was alone.

Shadow stood and dusted her self off as she looked toward the darkness outside the room. She whimpered and looked around for the men. She took a step and tripped over her goggles and landed hard on her knees.

Cursing under her breath, Shadow reached for her goggles and stood again. That's when she heard a moan. She grabbed her pistol with both hands and took hesitant steps toward the sound. She walked across the beams, listening. When she heard the moan, again, Shadow glanced down.

A man was lying on his back in a deep hole dug at least six feet down. She sucked in a breath. It was Raven. Shadow scrambled down the hole until she knelt beside him.

Pulling out her flashlight, she ran the light's beam across his face. His eyes were closed and he was unresponsive. She moved the flashlight lower and saw the reason. The hard landing was enough to knock him unconscious, but he had also been shot in the shoulder. Blood seeped out of the wound and on to the ground.

Shadow sobbed out, but went to work. She pulled off her backpack and reached inside for a bottle of water. Uncapping the bottle, she leaned over Raven, pulled him toward her and poured the water over his wound on both sides to cleanse away the dirt. He groaned, but never moved.

She reached back into her backpack and pulled out a long sleeve shirt she had packed in case the night grew cooler. She wrapped the shirt around his shoulder and arms and tied it as tight as she could with the arms of the shirt.

Wiping away tears, Shadow gently let his body rest back on the ground. She'd done all she could do for now. Standing, she glanced around the hole she was in and felt a shudder run down her back. She felt like she was standing in a grave. The top was several inches above her head and Raven was stretched out on his back with plenty of room around him to spare.

Getting down was a piece of cake. Climbing back up again would be the problem. Shadow glanced around for something to stand on and spotted her back pack. She was wondering what had happened to Raven's when she glimpsed the backpack lying between him and the wall.

Feeling like she was running a relay race, she grabbed up both packs and placed one on top of the other. Shadow placed one hand on the wall to steady herself as she climbed on top. She could have wept when she realized it had given her enough height to place both elbows on top of the floor. Using her feet, she was able to shimmy up the wall and climb out of the hole.

Shadow's arms and legs felt like rubber and she felt like her lungs would collapse from the exertion, but she didn't have time to stop and rest. She had to get Raven to the hospital and she was worried to death about Michael, Paul and Bob. They might be injured as well or even worse. She was afraid to call out their names, in case the other men were still around.

Shadow stood, pulled out her cell phone and called 911. She gave them their location and Raven's condition before disconnecting and then punching out the number for the police station. She left a message with the dispatcher to radio the deputy and send him to the site.

She made her way to the back wall and turned on her flashlight. She stepped out into the darkness. A hand fell on her shoulder. Shadow screamed, jerked away from the hand and took off running.

"Shadow, it's me," Michael called out.

Shadow stopped, turned around and ran back into his arms and held on tight. "Thank God, you're okay." Then she stepped back and whopped him on the shoulder. "Don't ever scare me like that, again."

Michael groaned and rubbed his shoulder. "I'm sorry. Damn, that hurt."

"Good. Have you seen Paul or Bob?"

"Yes. They're headed back this way. Where's Raven?"

"He's in a deep hole in there. He's been shot."

"Shit!" Michael followed Shadow back into the room and glanced down into the hole she was pointing toward.

"I've called the ambulance and the deputy. They should be here any minute."

"We lost 'em," Bob and Paul joined them. Bob noticed the worried look on Shadow's face. He glanced from Shadow to Michael. "What's wrong?"

"Raven's been shot in the shoulder and we need to get him out of there," Michael said.

Bob glanced into the hole and cursed. He'd never seen his boss down. Raven was always the one who got them out of scraps.

Bob jumped down beside Raven and knelt over him. He was still knocked out. He checked him over from head to foot. He didn't find anything broken, but there was no way to tell what type of internal injuries he may have.

"Shadow, see if you can find me a wide board about five or six feet long. Paul, I think between the both of us, we can lift him up on the board high enough for the medical team to grab him and pull him over when they get here," Bob ordered.

Paul jumped in beside Bob, ready to help.

"See if this will work," Shadow she slid a board from the back wall down to them.

Bob grabbed the board and laid it flat on the ground. He hoped the aged lumber would hold Raven's weight.

The sound of sirens pierced the silence as the ambulance pulled onto the site. Michael ran outside to meet them and brought the paramedics back to Raven.

The team lifted Raven onto the board. Raven moaned, but lay motionless. With a man on each end, they lifted Raven into the air and rested the board on the top edge of the hole. Michael and a paramedic pulled him away from the lip until he was resting flat on the ground.

Shadow knelt beside Raven and rechecked his bandage while Michael helped pull the other men out of the hole. Blood had soaked through the shirt she had wrapped around his shoulder and arm.

She rose and moved away from Raven, giving the two men and a woman room to work over Raven. They checked his vital signs before transferring him over to their gurney.

Shadow followed them outside to the ambulance and stood out of the way as they lifted him into the back and prepared him for the ride to the hospital.

She climbed in beside him and held his hand tight. She saw the deputy drive up as the paramedic closed the door on the ambulance.

Shadow reached over and with a gentleness brushed the dirt from Raven's face. She allowed the tears she'd been holding in check flow down her cheeks. "I love you," she whispered.

Maybe, just maybe he could hear her and know how she felt. She didn't know if she would ever be brave enough to tell him she loved him when he was conscious. She couldn't take the heartbreak of hearing him say he didn't feel the same way toward her.

Right now, she didn't care he didn't love her enough to be a permanent part of her life. He needed her and that was enough for now.

Shadow glanced down at her watch. It had been over a half an hour since she'd found him. It worried her that he had been unconscious for this long of a time. He landed hard on his back in the fall and it could've resulted in serious injuries.

The 'what ifs' began tumbling through her mind. What if he broke his neck or spine? What if he punctured a lung or damaged a kidney? What if he was bleeding internally? The gunshot wound and loss of blood was bad enough in itself. The wound could become infected causing major problems.

Oh Lord. Stop it, she told herself. Shadow straightened her spine and wiped away the tears with the back of her hand. She had to quit worrying about what might happen. Once again, she needed to be strong for a man she loved.

Her troubled thoughts were interrupted as the ambulance pulled up in front of the hospital. The paramedics opened the back doors and lifted Raven out of the ambulance. They rolled him inside where nurses were waiting to take him into an examination room.

Shadow climbed out of the ambulance and rushed into the hospital behind Raven. She tried to follow them into the room, but was stopped by a nurse who forced her to wait in the waiting room. She was filling out admission forms when Michael, Paul and Bob joined her.

"How is he?" Michael asked.

"About the same. They just wheeled him into an examination room. The nurse said the doctor on duty would be with him shortly."

"That's good."

After hearing Raven was with the doctor and there was nothing they could do for Raven at the time, Paul and Bob left the room.

Michael sat down beside Shadow. He gave her an affectionate squeeze around the shoulders. "How are you holding up?"

"I'm fine. I'll be better when we talk to the doctor."

"Yeah, me too."

Shadow heard the worry in Michael's voice and knew it echoed her own. She laid her head on his shoulder and whispered. "He'll be alright. He has to be."

Michael gave her an extra squeeze and nodded.

Bob and Paul returned with four cups of coffee from the vending machine.

"Here. I thought you might need this." Bob told Shadow as Paul handed a cup to Michael.

Shadow smiled her thanks and reached for the coffee. "I do. Thank you." She held the warm

Styrofoam cup between her hands.

Several nerve-racking minutes later, she heard, "Deveroux family?"

Shadow glanced up and stood as she saw a doctor standing in the doorway.

"How is he?" she asked after the introductions were made.

"He'll be fine. I'm sending him into surgery right now to remove the bullet fragments and check out any type of damage. He has a mild concussion, but he is conscious, now. He's lost a lot of blood and will need a couple pints put back in him. I want to keep him in the hospital for a couple of days to make sure no infection sets in the wound or any other complications that might crop up."

Shadow breathed a sigh of relief. His condition was bad enough, but it could've been a heck of a lot worse. "Can I see him before he goes into surgery?"

"Yes. But just for a minute. They've already given him a shot to knock him out."

"Thank you." Shadow said before walking into the room where Raven lay. She rushed to his side. His complexion was pale, but he looked a lot better than he did earlier. He glanced up and gave her a drugged smile. The shot was kicking in.

"How are you feeling?"

"Much better. I was worried about you." His voice was grainy.

"I'm fine. I can't stay long. I just wanted you to know I'll be here while you're in surgery."

Raven nodded. His body seemed to relax. Raven glanced up into Shadow's eyes and whispered, "I heard what you said."

Shadow held his gaze. "What did I say?"

Shadow's Justice

"You said "I love you."

Shadow's face turned red. "You heard that? You were unconscious."

"I heard you and for the record, I love you, too."

Raven's head fell to the side as the pain medicine knocked him out.

CHAPTER SEVENTEEN

Shadow slept in a chair beside Raven's hospital bed. She woke to find a young nurse standing over him checking his vital signs.

After two hours of surgery and an hour in the recovery room, they had installed him into a private room around five a.m.. She knew the nurses had been in and out, but she'd been too exhausted to waken.

Shadow glanced down at her watch. It was now eight o'clock. She yawned and spoke to the young nurse. "Good morning. How is he?"

The nurse glanced back at her and smiled warmly. "He's doing fine. The doctor will make his rounds around nine and talk to you, then." She put her stethoscope into her pocket. "We keep a pot of coffee going at the nurse's station if you would like a cup."

Shadow smiled. "I would love a cup." She followed the nurse out of the room and located the coffee pot. Pouring a Styrofoam cup full, she went straight back to Raven's room. She wanted to be with him when he woke.

Michael was standing beside Raven's bed when Shadow entered his room. She greeted him with a hug.

Shadow's Justice

"How is he?" he asked.

"He seems to be doing okay. He's still konked out, but at least he's not feeling any pain, right now. The nurse said the doctor makes his rounds around nine o'clock. Maybe, we can find out something by then."

"That's good." Michael stifled a yawn.

Shadow grinned. "Here, take my cup of coffee. I'll get some more."

"Thanks, but I need to get out to the site. I'll get some there. Oh, by the way, Mom is on her way here. She knew you wouldn't leave, so she said she was bringing you a change of clothes."

"Thank goodness. I know I look like I've been playing in the mud."

Michael laughed and teased. "You do. You might want to stay away from the mirror this morning."

Shadow moaned. "That's just great."

"It's not that bad. Will you call me when you talk to the doctor?"

"Sure. Do you want me to tell Raven anything when he wakes up?"

"Yeah. Tell him that damn shack is coming down, today."

"He'll be glad to hear that. The whole site has been like a bad omen since day one."

"Amen, to that." Michael leaned down and kissed her on the forehead. "Got to go. Call me."

"I will. You be careful out there."

"I will. Quit worrying. See ya."

"Bye." Shadow took a sip of coffee and watched Michael leave. She couldn't help but worry. First, it was John who was hurt and now Raven. She feared what would happen next.

"Shadow?"

Shadow's Justice

Shadow heard the weak voice behind her and swung around toward the bed. "You're awake." She hurried to his side. "How do you feel?"

Raven ran his tongue over his dry lips. "Like hell warmed over. Can I have some water?"

"Of course. The doctor said you could have a little." Shadow poured a glass of water and put his straw in the glass. She raised the head of the bed enough so that he could drink from the straw. "Here. Take small sips."

Raven drank a few sips before his head fell back on the pillow. He glanced around the hospital room. "What happened?"

"We were ambushed and you were shot in the shoulder. You had to go into surgery earlier this morning to have the bullet fragments removed and your shoulder repaired."

Raven cursed under his breath and asked, "Is it as bad as it feels?"

Shadow grinned. "Probably not. The doctor will be here in a few minutes and you can ask him yourself."

Raven stared up at Shadow's rumpled and dirty appearance, barely hearing her answer. "You stayed."

Shadow's brow rose. "I told you I would be here. Did you doubt it?"

Raven shook his head. "No. Come here and kiss me."

Shadow couldn't believe how shy she became when she heard his words, but wild horses couldn't have held her back. She leaned over to kiss him.

"Raven? Good, you're awake? How are you? Shadow, I brought you some more clothes." Rose swept into the room.

Shadow found herself straightening Raven's covers.

She turned and greeted Rose.

"Thank you. Thank you. You're a life saver."
Shadow took the clothes and her overnight bag from
Rose and leaned down to kiss her on the cheek. "I'll
go into the bathroom and get cleaned up while you
visit with Raven."

Shadow glanced at Raven and let her frustration
show. She felt a little better when she saw the same
look in his eyes.

Rose did have a way of making a grand entrance.
This was twice she had interrupted their intimacy.
Shadow gave Raven a smile and an "Oh well" shrug
before turning and walking into the bathroom.

Shadow felt one hundred percent better when she
walked out of the bathroom a few minutes later after
washing, putting on clean clothes and brushing her
teeth. She'd run a brush through her hair, added a
touch of makeup and gave herself a strong lecture
before leaving.

They had both confessed their love for each other
the night before and she'd be danged before she'd let
him fall out of love with her.

Rose wouldn't always be around to interrupt them.
Shadow was damned and determined to finish what
they started the next time and make him love it. She
smiled to herself. Seems like she always had a mission
to accomplish.

Rose was standing over Raven's bed doing what
she does best, Shadow noticed as she came out of the
bathroom. Her mothering skills were being displayed
as she plumped Raven's pillows.

"Do I look more presentable?" Shadow asked both
Raven and Rose. It was Raven's response she waited
for.

Shadow's Justice

"You look wonderful. Refreshed," Rose answered.

Shadow turned toward Raven. His gaze traveled up and down her body.

"Ditto." His sensual mouth turned up at the corner.

Shadow's brows narrowed. He knew she couldn't respond to that smile while Rose watched them.

Raven grinned.

Before Shadow could respond, she was interrupted by someone entering the room.

"Hello, everyone. How is our patient today?" The doctor swept into the room with his nurse at his heels.

"I'm doing just great. Good enough to go home today," Raven answered.

The doctor laughed. "That might be rushing things a little too much." The nurse handed him Raven's chart and he began looking it over.

"When can I go home?" Raven asked.

The doctor closed the chart and handed it back to the nurse. He moved to the bedside and checked the bandage on his shoulder before giving Raven an answer.

"Give it a couple more days and if no infection sets up in your shoulder, you can go home then. How does that sound?"

"Like a life sentence," Raven grumbled.

Shadow turned toward the doctor and laughed. "I can tell right now he's not going to be an easy patient to deal with."

The doctor smiled. "Most men aren't. We're too macho to be ill." He patted Raven on his foot at the end of the bed. "If you need anything, just call one of the nurses. I'll be back to check on you in the morning."

"Thank you, Doctor." Raven frowned, resigned to his fate.

Rose stood and prepared to leave. "I need to get back to John. I'll be back to check on you, though. Call me if you need me," she told them as she kissed Shadow's cheek and bent down and kissed Raven's. She whispered in his ear. "I love you and so does Shadow. She'll stay by your side if you'll let her."

Taken back, Raven could only say, "Believe me, I will."

* * *

Bob wandered the streets of McClane Ridge. For once, he was dressed as himself in his casual denim. He'd decided early this morning that he might get more information out of people if they knew he was Raven's friend. It was worth a shot to try, anyway.

He stopped at the pedestrian walk. While he waited for the light to change before crossing the street, his thoughts went back to last night. He was beyond frustration that the men they had captured had slipped right through their fingertips. Could they have been tipped off that they were being watched? He never did see the fourth man who had slipped up behind them. Or was it a woman? Things didn't add up and it was annoying the hell out of him.

Bob stepped off the curb and crossed the street in front of the police station. He wanted to check in with Paul. His men had dusted for fingerprints earlier that morning. Molds had been made off the shoe prints from the four men and blood samples had been collected from one of the shovels. It would take the lab a few days, but he hoped they came up with something, because Michael was determined to bring the shack down this evening.

Bob opened one of the double doors going into the Police Station. A gut instinct made him stop and turn around. His gaze narrowed as he saw Stacy standing on the steps in front of the newspaper office. She was staring at him with venom in her eyes. She shot him a one finger hello before turning and walking into the building.

Bob laughed out loud. She was one sassy lady. Sexy as hell, too. His laughter stopped. Too bad, she was conniving and dishonest. Was she also a killer?

He was depending on his sources to give him the answer. Several of acquaintances in their network were delving into the matter for him. Within a few hours he would know Stacy's life history. Hell, they could find out what she had for breakfast two years ago if he thought it would help the case.

Bob took one last look toward the door where Stacy had walked through. For the first time in his life, he questioned his gut-instinct. What if he was accusing an innocent woman of a horrible crime?

Reaching into his pocket, he pulled out a roll of antacids and popped one into his mouth. Indecision and heartburn had never affected his life, until now.

Hell, maybe he should think about retiring after this case was solved. He could move to Mexico and spend the rest of his life serenading the senoritas. He was almost, pretty damn sure they could take his mind off of the tall, sensuous, green-eyed blonde who had just shot him the finger.

Bob popped another antacid into his mouth, turned back toward the police station and entered through the doors.

* * *

Shadow's Justice

Stacy was livid. She paced her office floor, growing angrier with every step. Just seeing that man pissed her off.

She knew he was having her investigated. Four of her friends and two of her neighbors had called the day before reporting that a government official had stopped by their homes asking a lot of questions about her.

She wasn't worried, though. The only thing her friends and neighbors knew about her was that she worked long hours at the newspaper office, socialized very seldom and went to church every Sunday morning. The last time she looked, there was no crime in that.

Stacy's phone rang and she cursed at the interruption.

She grabbed the phone and barked into the receiver. "Hello." She listened to the person's deep voice on the other end of the line.

"When did this happen?"

The person answered.

"Shit." Stacy hung up the phone. She grabbed her purse, told her secretary she would be gone for awhile and hurried from the building.

Stacy headed to the hospital. Raven had been shot earlier that morning and she was just now finding out about it.

Why hadn't Shadow called her? What was Raven doing at the site that early in the morning? Questions flew through her mind and she wanted answers. Dammit! A big story had almost slipped through her fingers.

* * *

Shadow watched Raven sleep. He'd sipped on a

Shadow's Justice

few spoonfuls of beef broth and drank a glass of milk for his noon meal before sleep overtook him.

She hadn't left his side to eat anything all morning, but her stomach began to feel empty and she needed to stretch her legs. She stood, grabbed up her purse and left to find the cafeteria.

Once she was in the cafeteria, Shadow filled her tray and found an empty table to sit while she ate her meal. When she was through, she walked outside into the sunshine. She needed the warmth and solitude for a moment to ease her tension.

A short time later, feeling more relaxed, she headed back to Raven's room. With a full stomach, she might be able to catch a quick catnap before he awakened.

Raven was still sleeping when she entered. Putting her purse down, she eased down into her chair and twisted around until she was comfortable. Leaning her head against the back of the chair, she closed her eyes and attempted to sleep.

"Shadow. I have a bone to pick with you."

Shadow's eyes popped open. She saw Stacy glaring down at her. Her hands were on her hips.

"Shhhhhh. You'll wake up Raven," Shadow whispered her disapproval.

"Too late. She already has." Raven grumbled from his bed.

Shadow stood and glared at Stacy before she walked around her to stand beside Raven. "Can I get you anything?"

Raven shook his head. His eyes were already closing again in sleep.

Shadow turned around, grabbed Stacy's arm and pulled her out of the room and down the hall to an empty waiting room. She let go of Stacy and sat down.

"Now. What's your problem?" Shadow demanded.

Stacy threw her hands up at the obvious. "My problem is that you didn't have the decency to call to let me know about the shooting."

Shadow shook her head in disbelief. Maybe she didn't know her friend after all. "So, you're here to get a story. You don't even care that Raven almost died."

Hurt showed in Stacy's eyes. "You know that's not true. He's my friend, too. I may be pissed at him right now, but I still care deeply about him."

"Then show it," Shadow shot back.

Hurt changed to anger. Stacy stepped back and stared down at her friend. She hesitated, then shook her head. "This is to unfrickin' unbelievable. You believe them."

"I don't know what you're talking about." Shadow went on the defensive.

"You know damn well what I'm talking about. You think I actually hired someone to kill Bob. I guess you think I shot Raven, too. Well, I've got news for you, my friend..., I didn't." She glared at Shadow one more time before she turned and stormed out the door.

Shadow jumped up and ran to the door. "Stacy."

Her friend stopped, but didn't turn around.

"I'm sorry." Shadow ran a tired hand across her face. "I'm exhausted and worried to death about Raven. I didn't mean to snap at you. And, No. I don't think you're capable of doing any of those things. Come back and sit down and I'll tell you about last night."

Stacy did turn around then and stared a long time

at Shadow. "Yeah? Well, "sorry" doesn't cut it. We've been friends a long time and I don't deserve any of this crap. But, I also know the hell you've been going through and I understand your bitchiness."

She looked Shadow up and down before sighing and returning back to the waiting room. Shadow watched her sit down before she joined her.

Stacy was hurt by her words and Shadow didn't blame her. She deserved everything her friend had thrown at her. But, damn it, why hadn't Stacy denied the charges before? Her denial was all she'd been waiting for.

Tears began to form in her eyes. Maybe all Stacy had been waiting on was the absolute trust of a true friend.

Shadow believed her without a doubt and she would make things right with Stacy if she had to hog-tie her to a tree and make her listen to her apologies. She sat down beside Stacy and began filling her in on the night's events.

When she finished, Stacy reached for her hand and squeezed. Her strained features showed her worry. "You could have all been killed. Are you sure you're okay?"

Shadow nodded and wiped a few tears away. "I'm fine and the doctor says Raven can go home in a couple of days. With rest, he'll be okay."

"And you will be close by to make sure he gets the rest," Stacy teased.

Shadow grinned. "You can bet your sweet bottom I will."

Stacy laughed and stood. "That's what I thought. I've got to get back to the office, but I'll call you later. Okay?"

Shadow's Justice

Shadow stood, as well and hugged Stacy. "Thanks for stopping by. It means a lot to me."

Stacy grinned and replied. "That's what friends are for." She waved and swept out of the room.

Shadow wiped away the tears and walked to the bathroom in the hallway. She splashed cold water on her face to get rid of all the evidence of her earlier distress before leaving the bathroom and heading toward Raven's room.

* * *

Raven was jarred awake. Groggy from the pain medicine, his eyelids felt as heavy as a ton of bricks. But, a noise had awakened him. He felt vulnerable for once in his life and it made him edgy.

He forced his eyes open. The room was in total darkness except for a sliver of moonlight coming through the window shades. He knew the day had slipped by while he slept.

A slight movement made him glance to his side. He saw an outline of a person standing over him holding a long object in his hand.

Raven lay still, watching and waiting, never moving. He kept his breathing slow and steady as if he were still asleep. He noticed the person was wearing jeans and a t-shirt instead of any type of medical uniform.

His first thought was that it was Michael, Bob or Paul. But, he soon realized the person was no one he recognized.

The individual raised the object in the air and Raven saw the shiny metal tip's silhouette in the moonlight. Then, he saw a stream of liquid shooting out of the tip. He knew what the person was holding. He felt his heart rate elevate.

Raven saw the object coming toward him and

acted. With one swift motion, Raven jerked his covers back. His right foot shot out, kicking hard to the person's midriff, knocking him backwards into the wall. He heard the syringe hit the tiled floor.

Raven heard Shadow's screams and his heart almost stopped. Shadow was in the room with them and in danger, as well. His male, protective instincts took over and he became the hunter. Despite the pain in his shoulder and the IV's stuck into his veins, he swung his legs over to the side of the bed to rise.

Then, he heard the footsteps running from the room.

CHAPTER EIGHTEEN

Shadow flipped the light switch and moved to Raven's side. He was sitting on the side of the bed breathing hard, his ashen-colored face showing his pain. She helped him lie down, all the while assuring him she was fine.

Shadow heard several footsteps running toward their room. She stepped back as a doctor and two nurses rushed to Raven's side.

"What's all the commotion going on in here?" The doctor questioned. He took in Raven's weak condition as the nurses checked his bandages and I.V.

"Someone just tried to attack me. I fought him off and he ran out of the room. The syringe is lying on the floor over there."

Raven's statement was calm and matter-of-fact, but inside his anger was boiling. The bastard who attacked him was as good as dead for putting Shadow in danger.

"Call Security and get them up here." The doctor barked out an order to one of the nurses. "Then call the police."

He turned back to Raven, his expression grim. "I'll make sure that a security guard is outside your door until the police can bring someone in to take over. They'll want to collect the evidence. I promise you this won't happen again while you're in our care."

"I appreciate that, Doc."

"Do you need one of the nurses to bring you a pain pill?"

Raven shook his head. "No. I need to keep a clear head. I'll be alright."

Before the doctor could argue, the security guard walked into the room. The doctor and Raven filled him in on what happened.

The guard assured them he would station himself outside the door and not allow anyone in the room other than the nurses on duty until the police arrived.

The guard left the room and the doctor turned back to his patient. "Let's take another look at that shoulder."

Raven waited patiently as the doctor checked him over and was relieved when he said the stitches hadn't broke loose. No blood seeped through the bandages.

"The nurses will be checking back in with you, but use the call button if you need them." The doctor told him before leaving to make his way back to his office.

As soon as the door shut behind them, Raven spoke. "Shadow, will you come here?"

Shadow rose from her chair and moved to his side. "What do you need?"

Raven scooted over to the far side of the bed and with his good arm, he pulled the covers back. He patted the spot beside him "Lay beside me. I need you close to me." He allowed his vulnerability to be displayed wide open for her to see.

Without a word, Shadow kicked off her shoes and climbed in beside him. Turning to her side, she snuggled up against him in the small bed and wrapped her arm across his middle.

"Is that better?"

"Much better," Raven told her.

He leaned over and kissed her on the top of the head. "I was so worried about you. I don't know what I would do if I lost you." His anguished whispered confession warmed her soul.

Shadow raised herself up on one elbow and looked him in the eyes. Her hand tenderly cupped his jaw. "I'm fine. He never touched me. It was you he was after. I know my life would be over if I lost you. But, do you know what?"

Raven shook his head.

"There, in the darkness when I knew you were in danger, I felt an unbelievable calmness come over me." Shadow shrugged her shoulder while trying to find the right words. "I don't know. It was like I knew you could take care of yourself. And me. I thought to myself, that idiot doesn't stand a chance. Raven will kick his butt from here to eternity."

Raven grinned and leaned down to softly kiss her luscious lips. His expression grew serious. "Thank you for your complete trust in me, but I'm not superhuman. Lying in this hospital bed testifies to that. My fear is that I won't always be able to protect you."

Shadow smiled and threw his own words back at him. "That may be true, but like you said, you're not superhuman. And these aren't normal circumstances. I don't plan on going through life fighting off bad men. Hopefully, this nightmare will be over soon and we can get back to a normal life."

A knock sounded. Shadow and Raven looked up as

the security guard opened the door and stepped inside.

"Sir. Ma'am. The police officer has arrived. He will be guarding you for the rest of the night. There's also a detective talking with the doctor right now and he will be in shortly to gather the evidence and to ask you a few questions. I'll be going, now. If you need me at anytime, just call."

"Thank you for everything," Shadow told him as she self-consciously climbed back out of the bed.

"Thanks," Raven added.

A few minutes later the detective knocked and entered. He introduced himself as Detective Sharp. He asked them several questions about the night's events while he scribbled in his notebook.

Neither Raven nor Shadow could give him much information. The room had been too dark and everything had happened too fast to gather many details in their minds.

The detective sighed and closed his notebook. "Well, if either of you think of anything else, give me a call."

"We will," Raven told him.

"Good." Detective Sharp pulled out his rubber gloves and a clear bag. He walked over to the syringe and leaned down to scoop it into the bag.

Rising, he pulled off his gloves and put the bag into his satchel. "Well, if that's it, I'll be heading back to the station to deliver this evidence. Here's my card. My number is on it if you need me."

"Thank you." Shadow walked him to the door. As the detective left, she glanced out into the hallway and saw a young police officer who she knew by sight, sitting in a chair outside their door. She gave him a smile before closing the door.

She walked back to the bed and climbed in beside Raven. Snuggling against him, she felt his steady breathing and knew he was finally giving in to sleep. Her eyes closed and she soon joined him.

* * *

Bob sat in the corner booth waiting on his breakfast. He sipped on his coffee and casually looked around the crowded room.

The local diner was hopping with the breakfast crowd. Everyone from the local farmers dressed in overalls to the well-dressed men and women in business suits were there to eat. The noisy room burst with activity with the constant, friendly chatter among the customers.

Bob's gaze fell on the two men across the room. Randall Collins and Judge Ben Adams sat across the table from each other. They seemed to be arguing, but Bob was too far away to hear them.

Collins was Bob's prey. He had hid outside of Collins's mansion that morning and followed him to the diner. He had nothing solid on Collins other than Raven's unsettling gut feeling, but that had served them well in the past.

There were too many links connecting Collins and the murdered victims to completely ignore. He was definitely worth watching.

A pretty waitress around his own age appeared with his breakfast. She noticed the direction of his gaze. Distaste of the two men showed clearly on her face. "Humph. Looks like there's friction between the town's leading pricks," she muttered under her breath.

Bob heard her quiet words and he grinned. "I take

it that you don't care much for them."

The waitress glanced back at Bob. "That would be the nice way to put it." Her brows narrowed. "You're new around here. I don't remember seeing you in here before."

"First time here. I've been in town a few days, though. I'm visiting with a good friend of mine, Raven Deveroux. Know him?"

The waitress grinned. "I know Raven, well. We use to be an item back in our school days. I heard he'd come back for the funeral."

Bob nodded. "He did. He's staying with the McClane's."

"Tell him to stop in and see me before he leaves."

"I will." Bob glanced back at the two men. "Why do you have such a dislike for those two? They seem harmless enough."

She looked down at Bob and her voice hardened. "Look, mister. Those two are as harmless as a rattlesnake and they have the power in this town to get away with anything, especially when the Police Chief was still alive."

She glanced around the busy room and saw new customers walking in. "I've got to get back to work. Enjoy your meal and tell Raven I said, hello." She pulled out her order pad and rushed back to work.

Bob began eating his breakfast. He wondered about the harsh feelings the waitress harbored against Collins and the Judge. He wanted to ask her several more questions, but didn't get the chance.

He watched as the two men stood and threw some money down on the table. Bob got a glimpse of the red, angry flush on Collins's face before he walked out of the diner. "Things seem to be sour in

Paradise," Bob muttered.

His waitress appeared at his side. "Would you like some more coffee?" she asked him, but her hard gaze was on the door that had just closed on the two men.

"No, thanks. But I would like to ask you a few more questions about our earlier conversation. What time do you get off work?"

She glanced down at Bob and shook her head. "I don't have anything else to tell you." She pulled his bill from her apron pocket and laid it on the table. Without another word, she turned and walked off.

Bob swore under his breath and watched her walk through the swinging doors into the kitchen. Her last words had held as much fear as they did the anger. He wanted to know why, but now wasn't the time to press the issue.

Picking up the bill, he stood and walked to the counter. He looked to see the amount to pay and noticed that on the bottom of the bill his waitress had written, "Thank you. Mandy."

Bob grinned. Now, he knew her name.

After paying the cashier, Bob left the diner. Getting into his car, he drove straight to the hospital. He would ask Raven more about Mandy.

* * *

Raven finished the last of his coffee and placed it on the tray beside his breakfast plate. Shadow had gone downstairs a few minutes earlier to eat breakfast in the cafeteria. He expressed his worry about her leaving his side after the attack that morning. He relented when she argued no one would attack her in broad daylight with people all around her. She would be okay.

Raven heard a knock on the door. He glanced up

as the door opened and Paul entered.

Paul greeted him with, "Can't you go through at least one night without being shot at or attacked in some way?"

Raven grinned. "Morning to you, too. Guess you heard about what happened last night?"

"Yeah, I heard. I was sleeping pretty damn good when I got the call this morning," he grumbled.

"Sorry about that."

"No, you're not." Paul grinned when he heard Raven's laughter. His tone turned serious. "I'm just glad you weren't hurt. I came by to check on you and to tell you that I've been busy this morning."

Raven sat up straighter. "Have you learned anything?"

Paul nodded and grinned. "We got a fingerprint and blood off one of the shovels. We're running it through the computer now."

"Hot damn!" Raven laughed. "I was beginning to think we'd never get a good lead on this case."

Paul smiled, but warned, "You'd better hope he has a record listed in the computer to match his fingerprints or DNA to or we'll be back to square one."

A knock sounded on the door and the deputy stuck his head through the opening. "Do you know a Bob Green?"

"Yeah, send him in." Raven told him.

The deputy stepped back. "You can go in, now."

Bob walked into the room and shut the door. His confusion was apparent. His thumb pointed back toward the door. "What's up with the guard stationed outside?"

"Raven was attacked last night." Paul and Raven

began filling him in on everything that had happened from the attack the night before to finding the fingerprints and blood this morning.

"Man, you guys have been busy. The news about the evidence is the best thing I've heard in days. But, I have also been busy. I had a very interesting breakfast this morning."

Raven snickered. "Let me guess. You changed from the big breakfast with all the trimmings to the jumbo breakfast with double everything."

Raven turned to Paul. "Have you ever seen this boy eat? It takes three waitresses to keep the food coming."

Paul shook his head and grinned. "Remind me to hire one of your bulldozers when I invite him home for dinner."

"Ha ha. Very funny, boys. No wonder you and Mandy aren't an item any longer. She probably didn't think your jokes were funny, either."

"Mandy?" Raven thought for a moment and then his face cleared. His sappy smile said it all. "Wow, I haven't thought of her in years. Man, she was beautiful."

"Oh, yeah?" Shadow stood in the doorway. She wasn't smiling. "Tell me more."

Raven grinned and quickly added. "But, not as beautiful as you."

Shadow laughed. "Good answer." She glanced at Bob and Paul. "What's up, boys?"

Bob caught Shadow up on the news before adding with a grin, "I hate to bring Mandy's name up, again, but she plays a big part in what I learned this morning."

Bob, told the three what had happened at the

diner, earlier. When he was through, he turned to Raven. "Do you think you might be able to get more information out of Mandy? She might know something important that will help us out. I'd like to know why she has such a pure hatred against Collins and the Judge."

"Yeah, me too. I'm supposed to be released as soon as the doctor makes his rounds this morning. Maybe I..." Raven glanced over at Shadow and grinned. "...and Shadow can stop by the diner after the lunch crowd leaves today. Mandy might have more time to talk to us then."

"Sounds good. I'll get back with you later on tonight. Collins is supposed to be in court all day. That will give me a chance to get a little sleep before I need to start tailing him, again."

"I need to get back to work. I'll let you know about the fingerprints as soon as I get the results back," Paul told them.

Raven watched the two men leave. As soon as the door shut behind them, Shadow walked toward him. Suspicious of her actions, he watched her cautiously.

Shadow leaned down and gently placed her lips on his and began taking him on a journey of sensuality he'd never experienced in his life.

When her lips released his, she straightened and looked down at him. "That's to let you know I really don't think I will ever have a reason to be jealous of you and another woman ever again."

One eyelid came down slowly in a sensual wink before she turned and with a provocative saunter, Shadow walked out of the room.

* * *

Michael watched with deep satisfaction as the

bulldozers flattened the old shack until it was level with the ground. With the front end loader, the operator shoved the crushed remains into a pile to be loaded into a dump truck for removal.

Paul's phone call earlier giving him the okay to destroy the building had made his day. They were still behind schedule, but at least now they could start making up time.

Michael made his way back to the trailer to call John. He was in daily contact with his brother, who by phone, still called the different contractors and set up the schedules from his bed.

Michael knew his limitations in keeping the construction running like clockwork. He could draw the plans up with ease, but John was the expert in pulling it all together to become a reality.

Fifteen minutes later their phone conversation was interrupted by a knock on the door. Michael stood and opened the door to find the Foreman standing outside.

Holding his hardhat in his hands, the Foreman spoke with urgency in his voice. "Boss, I think you need to come and take a look at this."

Seeing the tension in the man's face, Michael spoke into the phone. "I'll call you back." He hung up the phone and followed the Foreman's hurried steps leading to where the shack had once stood.

The bulldozer had already started breaking ground. Now the heavy machinery stood silent. The operator and several of the other workers were standing around the newly dug area.

Michael noticed they were all staring down at the loose dirt and talking quietly among themselves.

The operator glanced up as Michael drew near. He

Shadow's Justice

pointed toward the ground. "What do you make of that?"

Michael looked down to where the man was pointing. At first, all he could see was white spots mixed in with the brown dirt. He knelt down and scooped up two handfuls. The dirt sifted through his fingers leaving the white remains of a human appendage.

The bones of a forefinger lay intact across the palm of his hand.

Michael cursed. He quickly laid the bone down beside him and ran his hand through the pile, again. His fingers brushed across a larger object. He pulled it to the top and watched as the dirt fell away leaving the blank stare from the empty eye sockets of a small, human skull.

Michael turned back to his Foreman. "Call the police."

CHAPTER NINETEEN

Shadow hung up the phone and turned to Raven. She watched as the nurse helped him into the wheelchair. The release papers had been signed and Raven was able to leave the hospital. He fussed with every breath saying he could leave the hospital under his own steam.

Shaken to the core, Shadow ignored Raven's fussing and managed to hold her tongue in front of the nurse. With hurried steps, she left the room and headed to the parking lot while the nurse pushed Raven toward the front entrance doors.

Pulling the car around to the front, she parked and ran around to put their luggage into the trunk. The nurse helped Raven into the passenger seat as Shadow resumed her seat inside the car.

Driving out of the parking lot, Shadow glanced toward Raven before turning her attention back to the road. She asked, "Feel like riding out to the site with me?"

Raven glanced sharply at Shadow. He adjusted his sling. "Sure. The pain medicine is working fine. What's going on?"

"The phone call I got a few minutes, ago, was from Michael. He's discovered the reason those three guys were doing all that digging at the shack."

Shadow saw Raven sit up straighter. His brow rose. "And?"

"The dozer operator dug up a body this morning."

"Damn!"

Shadow's gaze focused on the road. She grinned at Raven's excitement. "My thoughts, exactly."

A few minutes later, Shadow maneuvered the car into a spot at the site between two patrol cars and parked. Getting out, she hurried to the passenger side to help Raven who was stubbornly trying to get out on his own.

Together, they walked toward the area where the shack once stood. Now, a yellow crime scene tape was wrapped completely around the section being investigated. A team of men with the letters 'New Orleans Crime Lab' blazoned on their white coats was busy gathering evidence.

Paul, Michael and Detective Sharp who had showed up at the hospital the night before, stood talking together.

Shadow and Raven joined them.

"Any news?" she asked no one in particular.

Michael answered. "Not yet. They're still gathering all the bone, clothing and hair fragments they can find. Detective Sharp was asking me about the deed to the property. I told him I thought you had all the paperwork at the office."

Not really understanding why the detective was asking about the deed, Shadow still nodded. "I do. I can have my secretary bring it out here if you need it."

"If you don't mind, I would appreciate it."

Detective Sharp replied.

Raven spoke up. "I think I know where you're leading with this. I might be able to save you some time, Detective. I've read the deed. This land was purchased in 1879 by the Fletcher family and has stayed in the family until our client bought it last December. The son, Jake Fletcher built that home for him and his new bride close to fifty years ago."

The detective stopped scribbling in his notebook and glanced quickly at the crime scene and then back at Raven. "Are you saying the body has been buried there for at least fifty years?"

Raven nodded. "That's what I'm saying. I think I also know who was buried there."

"Who?"

"A fifteen year old girl by the name of Karen Jacobs. She came up missing fifty years ago and was never found."

Shadow sucked in a harsh breath. "My God, you're right. It has to be her."

"If it is, we should be able to match it up with her dental records that are still on our archived file," Paul inserted.

"Great. Let's check into that right away," the detective said before turning back to Raven and grinning. "It sure would save me a whole lot of time and energy if you happened to know who killed her, too."

Raven laughed. "I'm afraid I can't help you there. I'll keep my suspicions to myself."

"Oh well. Can't win 'em all. I guess I'd better get to work, then. Let me know if you think of anything else."

"I will."

Shadow's Justice

Detective Sharp closed his notebook, raised his hand in a wave and walked toward the crime scene where the crime unit was busily taking samples.

Shadow turned back to Raven. She shook her head, her thoughts racing. "Surely, Fletcher didn't kill that girl and then build his home on top of the grave."

"It's a possibility, but I really don't think that's what happened. I'd bet you top money someone else buried the body there, never dreaming someone would build a home right in this very spot."

"Or, maybe they did know," Paul interjected. "Hide your crime where you know it will be buried beneath a house that might stand for over a hundred years? What could be a better plot?"

"You guys do realize the murderer may be dead by now, don't you?" Michael pointed out.

Raven shook his head. "I don't think so. We scared the crap out of someone when we began the construction here. They went to a lot of trouble to keep their secret safe. First, they tried to warn everyone away with the explosions and when that didn't work, they decided to have the body dug up and moved before it was found."

Shadow agreed. The murderer was still alive. And dangerous. She glanced over at the grave and wondered what the poor girl had suffered before succumbing to the hands of death.

The burial spot was miles away from where she was last seen leaving the party. Hours could have gone by before she was finally killed. Was she tortured or raped or both? Was her last breath a scream of terror?

Shadow shook her head to ward away her terrifying images. She rubbed her arms vigorously as she felt a cold chill run through her at the thought of the murderer still on the loose. Another thought lingered. Was Karen Jacobs his only victim or had he struck again and again?

There was one thing they did know and she voiced her thoughts out loud. "The suspect can be narrowed down by his age. It has to be someone in their sixties or older. If it's like you say, he knew the house was being built in that spot, he would have lived in McClane Ridge at that time and not someone just passing through."

Raven nodded. "Good point. I'll have Bob check out the court house records and get a list of who was born around the 1950's to maybe 1955 or somewhere around then. That time period would put them in their early teens and older. Or, better yet, see if Bob can locate a school yearbook from fifty years, ago. "

"I bet the school will have the yearbook on a CD somewhere. They archive everything. Bob might have a long list to go through," Shadow said.

"He won't mind. He thrives on mysteries."

Paul grinned. "He may be wasting his time. You and I both know this case will probably be turned over to the FBI and they'll want to do their own investigation."

Raven shrugged his shoulder. "So, let 'em. I don't know about you, but I don't have time to wait on them to cut through the red tape before releasing the crime scene. We have a hotel that needs to be built. Now."

Paul nodded and warned. "Just don't be stepping down hard on anyone's toes. In the meantime, I'm heading back to the office to see if anything has come through on those fingerprints and blood samples. I'll talk to you guys later."

Shadow watched Paul walk away before turning back to Raven. She noticed the white strain around his eyes and mouth and knew he was growing tired and in pain. She also knew he would never admit it. "There's nothing else we can do here. Let's head home. You can catch Bob there before he leaves, again."

Raven agreed a little too quickly. "Sounds good. Let's go."

They said their goodbyes to Michael and left.

* * *

Stacy Chandler knew the golden rules. A person didn't get anywhere these days by stepping on the wrong toes. She had a story to do, even if it meant kissing the whole McClane family's butt and she would if she had to.

She gave instructions to her photographer before she plastered a huge, fake smile on her face and headed toward Michael inside the trailer.

"Hey, Michael. What do we have, here?" she said as she stepped through the doorway.

Michael looked up from his work and smiled. "Well, look who's showed up. The assassin's accomplice, herself."

Stacy's bright smile dropped. She raised her hand to slap the crap out of Michael. "You sorry piece of shit."

Michael grabbed her hand and held it back. In between bouts of laughter, he managed to say, "I'm sorry. I'm sorry. I know you didn't do it. I just couldn't resist teasing you. Payback is hell, you know."

Stacy grabbed her hand out of his grasp and gave

him a go to hell look. "It's not a laughing matter."

Michael tried to look duly chastised, but another burst of laughter erupted.

Stacy felt a grin emerge. She rolled her eyes and gave up. "You're still a piece of shit, but at least you believe in my innocence. And, Shadow."

Michael's laughter faded at her last words. "Of course, we do. So does everyone else. If you would stop and think about it clearly for a minute, you would know Raven had the obligation to check everything and everyone out. When it comes to his loved ones in danger, he can't leave any stones unturned."

Stacy sighed and nodded. "I know you're right, but it still hurt to be accused of such a terrible crime. Especially, by your best friends who should know you better than anyone in this world."

"I agree, but give them a chance to make it up to you, okay? Make 'em grovel."

Stacy laughed, her eyes twinkled. "You're my kind of man, Michael. Now, how about taking me out to the crime scene and filling me in on everything that's happened. Even though you have the time to stand around and chit chat, I don't. I've got a job to do."

Michael chortled. "Yeah, right. If you want to call what you do a job," he teased as he led the way out of the trailer and out to the scene that wasn't taped off. The media would be all over the story, anyway. It was newsworthy. Stacy might as well get first shot at anything the detective didn't believe would hinder the case.

Stacy listened, asked questions and took notes as he told her all the details about the morning's events leading to the police and detective being called in.

When he finished, she closed her notebook. She was anxious to get back to her office to type up the story. She knew this would end up a front pager.

Glancing around, she noticed her photographer was still busy taking pictures of the scene. He looked up for a moment and she signaled to him that it was time to leave.

Turning back to Michael, she thanked him sincerely for everything.

He pulled her to him and gave her a warm hug. "Keep that chin up, kiddo."

Stacy raised her chin skyward before looking back down at Michael. She squeezed him hard and winked. "You bet." She stepped out of his arms, turned to walk off and came face to face with Bob.

**

Bob watched the intimate scene between Stacy and Michael. He felt his gut clench. His heart hardened, once again. Looks like I'd get use to seeing the woman I care about in another man's arms. With the evidence uncovered at the site, he no longer believed she could be involved in hiring the hit man to kill him. Whoever killed the young girl buried here was behind everything. Stacy would never forgive him.

Resolved to his loss, Bob greeted her with a simple nod and spoke. "Stacy. How are you?" He saw a fleeting look of sadness cross her eyes. He hesitated, unsure. Then, the shutter came back down and her eyes grew glacier.

"I'm doing just fine. How are you?"

"Good. Good. Raven sent me to check out some things. So, I won't keep you."

He didn't want to see another intimate goodbye between Stacy and Michael, so he retreated. He

Shadow's Justice

nodded a greeting to Michael before turning his back on her and walking toward the crime scene.

Everyone except for one suited man had left. Bob eased beneath the yellow tape as if he belonged there. He walked over and introduced himself, giving his credentials to the man he learned was Detective Sharp. He explained why he was there.

The detective looked around the area and then back at Bob. "All right. The other team has gathered all the vital evidence they need or I wouldn't let you in here. Hell, I wouldn't be in here. I don't know what you hope to find that they didn't, but be my guest. I need all the help I can get."

"Thank you. I won't be long." Bob dropped his satchel on the ground, knelt down and pulled out a long, slender instrument that extended out to three feet. The needle's cable was plugged into his laptop.

The Detective cocked his head to the side. "Do you mind if I stick around and watch you? I don't believe I've seen a gadget like that before."

Distracted, Bob glanced up. "Not at all." He went on to explain what he was doing. "This needle will detect any blood still lingering in the ground. It will send all of the information to the computer to be analyzed and run through the database.

Since this is probably around fifty years old, it won't be on the database, but we can at least get a quick DNA. What we are hoping for is that it will detect the killer's blood, as well. One good thing about this equipment is that it can detect the chemicals of the blood from a circumference and depth of five feet."

"Humph. All this new finangling stuff always amazes me."

Shadow's Justice

Bob grinned at the Detective's assessment as he watched the thin strip of calculations running from his printer. He pulled the needle from the ground and moved to the opposite side of the taped off area and repeated the operation.

His needle hit against something solid about a foot down. He pulled the instrument out and dug with his hands until he found the culprit. He pulled out a large, oblong rock. He raised it in the air and showed it to the Detective. "This may very well be your murder weapon."

* * *

Randall Collins quietly whimpered and muttered incoherently to himself. Wild eyed, he frantically paced the wet ground beneath his feet.

He stopped and took another swig out of the near empty whiskey bottle. His whimper turned into a sob as he saw an alligator slip into the water.

Damn, but he hated the swamp. It could suck your soul to the very depth of hell.

He glanced down at his watch. His hand was shaking uncontrollably, but he was still able to read the letters on the dial. 3:00 o'clock. Ben was an hour late. Where in the hell was he?

He raised the bottle to his lips and heard the sound of a car's motor. He lowered the bottle, wiped the excess liquid off his lips with the sleeve of his shirt and watched as Judge Ben Adam's car appeared around the curve.

Randall's exultant laugh turned into a drunken giggle. Finally. They could talk without being heard and then get the hell out of there.

He weaved his way over to the Judge's car as his friend parked and got out. "It's about damn time you got here. I was getting ready to get in my car and leave."

"That would've been stupid on your part." The Judge told him as he eyed the bottle still in his hand. "I thought I told you to stop drinking. Drunks talks too much."

"Yeah? Well, I do as I damn well please. There's no way in hell I can face this sober."

The Judge rammed his hands into his pant's pockets, but said nothing. His gaze turned toward the swamp. Through gritted teeth, he ordered, "Tell me what has happened."

"They found the body."

"Shit!" The Judge stormed away, and then he turned back to Collins. "When did this happen?"

"This morning. Cops are swarming the place."

The Judge cursed beneath his breath. "You idiot. I thought you were going to take care of this."

Collins straightened his spine. He had been to hell and back for years trying to take care of the problem. He felt his mind sobering. His thoughts became clear for the first time in fifty years. He was at his limit.

Turning back to his friend, his voice was solemn. "Don't worry. I have it taken care of."

The Judge hesitated and then smiled. "Good. Good. I knew I could count on you. You've always come through." He glanced down at his watch. "I have to get back to court. Let me know the results, will you?"

Collins nodded. "You bet."

The Judge stuffed his huge frame back into his car and started the motor. He put it into drive and waved as the car moved forward.

The Judge never knew when Collins pulled a pistol

out of his coat pocket, aimed it at the side of his head through the window and pulled the trigger.

Collins watched the car plow into the swamp flinging the Judge through the windshield. The frenzied splash from the alligators was deafening.

CHAPTER TWENTY

Shadow sat across the dining table from Rose. She sipped on her coffee, her breakfast forgotten. She had a lot on her mind this morning, the main thing being Raven.

Her fingers did a continuous rat-a-tat-tat on the table as she thought her feelings through.

Startled, she glanced up as Rose placed her fork on her plate and sat back. She had that familiar 'Mother knows all' look in her eyes.

Rose spoke. "You love him, don't you?"

Shadow's fingers stilled. Her heart almost stopped. She glanced down at the table. "Who are you talking about?" She hedged.

"Shadow Renee McClane. You know good and well I'm talking about Raven. Look me in the eyes, so I can see the truth."

Shadow shifted in her seat, but raised her eyes to meet Rose's. She was bursting to share the news with Rose. Finally, she nodded. "Yes. I love him."

Rose grinned. "I thought so. I could tell by the way you were acting around him. Now tell me, does he love you?"

A slow smile emerged. "He says he does."

"That's wonderful, honey. Why haven't you told

me?"

Shadow shrugged. "I don't know. I guess our feelings are too new, so we haven't told anyone. And, to be honest, we still have a lot of issues to be worked out."

Rose cocked her head to one side and studied Shadow. "Such as?"

She shrugged. "Such as his life as a mercenary. I keep telling myself he can take care of himself and he would always come home to me. Part of me believes that, but another part worries I won't be strong enough to conquer my fears that he won't come home one day."

Rose leaned forward and placed her hand on top of Shadow's. "Honey, take it from me. You have to take life as it's dished out. Believe me, I know how you feel. I had a husband who never came home. I won't say it's easy. The pain will last a long time, but you will survive. I will survive."

Shadow felt the tears welling in her eyes. She stood and rounded the table. Leaning over, she wrapped her arms around Rose and hugged her tight. "That's for being the wisest, strongest, sweetest woman I know. I love you very much. Thank you for clearing a lot of things up in my mind."

Rose sniffed. "I don't know about all that praise and I'm not sure how much help I was, but I do know for certain that I love you too, honey."

Shadow kissed her on the cheek. "I think I'll go up and check on Raven."

Rose glanced up. "Oh, I thought you knew. He left out early this morning. He said he might be late getting in this evening."

Shadow felt her temper rise. That idiot was out of

the hospital less than a day after being shot and here he was, out by himself running around doing God knows what. Besides, they were supposed to be working on this case together. If she didn't love him, she'd kill him.

"Did he say where he was going?" Shadow asked through gritted teeth.

"No. He just said he had some things to check out. Is anything wrong?" Rose asked with a frown.

Shadow shook her head and sighed. "No. I just wish he'd wakened me. I would've gone with him."

Rose grinned. "Ain't love wonderful?"

* * *

Raven slid into the diner's booth against the wall. He wanted to observe the customers as they came in and out while he waited on Mandy to take her break.

He was hoping the Judge and Collins would be eating there again this morning. So far, according to Mandy, they hadn't showed up, but that wasn't unusual. They only ate there once or twice a week, she'd told him.

A few minutes later, Mandy placed a cup of coffee in front of him before sliding in the seat across from him.

She smiled. Her flirty, soft voice said, "I'm glad you stopped by. I'd heard you were in town."

Mandy leaned over, crossing her arms on top of the table. Her full breast overfilled her uniform, giving him a glimpse of a forgotten past.

Raven grinned and took a sip from his coffee cup. Mandy had only supported his reasoning for not bringing Shadow with him. Shadow wouldn't understand at this point in their relationship, that in his eyes, Mandy's luscious view was nothing compared to hers.

Deciding it was time to get down to business, Raven placed his coffee cup on the table. "I've been back for a few days. My friend Bob said he'd talked to you yesterday morning and you had seemed a little upset over a couple of customers."

Mandy sighed and sat back. Her nervous glance scanned the room before she answered. "If you're talking about the Judge and Randall Collins, I'll tell you like I told your friend. I have nothing to say on the matter."

Raven leaned closer and lowered his voice. "What are you afraid of, Mandy?"

She became defensive. "It's not what, it's who. Look, I've got to get back to work." She moved to slide out of the booth.

Raven caught her hand with his to stop her. "Mandy, I need your help, here. A man, who was like a second dad to me was sentenced to death and then executed for a murder he didn't commit. I think Collins is involved up to his eyeballs, but I need proof. Mandy, I need to find the real murderer so Jack McClane's family and I can have some type of closure. Will you help me?"

Mandy glanced around the room one more time before giving him a reluctant nod. "But, not here. I don't want anyone to see me talking to you for any longer than a simple reunion between friends. I'll meet you tonight at 10:00 at the old feed mill outside of town. It's been closed down for years. No one will be there."

"I'll see you then. Thank you." Raven watched her slide out of the booth and stand beside him with a sad smile.

"I was stupid for ever letting you slip through my fingers back in high school," she told him.

Raven grinned. "No, you weren't. You were lucky to get rid of me. I would've never settled down back then."

"And, now?"

"And now, I've found the woman I want to spend the rest of my life with. I love her very much."

"I see," she told him. Regret softened her voice. "I envy her, but I wish you both all the happiness in the world."

He gave her hand an affectionate squeeze. "Thank you, Mandy. I'll see you tonight."

She nodded and Raven watched her walk away before he stood, dropped some money on the table and left the diner.

Raven walked without delay toward the area where he was to meet Bob. He called earlier saying he'd followed Collins from his home and wanted Raven to meet him across the street from the courthouse.

Reaching his destination, Raven walked up to stand beside Bob who was pacing back and forth with impatience.

"Hey, what's up?" Raven questioned.

"I'm not sure. About an hour after we arrived, I noticed several groups of people were leaving. I stopped one lady who I learned was a juror and asked her what was going on. She said court had been adjourned for the day. Evidently, no one can find the Judge."

"Are you serious? Have they checked his home?"

"Yes. The housekeeper said he didn't come home the day before and he hasn't called. That's about all I could find out. I don't know about you, but I have a sick feeling about this and I think Collins is involved up to his ass."

Bob glanced over toward the courthouse before he continued, his tone somber. "I'll tell you something else, boss. You're going to think I'm crazy, but I believe the evidence will show everything that has been happening in McClane Ridge lately connects together."

Raven never questioned Bob's analysis on any job they were on. He always backed his thoughts with facts. But, this time he was taken back by his hesitant words.

"How?"

Bob shrugged one shoulder. "I'm not sure. I don't have everything clear in my mind, yet. But, I'm almost willing to bet you good money on this one. I think both Steven Tucker and his father's murder, which led to Shadow's father's arrest is somehow linked to the girl's body that was found yesterday."

Raven shook his head as Bob's words sunk in. "You're saying the recent murders happened because the victims witnessed what happened fifty years, ago? Damn, if it don't make sense, but there's one hole in the theory. Steven wasn't even born back then."

Bob shrugged again. "I don't know. Maybe his father told him what he saw before he was murdered. Or, maybe he stumbled up on something that disclosed the murder. Either way, it scared the hell out of someone and they eliminated the threat by killing Steven and destroying any type of evidence in the fire."

"Well, I'll be damned. You may have something there. That would explain why Collins hired a private detective to follow Tucker. He was trying to find the evidence." Raven said as the pieces began falling into place.

Bob nodded his head. "He couldn't find it so, Collin's had it destroyed."

"That has to be what happened. Where's Collin's now?"

"He's still inside. I wanted to stick around and follow him when he came out."

"Good. While you're doing that, I'll stop in on the housekeeper to see if I can learn anymore news about the Judge. I've got a bad feeling Collins has struck, again. I'll call Paul on the way and tell him our theories, so he'll know what's going on."

Raven turned to leave and then turned back. "Oh, I forgot to tell you. I met with Mandy this morning. She wouldn't talk to me there. I'm meeting her at 10:00 tonight at the old feed mill outside of town. Maybe she can give me some more information."

"Want me to come along, boss?"

Raven shook his head. "No. She'd open up more if I was alone."

Bob's wolf grin appeared. "Yeah, I bet. I'm just wondering which part you want opened up."

Raven grinned and nodded his head toward the courthouse. "You better get your butt in gear if you're going to tail Collins. He's half way down the street."

Bob's grin faded. He cursed and took off running after the lawyer.

Raven laughed at his friend as he pulled out his cell phone. Before he could dial Paul's number, his phone rang.

"Hello."

"You're a sleezeball, Deveroux."

"Hello, Shadow. I love you, too." The amusement

sounded in his voice. He heard the hesitation before she continued.

"I'll never get tired of hearing you say that. I love you, too. I wish you were here. I would show you how much."

Raven groaned. "Sweet heaven. Say that to me when we're together."

"Uh, uh. You're a sleezeball. Did Mandy serve you anything more than breakfast, this morning?"

"Ah ha. You're jealous. I knew it." Raven said as he got into his car.

"I am not."

"You have no reason to be."

He heard a loud sigh before she said. "I know."

"Good. What are you doing, right now?"

"I'm headed to the office."

"Why don't you meet me in front of the Judge's house?"

"Why?"

Raven clued her in on the conversation between himself and Bob while he started the motor and headed out of town.

"I'll meet you there in five minutes." Shadow told him.

A few minutes later they parked in front of the Judge's mansion. Raven led the way to the front door and rang the doorbell.

When the housekeeper answered the door, Raven introduced himself and Shadow. He explained the investigation they were conducting and the reason they were there.

The young housekeeper ushered them into the elegant and modern sitting room and motioned for them to sit on the settee. She sat across from them in an overstuffed chair and pulled down on the hem of the short uniform she wore. She sat up straight with her hands clasped in her lap.

"I'm not sure how I can help you or what the Judge missing has to do with your investigation," she told them.

Raven noticed a huge oil painting of the Judge from his earlier years hanging above the fireplace. The Judge's home spoke of money.

He asked, "How long have you worked for the Judge?"

"About two months, more or less. I moved here from Alabama less than four months ago and started working for him right after that."

"Does he make it a habit to leave for a long time without telling anyone?"

"No. He always lets me know where he's going and when he'll be back in case there's an emergency."

"Where was he going yesterday when he left?"

"He said he was going to his office to catch up on the paperwork from the morning's cases. He told me he wouldn't be gone long and he would have dinner at 7:00 o'clock, his usual time."

"Did you call his office yesterday to check on him?" Shadow asked.

"Yes. No one answered. His secretary leaves around 5:00 every evening. I called her home and she said he never showed back up at the office. I've been calling his cell phone, but he must have it turned off. I'm afraid that's all I know to tell you."

Realizing they had gotten all of the information the housekeeper knew, he smiled and said, "Well, thank you very much for your time." He stood and handed her his business card. "If you think of anything else, I would appreciate it if you would call me at that number."

The housekeeper nodded and stood to show them out. "I will. And please, let me know when you find him. I need to know if I still have a job or not."

"We will. The police department won't officially report him missing for twenty-four hours, but I'm sure the Police Chief is already on the job. He'll want to stop by and ask you some questions."

"Okay. I'll be here. I have nowhere else to go."

Raven turned to follow Shadow to the car, but turned back to the housekeeper and asked one more question. "Tell me, how did you get along with the Judge?"

The friendliness disappeared from her face. "I didn't get rid of him, if that's what you mean."

Raven shook his head. "No, that's not why I'm asking. I'm trying to find out more about his character."

The housekeeper shrugged her shoulder. "I haven't known him for long, but it didn't take me long to find out that he's a bastard, but he pays good money. If I wasn't desperate for the money, I wouldn't be here."

"Why do you think he's a bastard? What has he done?"

The housekeeper shook her head and started backing up. "Look, I still have to work for the guy. I'm not going to say anything that would get me fired." She closed the door in his face.

Raven cursed before he turned and walked over to Shadow's car. He leaned down to talk to her through the open window. "I'm beginning to think the Judge is not as upstanding as he has everyone believing."

Shadow nodded. She had overheard the

housekeeper's harsh words describing her true feelings about her boss. She had also seen the expression that crossed her face for a brief moment before it was replaced with the look of reserved coolness.

"That's two different women who seem to hate him. They fear him, as well." Shadow told him.

Raven glanced back toward the house in deep thought. Their fear was what worried him. He knew he wouldn't rest easy until he found out why they were frightened of him. Coming to a decision, he turned back to Shadow. "Feel like going on a little rendezvous with me later tonight?"

"Sure. Where to?" she asked.

"The old feed mill outside of town."

"Okay. Mind telling me why?"

"Not now. I'll meet you back at the house for dinner tonight. I'll explain everything then. Right now, I need to find Bob to see if he's learned anything else."

Raven saw her lips begin to turn down in a pout. Before she could complain about being left behind, he leaned in closer and kissed her long and with a built-up passion.

When he drew back, he noticed the pout was gone. He grinned, told her bye and headed to his car. He heard her curse and then the words, "That man doesn't play fair, but two can play that game, buster."

CHAPTER TWENTY-ONE

Stacy knocked and entered her boss's office. "Good morning, Charles. You wanted to see me?"

The elderly, senior editor looked up and scowled at being interrupted. He pulled off his wire-framed glasses and motioned her toward a chair. "Sit."

Stacy grinned and did as she was told. She'd worked for Charles Tallant for six years and knew he was a teddy bear behind his rough exterior and mannerism. She loved the old man.

Her boss steepled his fingers beneath his chin and studied her from across his desk. "Where are you at on your follow up article about the dead body that was found? We're going to need something by this evening."

"I'll have you something on it before then. We have a good idea who it is, but I'm waiting on a positive I.D. from Paul. They're comparing the dental records, now. Sounds like it might turn into a fifty year old unsolved mystery." She filled him in on the case of Karen Jacobs.

Charles nodded. "I remember when that happened. I was a young teenager, myself and I met her a couple of times. She was a sweet and pretty young girl. I was at the party being held when she came up missing. We searched for days, but she was never found. I've often wondered what happened to her."

Stacy was elated over this bit of news. She hadn't thought about her boss knowing the girl. She leaned forward and asked, "Do you remember anything else about the night of the party? Did you see her having an argument with anyone or see her when she left?"

Her boss shook his head. "No. To tell you the truth, a few of us guys had snuck out the back door and enjoyed a full fifth of whiskey before going back inside. I never knew when she left. I just remember sobering up in an instant when the grandfather showed up to pick her up and she wasn't there."

Disappointed, Stacy sat back in her chair, her hopes dashed. "Do you think you might be able to give me some names of other kids that were there? Maybe they saw or remember something."

"It's been fifty years and my memory isn't as sharp as it use to be, but sure. I'll try to gather a list of names and call you."

"Thanks. That will help and in the mean time, I'll get some type of article written up by this evening," Stacy promised as she stood and walked to the door.

"Great. Oh, by the way, I meant to ask you and forgot. Did that man ever find your friend, Bob?"

Stacy stopped, her hand on the doorknob. She shook her head in puzzlement. "I don't know what man you're talking about. I don't know Bob well enough for anyone to be calling me to look for him."

Her boss frowned. "He said it was important and he described Bob. I walked by your office and saw a man who fit his description. I told him I believed this "Bob" was with you at the moment."

"Did he give you his name?"

"No. I asked him and he hung up."

Stacy felt her stomach turning queasy. "Do you remember what day it was?"

Charles thought for a moment and then nodded. "Yes. I remember, now. It was the same day the guy shot the man who was stalking him. I believe the stalker pulled a gun on him and the guy shot him in self-defense. You did the article on it. What was the guy's name?"

Stacy swallowed hard. "His name was Bob."

* * *

Raven pulled up into the dark parking lot and killed the motor. The old abandoned feed mill stood in the shadows looking neglected and defeated in the moonlight.

It was almost eerie how the sad looking building reminded him of an old, isolated graveyard he'd once visited. Weeds covered the overturned headstones and the carved words were faded and barely legible telling of forgotten loved ones.

Raven shook off his gloom and turned the car key over to look at the clock on the dash. Five minutes after ten and a no show for Mandy. He glanced over at Shadow. "She must have been held up. We'll give her a few more minutes."

Shadow nodded and reached over to lock her door. "I hope she shows up, soon. It's spooky out here."

Raven grinned, but locked his own door. There had been too many murders of late to be careless with Shadow sitting beside him.

He cracked his window a couple of inches to listen for Mandy's car, but all he heard was the chirping of crickets and the rustling of leaves as unseen animals scurried about.

Raven glanced over at Shadow. She was still sitting in the same stiff position. Her head jerked toward a noise outside her window.

"It was just a 'possum." Raven told her.

"Oh." She settled back in her seat a little, but kept a vigilant watch.

Raven couldn't resist. His eyes gleamed in the darkness as his storytelling voice began. "The bodyless hand came out of the darkness wielding a long, sharp machete…"

Wham. Shadow's open hand slapped him across his shoulder. "You sorry piece of…" She slapped him again as his laughter rang out.

"That wasn't funny," she told him.

"Sorry. I couldn't resist. I…," His voice trailed off when he heard a car's motor in the distance. Then he saw the headlights drawing near.

A car pulled up beside them and parked. Raven opened his door and got out so Mandy would know for sure it was him. He watched as she got out and come around her car. Greeting her, he opened the back door of the S.U.V. and waited for her to climb in.

Shadow and Mandy greeted each other. If Mandy was uncomfortable with Shadow being with him, she didn't let on.

"Sorry I'm late. I had to fill in at the diner for a few hours tonight." Mandy explained.

"No problem. I'm just glad you were able to show up. We're very curious about your harsh reaction toward Collins and the Judge. What have they done to make you hate them the way you do?" Raven asked her as he and Shadow turned toward the backseat.

Mandy hesitated and looked through the window

into the darkness before a resigned sigh escaped. She turned back to the front and faced Raven and Shadow. Her voice was above a whisper as she began her story.

"Three years, fourteen days and two hours ago, I was viciously raped."

"Oh my, God." Shadow reached back and squeezed Mandy's hand. She held on as Raven said with concern. "Tell us what happened."

Mandy gave a nonchalant shrug, but the anger and pain showed clear in her eyes. "It's a short story, really. I went to work as a housekeeper for the Judge about two months before it happened. I had a room there at his home. He came in my bedroom one night and raped me."

"Son of a bitch!" Raven turned and his fist slammed into the dash. He was silent as he forced his rage to calm. He took a deep breath and turned back to Mandy. Through tight lips, he asked. "Did you report the rape?"

Mandy shook her head. Tears ran down her cheeks.

"Mandy, why didn't you turn the bastard in?"

She took the back of her hand and wiped away the tears. "He threatened me. Judge said if I tried to go to the cops, he would tell them I lied and that he was the real victim. He was going to tell them I stole expensive jewelry and other items from him and the Police Chief Walker and Randall Collins would testify on his behalf. He said he would make damn sure I spent a few years in prison on felony charges. That's when he laughed and told me I was fired and to get my ass out of his house."

Mandy's head fell back against the seat. She blew out a harsh breath. "You two are the only living souls

I've told this to."

Shadow squeezed her hand, again. "I'm so sorry, Mandy."

Mandy straightened. "Thanks, but I survived. I left his house that night and went to my parents. When I drove up into their driveway, I watched as Walker drove by in his police car and slowed to a crawl behind me to let me know he was there. Then, he drove on. I knew then the Judge's threats weren't idle. He meant what he said and he has the power in town to make it happen."

"I'm glad you told us, Mandy. I've got a feeling you're not his only victim." Raven told her about the Judge who came up missing and their interview with his latest housekeeper that morning.

"I hope the bastard is dead. Maybe one of the other housekeepers had the guts to kill him off," Mandy said with a vengeance.

"It's a possibility. Something's happened to him. He still hadn't shown up when I called and checked about an hour, ago." Raven told her.

He understood Mandy's feelings of wanting the Judge dead after what he put her through. He had the morals and decency of a vicious animal. He deserved to be put away for life for the things he had done.

First thing in the morning, he wanted to find out the names of all the housekeepers the Judge had employed. Perhaps, he could get some of them to talk.

"Mandy, I'm going to ask you for one more difficult favor. Will you give me permission to tell your story to the Deputy Police Chief? Paul is nothing like Walker and would protect you from anything the Judge or Collins could do to you. He needs to know.

For all we know, he may have skipped the country if one of the women has turned him in to the police in another county or state."

Mandy started shaking her head and then her spine stiffened. "Yes, you can tell him. I'm sick and tired of living with this hatred and knowing he's getting off scot-free. Seeing him in the diner with that damn smirk on his face is enough to make me puke. He needs to be put away before there's anymore victims."

Raven nodded in agreement. "Knowing Paul, he will do everything in his power to see it happen. Thank you for telling us, Mandy. I know this wasn't an easy story to tell."

Mandy shrugged her shoulders and simply said, "It needed to be told.

* * *

The next morning, Stacy planted her feet firm on the sidewalk and stopped Bob dead in his tracks. With hands on her hips, she stared him down. "We need to talk. Now."

Bob nodded. If he was surprised at her audaciousness, he didn't let it show. "I agree. Where?"

"My office." Without giving him a chance to change his mind, Stacy turned and headed back to her office a block away. When they arrived, she closed the door behind them. Motioning him toward a chair, she rounded her desk and sat across from him.

Stacy leaned forward and rested her crossed arms on the desk and gazed straight into his eyes. "We're going to get this mess straightened out, once and for all. I did not inform a hired assassin that you were in my office that day. Understand?"

Bob leaned back and crossed his arms across his

chest. One eyebrow rose. "Prove it," he shot back.

Stacy leaned forward. "I will. Has it ever occurred to that mulish, bullheaded mind of yours that I'm not the only person working in this building?"

Bob's lips curled into a grin. "Yep. It occurred to me. But, no one else saw me here that morning."

"Are you sure?"

"Yep."

"Then let me add blind, stupid and asinine asshole to your description. Someone did see you that morning." Stacy went on to fill him in on the conversation she'd had earlier with her boss.

Bob sat forward. He ran his hand across the top of his head and then he stood and began pacing.

Stacy watched as he stopped and stood in front of her. He placed both hands palm down on the top of her desk and said, "I still don't understand how he even knew I was coming here. Why call your boss on a hunch that I might show up?"

Stacy shrugged. "I don't know. Maybe he called around to several places, hoping to luck out. I don't think he followed you here. I mean, why would he bother calling if he already knew where you were?"

"It might explain that part of it, but how would he know it was me coming out of the building after I changed clothes in the bathroom? My disguises are made to conceal. No one would have recognized me."

"Maybe he was close enough that when he called and found out you were here, he had time enough to get here and see you walk into the bathroom and see you come out. He might have walked into the bathroom while you were in a stall and saw no one else was in there, but you. That's the only explanation I can think of that makes any sense."

Bob nodded his head. "It's possible it happened that way. I didn't hear anyone enter the bathroom, but I wasn't trying to be quiet while I dressed. He was a trained professional. He could've been in there and out and I would've never known."

Stacy sat back and steepled her fingers beneath her chin. She felt the ice around her heart melting away. He had come very close to admitting he believed her without actually saying the words.

A slow grin emerged. "So, does this mean you owe me a big time apology?"

Bob glanced down at her and his mouth twitched with amusement. "Sorry."

Stacy brushed her hair back from her shoulder and crossed her legs. Her skirt hiked up mid-thigh. She watched as Bob's gaze followed the movements. A simmering smile appeared. "Uh uh. That won't get it. Try again."

An answering smile appeared on his face. Before she could react he rounded her desk and leaned over to capture her smile with his lips.

The kiss deepened and before she knew it, she was standing inside his arms giving back as well as she was receiving. Her arms rounded his neck to pull him closer.

She felt his hand rubbing against the silky material of her skirt draped over her thigh. The material rose higher and higher until her black satin panties were revealed.

She found the strength to step back and break the sensual kiss. She shook her head in confusion, wanting nothing more than to step back into his arms and finish what she had started. But she didn't.

Stacy felt him pulling her close, again. She resisted

with her hands wandering over his chest and muttered against his lips. "Please. Not here. Someone might see us."

Breathing hard, Bob stepped back and rested his forehead against hers. "You're right. Your office is not where I want our first time to happen."

He stepped back and gazed into her eyes. He pushed a stray strand of hair from her face and asked, "Will you have dinner with me tonight?"

"Yes."

Bob's smile gleamed. "Great. I'll pick you up at seven, if that's a good time for you."

Stacy watched as a more intimate invitation showed in the smoldering depths of his eyes. She managed to nod her head and answer, "Yes. That will be fine."

"Good. I'll see you, then." Bob leaned down and kissed her one more time, leaving her weak in the knees. She clung to his neck to hold on for dear life. Lord, help her, but that man knew how to kiss. His tongue was a natural weapon against her senses.

He broke off the kiss and held her with firm hands on her shoulders. She felt his tremors and knew he was equally affected by their kiss.

When he stared into her eyes, Stacy thought she saw something in the blue depths indicating an emotion much stronger than lust. But, then the shutters came down, hiding his true feelings.

She hadn't been mistaken. For one short moment, she had seen his growing love for her. She realized then, she had one heck of a battle in front of her. A woman's intuition told her his heart had been broken before by some woman. He would fight to keep the pain from happening again.

Stacy was disappointed, but not discouraged. He

hadn't dealt with her form of persuasion before now. She was determined to break the hard shell surrounding his heart. He'd put his unbreakable barrier in place, but he would soon realize how strong her new found love could be.

She didn't know what had happened in his past to make him distrust the true meaning of love, but she would get to the bottom of the reason. When she was through with him, he would no longer be able to deny her his growing love. She didn't care that it had only been a few days since they'd met. She knew in her heart they were meant to be.

Stacy's thoughts came back to the present as she heard his sultry words spoken.

"I promise you, I will show you tonight exactly how truly sorry I am that I ever doubted you. Will you let me make it up to you?"

Stacy smiled. "Oh yeah. Believe me, I plan on enjoying every minute of it."

Bob's wolfish grin appeared. "I plan on seeing that you do."

CHAPTER TWENTY-TWO

For once, Shadow lingered over her morning ritual. The long, relaxing soak in the tub, a little extra makeup and added curls to her hair made her feel more feminine than she'd felt in a long time.

She rubbed lotion onto her body before slipping a strapless sundress over her head. Looking into the full length mirror, Shadow smoothed the mid-length, cotton material over her hips. She liked the way the light peach color brought out her dark tan.

She swiveled side to side, watching as the full skirt danced around her legs. Satisfied she looked her best, she slipped on a pair of matching sandals and glanced once again into the mirror. She grinned and patted her hair. Blowing a kiss at the mirror, she winked before saying, "Raven won't know what hit him."

Shadow left her bedroom and walked downstairs to the dining room. She was delighted to see John sitting at the breakfast table. A crutch leaned against the chair next to him. Rose sat across from him with Raven seated at the end.

"Good morning, everyone." Her glance lingered on Raven. Leaning down, she hugged John's shoulders and teased. "Hey, this is a surprise. What's your lazy tail doing up? I thought you'd still be in bed moaning for sympathy over that minor cut on your leg."

John grinned and waited until she was seated before replying, "The major cut on my leg is healing up, nicely. Thank you for asking. I thought I'd hitch a ride with you out to the site this morning. But, since you look like you're all dolled up for a hot date instead of work, I'll call Michael to stop by and pick me up."

Shadow's cheeks burned as she glanced up at Raven and then back at him.

"No. I don't mind driving you. I was planning on stopping by there anyway and picking up some papers to take to the office," Shadow fabricated.

There was no way she would've said, No, I'd planned on getting Raven alone today and making sizzling, erotically wild love to him.

Which was her original plan. Dammit!

Shadow glanced at Raven with a pout on her lips. She knew from the answering frustrated look on his face he knew what she had on her mind.

Shadow turned her attention to Rose and asked, "What are your plans for today?" She sat back as Carol brought in their breakfast plates.

"Thank you, Carol," Rose said as a plate was placed in front of her. She turned back to Shadow. "I'm having lunch with Joan," she said, mentioning one of her life time friends. "Then, we plan on doing a little shopping. Would you like to join us?"

"Sounds like fun, but I have some work to do at the office. I'm really glad you've decided to get out of the house and enjoying yourself for a change. It will do you good to get your mind off things for a while. Even though I would prefer you stay inside."

"Joan insisted or I wouldn't be going. I'll enjoy it,

though. I can't stay cooped up all of the time and I will be surrounded by people at lunch and in the shops. I'll be fine." Rose took a bite of her egg before turning to Raven, the matter closed. "How about you? What's on your agenda?"

Raven took a swallow of coffee and set his cup back down before answering. "I have some phone calls to make and then I'll probably check in with Paul and Bob to see if either has had any luck finding the Judge." He looked up at Shadow. "Can you join me later?"

"Sure." Shadow answered a little too quick. She flushed as two sets of brows rose.

* * *

"Just in time, boys. Have a seat." Paul said as Raven and Bob entered his office a couple of hours later. He leaned back in his chair and waved two sheets of paper in the air.

"What do you have?" Raven asked.

"I have the report back on the DNA samples from the blood we found at the site and a positive I.D on the body. The dental records shows the remains were indeed Karen Jacobs. She died from one blow to the head by a blunt instrument. The rock Bob found where she was buried has been listed as the murder weapon."

"Well, that's part of the mystery solved. What about the new DNA samples found in the shed?" Raven asked.

"Believe it or not, we have a match." Paul glanced down at the sheet of paper in his hand and read. "The blood samples belong to a Simon Duprue who has a rap sheet a mile long. He's done time for breaking and entering, his third offence in less than ten years.

He's been out of the pen for less than a month for brutally beating an old man in his home while he was robbing him."

"Do you know where he is now?" Bob asked.

"Yes. He's staying with his sister in New Orleans. The police there have picked him up. I plan on going there later on today to question him."

"What about the other two men who were with him that night and the mysterious person who shot me? Did you find anything on them?" Raven asked.

"No. Nothing. We're hoping Duprue can be convinced to squeal out some names to help us out. In particular, the name of the person who hired him. He didn't do this on his own. It's not his typical M.O."

"Would you mind if Bob and I drove down with you and watched behind the one-way mirror while you're doing the interrogation?"

"No, it won't be a problem. As a matter of fact, it might help me. You might see something in his expression or a deviation in his voice during the questioning where I might need to hammer him harder on. I'll give you a call before I go."

"Great. Have you found out anything on the Judge?"

"No. Nothing. We don't think he was planning on being gone this long. His housekeeper said his suitcases and all of his clothes are still in his closet. We've been running his license plate number through the system, but so far no one has seen his car."

"Have you checked the bank to see if he's withdrawn a large amount of money in recent days?"

"Yes, we checked yesterday. He hasn't pulled out any money other than his monthly payments made earlier for his utilities."

"Well, that blew one theory all to hell," Raven said.

"What theory was that?"

Raven filled him and Bob on the meeting he and Shadow had with Mandy the night before.

"Damn." Paul's expletive conveyed his shock.

Bob cursed, as well. "I knew she was hiding something. I didn't think I imagined her look of pure hatred towards them. If looks could kill, the Judge would be a dead man when she watched him and Collins walk out the door that morning at the diner. Do you think she may have killed him?"

"She has plenty of reasons to hate him, but I don't believe she killed him. We don't know for sure he's dead. I made a few phone calls this morning trying to locate some of his former housekeepers. Mandy gave me a couple of names to start searching."

"Any luck?" Paul asked.

"No. They've both moved out of state. The mother of one gave me her daughter's phone number. I got her on the phone, but she wouldn't talk. She hung up on me when I tried to pressure her."

"What about the other one?"

"I wasn't able to contact her. No one, her family or friends seems to know where she moved. They're not telling, anyway."

"We may have to find her if anything has happened to the Judge. They would both be possible suspects," Paul informed them. He hesitated for a moment and then added. "Mandy would be, too. You know I can't go on your gut instincts."

"I understand. You're just doing your job unlike the former Police Chief. One other thing, you might as well add the new housekeeper to the list. Believe me, she's not too fond of him herself," Raven told them.

"In that case, maybe I need to have a talk with her," Paul made a note.

Bob shifted in his seat. He'd been silent throughout most of the conversation. He finally spoke up, his voice thoughtful, as if testing an idea. "Let's go back to the Karen Jacobs murder, for a minute. Will there be an in-depth investigation conducted?"

Paul shook his head. "No, nothing other than checking blood samples and questioning a few of the guests at the party. The ones still living, anyway. We really don't have the manpower to reopen a fifty year old case. Why? What's on your mind?"

Bob shrugged. "I keep thinking back to the old newspaper article. There wasn't much of an investigation back then, according to Stacy."

Raven looked up in surprise. "You've talked to Stacy?"

Bob's face turned red. "Yeah, I talked to her. She proved her innocence. I believe her, now." He told them about the phone call from the stranger Stacy's boss received and about her boss being at the party fifty years ago when Karen Jacobs came up missing. He left out the more intimate exchange between himself and Stacy.

He summed it up by saying, "Her boss is going to give her a list of names of the ones at the party that he can remember."

Paul sat back in his chair. "Well, that explains how the thug knew where you were that day. I just wish we knew who hired him to kill you and why."

"I think it was out of fear that I might've stumbled up on the truth about the murders."

"You may be right. Maybe, we'll find out the answers, soon. Before something else happens." Paul said before adding. "Can you get me a copy of those names on the list when Stacy's boss gathers the information for her," Paul requested.

"Sure. I'll get a copy to you right away."

"Great. I'll call you two when I'm ready to leave for New Orleans."

"Thanks Paul. I'll owe you one." Raven stood as they readied to leave. His right hand delved into his pant's front pocket for his keys. Instead, it came in contact with the set of cufflinks he had put in there that morning. "Damn. I forgot all about the cufflinks." He said as he pulled them out and held them in the palm of his hand.

Paul looked at them with a questioning eye. One of the matching pair was shiny and new looking where as the other one was black with grime. "Cufflinks?"

"Yes. I meant to tell you, earlier. I found the charred one in front of Tucker's home when it got torched." Raven held up the shiny one. "This one, I found in Collin's bedroom."

Paul shook his head. "Please tell me he invited you into his home and there was no breaking and entering involved."

Raven stayed silent.

Bob grinned.

Paul looked at one and then the other before a loud sigh escaped. He looked down at the cufflinks. "This doesn't mean a thing. Collins could've lost that cufflink at anytime before the fire. This would never stand up in a court of law."

"Maybe not, but you know as well as I do Collin's is involved up to his ass in all of this. I would bet your...," Raven stopped in mid-sentence as a thought struck him. He turned to Bob. "Do me a favor and call Stacy. Have her talk to her boss to see if he remembers whether Collin's or the Judge attended that party where the Jacobs girl came up missing."

Bob's eyes widened. "Damn. I never placed them at the party, but you may be right. They would be the right age. I'll get right on it." Bob pulled out his cell phone and dialed Stacy's office number.

A few minutes later, he hung up. He turned back to Raven and Paul with a wide grin on his face. "Bingo. They were both there, plus their side kick, Walker. Her boss said one never went anywhere without the other two."

Paul nodded. "The last part doesn't surprise me in the least. From what I've heard, the three of them have been inseparable all of their lives."

"Until now." Raven added.

"Until now." Paul agreed as Raven and Bob made their way to the door and said their goodbyes.

Raven opened the door and let Bob go through first. "So, you had to eat crow with Stacy, huh?" Raven twisted the barb in deeper with his teasing as they left Paul's office.

Bob's laughter rang out. "Hell, yes. But, for once, I enjoyed the hell out of it."

* * *

Collin's was cold sober. For once, in a long while, he was able to rationalize without all the clouded, spider web thoughts running through his head. His ulcers hadn't bothered him all morning.

Happiness bubbling up inside him. He felt free and it felt good. He'd had a wonderful dream that night. He'd dreamt that Walker and Ben had roasted in hell.

He had stood on the sidelines laughing as flames billowed out around them while they turned around and around in a circle. They reminded him of a rotisserie chicken and it had been enjoyable as hell to watch .

Collins brought his thoughts back to the moment. He stood in front of his mirror adjusting his tie as his smile faded.

He'd followed his normal routine that morning. He'd gotten out of bed, dressed, ate breakfast and now he was ready to drive to the courthouse at his usual time.

His actual court case wouldn't start until after they broke for lunch, but they still had to pick their jury members. The damn Prosecuting Attorney and his client refused to settle out of court.

His secretary called him earlier and informed him that Judge Brackett would preside this morning in the place of Judge Adam's.

Brackett was a tough bastard with balls of steel. He would have to be on his toes if he wanted to win this case. Collins grinned. "But, this isn't my day to give a shit."

He pulled up to the curb and parked. Whistling, he reached over to the passenger seat and grabbed his satchel. Stepping out of his car, he strolled toward the courthouse.

He pulled up short as Raven and his friend, Bob stepped in front of him.

"Hello, Collins. How are you?" Raven asked, cordially.

Collins was forced to stop and speak. "I'm doing great, Raven." He glanced down at his watch. "I'm running a little late, though. Please, give my bests to

Rose and Shadow." Collins moved to go around the two men.

Raven sidestepped with him. "I heard that the Judge was missing. Seeing as how the two of you were such good friends, I bet you've been worried to death."

Collins nodded. "Yes. I've been beside myself with worry. Now, if you'll excuse me."

"I don't guess he told you where he was going or if anything has been bothering him, lately."

Collins sighed, letting his impatients show. "No. He didn't. If he had, I would have already informed the police. I've been doing everything I can to help them with their investigation."

"I'm sure you have." Raven told him. He smiled. "Well, let's hope they will find him unharmed."

"I'm praying so." Collins told him.

"Well, we'll let you get on into the courthouse. I know you have work to do." Raven reached into his pocket as if he was pulling out his car keys. Instead, he pulled his hand back out and opened his hand wide. The set of cufflinks lay in the flat of his palm. "Damn. I meant to leave these with Paul."

Collins felt the blood rush from his face as he saw what Raven was holding. His heart rate accelerated.

"Excuse me." Collins rushed toward the court house and into the bathroom where he lost his breakfast.

* * *

Raven grinned. He glanced back at Bob as Collins disappeared into the building. Collin's frightened reaction confirmed his guilt in Raven's mind. "Did you see his face when I pulled those cufflinks out of my pocket? It was like he'd seen a ghost."

Bob laughed. "I think he would've preferred to have seen a ghost, instead of those cufflinks you shoved in his face."

"I'm sure he would. I wanted to see his reaction to them and I got the one I was expecting. They scared the hell out of him."

Bob looked back at the courthouse doors with a frown on his face. "I just hope it scared him enough to become careless, but not crazy. He knows you're on to him, now. There's not much telling what he might do. You might want to watch your back, my friend."

Raven nodded with a solemn look on his face. "Believe me, I will."

CHAPTER TWENTY-THREE

Shadow hung up the phone. "Damn!" She leaned forward in her chair and laid her torso with arms stretched out across her desk. "Damn," she repeated.

Raven's phone call dashed all hopes of meeting with him later for a little private time. He called to tell her he and Bob were riding to New Orleans with Paul to listen in on a possible suspect being questioned.

Shadow blew out a frustrated sigh and sat back in her seat. She was excited they caught Duprue. He might be able to help them with their investigation.

All they needed was one good lead. The only thing they had so far was one mystery after another piled on top of each other. She had a gut feeling they all linked back to her father's imprisonment somehow, but they didn't have one ounce of proof to show for it. Yet.

She moaned. Perhaps, all the mysteries, murders and mayhem were coming to an end. She knew they were coming close to finding out who was behind it all and only then would everything be over with. Then maybe, just maybe they could get down to having a normal life for a change.

When this was all over she planned on kidnapping Raven and taking him somewhere secluded and very private. Then, she planned on having her way with him. Over and over and over. For days. Amen!

* * *

Raven thought of the sexy sundress Shadow wore that morning as he and Bob joined Paul in his patrol car. He'd had big plans on removing that dress and admiring the body beneath it with his hands and mouth until they both begged for mercy.

Damn it to hell. Instead, he was headed to New Orleans to observe Paul interrogating Simon Duprue. This was their big break. Duprue's testimony could easily end their investigation as early as today.

Raven grinned. Then, nothing or no one would keep him from ridding Shadow of her sexy sundress and doing to her everything his imaginative mind had conjured up for the past week.

An hour later, Paul pulled up into a fast food restaurant outside of New Orleans. They ate a quick lunch before heading straight to the police station. They were to meet the Detective assigned to the case at 1:00.

Paul drove into the parking lot and the three men got out of the car. He led them inside where he introduced them to the clerk on duty.

The clerk smiled a greeting and stood. "Right this way. Detective Jarrett is expecting you." She led them down a hall and into a large area where several desks were placed around the room. The chaotic atmosphere of ringing phones and the smell of day old coffee penetrated the room.

A man who looked to be in his late fifties rose and greeted them as they made their way to his desk. Rick Jarrett's suit was wrinkled, his tie undone and the bags under his eyes attested he hadn't seen his bed for a long while.

After introductions were made Jarrett said. "Just in time, boys. They're bringing him down to the interrogation room as we speak. If you'll follow me." He led them down the hallway and into a stark room void of any furniture. A wide one-way mirror covered one wall.

"Duprue has already confessed to being at the shack the night you guys set up a surveillance. He didn't have much of a choice since we had the blood samples back from the lab. But, he's not admitting to anything else or squealing any names. We've been watching Duprue for a long time, now. Some of our undercovers have been trying to connect him to a rash of car thefts, but haven't been able to pin anything on him. He's a slippery S.O.B. You don't know how happy we were to have his DNA show up in McClane Ridge. It gave us a reason to haul his ass in." Jarrett told them.

"Looks like we both need him to do some confessing." Raven said as he walked toward the mirror and gazed into the next room where a table and chairs were set up. His attention was averted as the door opened into the interrogation room.

A police officer motioned a man dressed in orange into the room. Duprue looked to be of a medium build and around forty years old with multiple tattoos covering his face and arms. He walked with arrogance toward a table and sprawled down into the seat. A smirk emerged on his face.

In an instant, Raven recognized the man as being one of the three digging at the shack that night. "That's him."

"Are you sure?" Jarrett asked.

"It's him alright."

"Well, it looks like it's showtime, boy's. This should be fun," Jarrett told them as he and Paul left the room.

Raven and Bob watched as Jarrett entered the interrogation room and greeted Duprue before sitting opposite him at the table. Paul placed one foot in a chair and leaned forward with his arms lying on his knee.

Jarrett began. "I'm Detective Jarrett and this is McClane Ridge's Police Chief, Paul LaCroix. We want to ask you a few questions."

Duprue shrugged with insolence. "Got a cigarette?"

Jarrett glanced at Paul and then back to Duprue. He stared him down. "No. Who hired you to dig up the body in McClane Ridge?"

Duprue's grin was contemptible. "What body? I don't know what you're talking about."

Jarrett leaned back in his chair. He steepled his fingers beneath his chin and studied Duprue. Finally, he sighed and looked toward Paul. His soft spoken words belied the iron will behind the meaning. "I'm really not up to playing any damn games with this guy. It's been thirty-six hours since I last saw my bed. I've had nothing to eat for hours except dry donuts and cold coffee. I'm exhausted. I have heartburn and my temper is close to blowing the Richter scale right off the frickin' universe. You might want to leave and let me conduct this interview by myself. Cause it ain't gonna be pretty."

Paul grinned and sat down, making himself comfortable. "Uh uh. I wouldn't miss this for the world."

Shadow's Justice

Duprue sat up straight in his chair. His nervous gaze went from one man to the next. Then he sat back and laughed. He pointed a finger at Jarrett. "I get it. Good cop. Bad cop act. I have to hand it to you. You're good." He glanced at Paul and repeated. "He's good."

Jarrett laughed and stood. He pulled his tie off and threw it on the table. He walked toward Duprue and stood beside him. "You're right. You're a smart one for catching on so fast."

Jarrett's hand landed on Duprue's shoulder blade. His fingers dug into the sensitive area and he pushed downward until Duprue was on his knees beside his chair whimpering in pain.

"I'm going to ask you one more time. Who hired you?"

"Go to hell, you bastard. This is police brutality. I'll have your fucking job for this, Jarrett."

Jarrett's fingers tightened and his knee pressed hard into his spine. He glanced up at Paul. "Am I being brutal to this scumbag?"

Paul shook his head. "Nope. I haven't seen you do anything, but ask him some questions and the camera is turned off. Maybe he will do better if I ask the questions."

Paul stood and walked around the table. He towered over the suspect. He cupped one hand under Duprue's chin and raised his head until they were eyelevel with each other. "Jarrett asked you a question. It would be in your best interest to answer him."

Duprue whimpered as Paul's six foot frame towered over him. He bowed his head and nodded. "Let me up and I'll tell you."

"Good choice. Let him up, Jarrett."

Jarrett stepped back and then reached one hand under Duprue's arm to help him up. When he was seated, Jarrett and Paul resumed their seats.

"Start talking," Paul ordered.

Duprue rubbed his shoulder blade. He shook his head in resignation. "Man, you know if it gets out that I squealed, I'm a dead man."

"You're a dead man, either way, Duprue. You know good and well the one who hired you won't take the chance you might talk later on. Your only hope is we capture this guy and put him away for a long time. He won't be able to hurt you, then," Paul told him.

Duprue nodded. His insolence and bravery had evaporated into an uneasy willingness to cooperate. "Okay. I got a call one night about two weeks ago, from a guy I'd done some jobs for a few years back. He wanted me to get a couple of guys together and meet up outside of town late that night. I was surprised, because this guy never wanted his face seen or his name known, which never made me a diddly shit, since he always paid good and paid with cash.

Anyway, I gathered up two of my buddies and we met this guy right where he told us to. He told us he would pay us five hundred dollars a piece up front and five hundred each when the job was completed. He handed us a rough drawing of this old shack and a map of how to get there. He told us there was a body buried there and he wanted it dug up and disposed of proper like. He laughed and said a cremation of some sorts would be perfect. He showed us on the drawing the exact spot where we' needed to begin digging."

"Did you start digging that night?" Paul asked.

"No, we waited until the next night. The bastard failed to tell us their were armed guards patrolling the area. We had to sneak around back and it took us most of the night just pulling off the boards and the flooring to get to the ground. We were able to dig some, but we had to leave right before daylight."

"Were you able to go back the next night?"

"Yeah, we went back and that was when you guys showed up and put a stop to everything."

Paul thought through everything Duprue had said. One part bothered him. "You said you only brought two guys with you. We had our guns pointed at the three of you, so who was it that pulled off the shot behind us?"

"The man who hired us. I guess he didn't trust us enough to do the job, so he followed us. I saw him raise his gun and fire and that one guy went down. That's when we lit out of there. The sorry bastard refused to pay us the rest of the money."

"This man who hired you. Did he ever give you his name?"

"Nope. But, I recognized his face as soon as I saw him. He's been in the newspapers so many times it would be hard not to know him."

Paul felt the excitement gush through him. "What's his name?"

"He's that hot shot lawyer in McClane Ridge. His name is Randall Collins."

"Son-of-a-bitch!" Paul's curse sounded throughout the room, matching Raven's exact words from the room next door.

CHAPTER TWENTY-FOUR

Shadow left her office around four o'clock and drove straight home. She wanted to be there when Raven arrived back from New Orleans. He'd called a few minutes before to tell her they were on their way back to McClane Ridge.

Their bad cell phone connection cut them off before she was able to ask him any questions. She was anxious to find out what Duprue had told them. They had a lot at stake that was depending on one convicts testimony.

Shadow drove Raven's car into the garage and parked beside Rose's SUV. Good. Rose is back from her luncheon. She'll be here when Raven arrives.

Shadow entered the house through the kitchen and called out a greeting. She shrugged her shoulders when she found the room empty.

She opened the refrigerator to pull out the iced tea pitcher, but there was none. Puzzled, she closed the refrigerator door and glanced around. That was odd. Carol always had fresh tea made and she was usually in the kitchen making preparations for dinner at this time.

Concerned that Carol might be sick, Shadow

turned and left the kitchen to find Rose. Hearing voices coming from the sitting room, she headed toward the door. Shadow was relieved to note one of the voices sounded like Carols. Rose was more than likely talking her ear off about her luncheon and shopping spree.

"Hey, you guys. I'm home." Shadow said as she opened the door and stepped into the room. Her steps faltered and then came to a complete stop as her gaze took in the scene before her.

Randall Collins stood in the middle of the room facing Rose and Carol who was sitting on the divan. Tears were running like a river down both women's faces.

"What's wrong? Has something happened to Raven?"

Collin's upper body turned toward her as she entered. His unsteady hand held a pistol at arms length and it was pointed straight at her.

Shadow inhaled. "Rose? Carol? Are you alright?" she asked without taking her eyes off of Collins.

"He hasn't hurt us." Rose answered. Shadow heard the controlled sob in her voice.

She felt the lump in her throat disappear. "He's lucky," she said, matter-of-fact as she took in his unusual rumpled condition. His suit was wrinkled and his hair looked like he had run both hands several times through the normal stylish cut. His sleepless eyes bore down on her with a wild, cornered look.

With jerky movements, Collins pointed his gun toward the divan. "Get over there beside the other two where I can see all of you," he ordered.

Shadow stood her ground. "Put the gun down, Randall."

"Do it. Now," he screamed out.

Shadow hurried to do as he bidded. She sat down beside Rose and gave her a quick hug. Her step-mother and Carol were scared, but holding up okay, she noticed.

Shadow's attention returned to Randall. He was clearly beyond being mentally distraught and was now very dangerous. No, she thought. Raven's been right all along. Randall has always been dangerous.

She moved to the edge of the seat and began talking with a quiet and soothing voice. She hoped to bide their time until Raven had time to get home.

"Randall, whatever the problem is we can work through this. I will help you, I promise. Please, talk to me and tell me why you are doing this."

His sudden laughter turned bitter. "Now, that is hysterical. You of all people want to help me. You bitch, you don't have a clue." The gun waved in her face.

Shadow flinched at his harsh words and altered actions. Her mind struggled to find a way to calm him down. Words were the only weapon she had at the moment.

"Then tell me, Randall."

Her pleading words fell on deaf ears. Collins was staring at Rose, his expression softened. "Do you know that I've always loved you?"

A quiet sob escaped from Rose. With a quick, nervous shake of her head, she answered in a quiet voice. "No, Randall. I didn't know."

"Well, I have. I fell deeply in love with you in high school. But, you never even saw me as a lover, only as a friend. I came close to hating you when you married Tolliver." His eyes glazed over as if his mind had taken him back to those days.

He shook his head and his soft laughter bordered on insanity. "And, then to top it all off when the bastard finally died, I was married to that damn frigid wife of mine who refused to give me a divorce. But, I fixed her self-righteous ass. Then you up and married McClane. When I found out the date McClane would make you a widow once again, I was determined nothing would stand in my way with you."

Rose's hand went to her mouth to stifle a scream. Shadow heard Carol's quiet sobs. She shook her head in disbelief. "You killed your wife." Her controlled statement was whispered, but seemed to echo across the room.

Collin's gaze jerked toward her. A sadistic smile appeared. "Of course, I killed her. It was easy, really. It didn't take but a minute to snip the brake line on her car and only a few miles before the fluid drained out of the brakes. I've told the bitch for years she was going to take a curve too fast, once too often."

"You bastard." The words flew out of Shadow's mouth. "How did you get away with it?"

"My dear, surely you don't think my good friend, Chief Walker would ever let a minor thing like a cut brake line get out to the public, do you? He protected the Brotherhood a hell of a lot more aggressive than he ever did the law. I believe the cause of her accident went on record as speeding and reckless driving."

Shadow's mind reeled from his confessions. She fought down the bile rising in her throat as she thought of his wife's horrible death.

None of them had ever known the true Randall Collins. They had always considered him a brilliant lawyer and a true friend. Instead, he was an insane murderer.

Shadow's head jerked up. One part of his statement finally sunk into her dazed mind. He had mentioned the Brotherhood. Old man Sanders had told her to look toward the Brotherhood to find the truth of her father's innocence. "I don't believe this. You killed old man Tucker, didn't you? Then you framed my father for the murder."

Shadow shook her head in disbelief. "Three people dead, just because of your love for Rose. You're insane."

Shadow watched the rage cross his face and flinched as his finger moved closer to the trigger. It dawned on her that he would never leave any witnesses to his confessions. He planned on killing them.

"If you love Rose so much, please let her and Carol leave. I'll stay here with you." Shadow pleaded over Rose's and Carol's objections.

Collin's visibly relaxed. He laughed out loud. "You don't have a damn clue about anything. My loving Rose doesn't have anything to do with why I'm here."

"Then tell me why you're doing this."

"All in good time, my dear. All in good time. Now, shut the hell up and tell me when Raven will be back."

Shadow shook her head. "I don't know."

His thumb cocked the gun. "When will Raven be back?" His threatening tone stressed each word.

"I'm telling the truth. I don't know. A half an hour or so, maybe. Leave him out of this." Shadow worked hard to keep the quiver from her voice. She didn't want to appear weak or cowardly in front of him. Dammit. Why did she leave her gun in her bedroom this morning? She had to think of someway to get Rose and Carol safely out of the house. Then, they could warn Raven.

Collins interrupted her thoughts. "I'm afraid Raven has to be here before I can finish what I've started. He's played a major part in everything."

Rose's soft voice pleaded. "Randall, you don't want to do this. Walk away, right now, move out of the country. We won't try to stop you. Please, Randall, let us go."

A flicker of regret and pain showed in his eyes for a moment. "I can't Rose. Don't you understand? It's too late."

Rose shook her head with vigorous intent. "No. It's not, Randall. You would have at least an hour's head start before anyone would know to look for you. If you harm us now, there is no way my sons would let you get away with it. They wouldn't stop until they made sure you paid for your crimes."

"She's right, Collins. You'd have a better chance of escaping capture if you leave, now." Shadow added.

Collins grinned as he waved his gun back and forth. "You don't understand. I can kill the four of you who knows too much and then I can go back to living my life the way I always have. No one will ever suspect it was me. They never have."

Shadow grasped at straws, trying to draw out more information. She was hoping to find out how many more members made up the Brotherhood. "That's because the Brotherhood has always protected you. Who's going to protect you, now?"

"I won't need any protection from anyone, nor will I have to protect the other two, anymore. Don't you get it? This is the end of the line. With the four of you dead, no one will be snooping around trying to dig up ancient history. It will all be over."

"No, it won't. Rose told you the truth. John and Michael won't stop at anything to find out who killed their mother and the rest of us. And, you're forgetting about Paul and Bob. You've been their number one suspect since day one. They may be driving back from New Orleans right this minute with the information to convict you and put you away for life."

"What are you talking about?" Both hands were now on the gun pointed at her heart.

"Let Rose and Carol go." Shadow hedged.

The caged, animal look came back into his eyes. "Don't make me shoot you right now. What information are you talking about?" he screamed.

Shadow sat back. She had pushed him too far.

The shrill sound of the phone ringing jarred across the room. Shadow glanced up at Collins. His panic-stricken gaze was focused on the telephone on the table beside her.

"That might be Raven. He will know something is wrong if I don't answer."

"No."

The phone rang with an eerie steadiness.

"He'll bring the Calvary with him. Paul and Bob are with him. You won't be able to shoot us all before one of them is able to get a bullet straight into your heart."

Collins began pacing. "Dammit. I just want Raven." He stopped in the middle of the room and pointed at the phone with his gun. "Answer it and do whatever you have to do to convince him to come home alone. You give me away and I'll shoot you as you speak to your lover boy. Got me?"

Shadow's Justice

Shadow nodded and reached for the phone. "Raven?" She spoke quickly.

"Yeah, babe, it's me. What took you so long to answer?"

"Where are you?"

The silence on the other end had her nerves stretched to the limit. She glanced up at Collins.

"We're on the outskirts of town. What's wrong?"

"As soon as you drop the other two off, will you be coming straight home?"

"Bob will drop me off. You do remember that you have my car and I'll have to hitch a ride home with Bob, don't you?"

"Yes, of course. Tell Bob I'll see him the next time he's in town."

Silence. "Bob's not leaving town. Shadow, what's wrong?"

"I hope you have good news to tell us when you get home. Raven, be very careful." Shadow hung up the phone. Her heart felt like it was beating out of her chest. She had done everything she could think of to let Raven know something was up, without giving herself away. And yet, she was petrified he would walk straight into an ambush.

"Well, what time will he be here?" Collins asked.

"He said it would be another half hour or so before he could make it home," she lied. Hopefully, he would be there a lot sooner than Collins expected.

* * *

Raven put his cell phone back into his pocket. He stared out of the window as he thought about Shadow's weird phone conversation. He was tuned into Shadow enough by now to know there was a hidden sound of fear in her voice.

A cold chill suddenly ran down his spine. He sat up straight and glanced over at Paul. "Something's wrong. Take me home."

"What's wrong?" Bob asked from the back seat.

Raven told them what Shadow had said over the phone. "She was trying to warn me about something. I don't know what in the hell it was. I just know she's in danger."

"It sounded like she needed you to come straight home, but alone." Paul said.

Raven nodded. "That's what I thought, too."

"What do you want us to do?" Bob asked.

"If someone is in the house with her, they will think it will take us at least fifteen minutes longer if we go by the Police Station and switch cars. That will give us time to park a block away and go up on foot. We can enter the house from the basement door."

Raven felt the adrenaline pumping through his body. He reached inside his jacket and pulled out his pistol. Opening the chamber, he reassured himself it was loaded. He could hear Bob in the backseat going through the same procedure. Paul was on the radio asking for backup. He told them to stay out of sight until given further orders.

Every muscle in Raven's body tensed as Paul pulled up beside the curve and parked. Raven glanced over at Paul. His gaze was hard as steel. "You might want to stay here and not be a witness to any of this. Because I swear, if anyone has hurt Shadow or the rest of the family, I will kill the bastard."

Paul stared at his friend for a long time. He sighed and opened his door and stepped out. He leaned down and spoke through the open door. "You never know what a man will have to do in self-defense to protect himself or the ones he loves. I know what I would do. Time's a-wasting. Let's go."

Raven nodded and got out of the car to stand beside Bob. He knew what his friend, Paul was trying to tell him. Murder in self-defense was protected under the law. He would just have to make sure it looked that way if the worst case scenario happened.

The three men jogged toward the house. They veered off the sidewalk a few yards from the house and cut through the neighbor's shrubs to enter into the backyard.

Each man gripped a gun in their hand as they crept toward the small door leading into the basement. Raven's hand moved across the ledge until he felt the key. Unlocking the door, they climbed down the steps until they were standing in the dark room.

On silent feet, they moved across the basement floor to climb the steps leading into the kitchen. With gun drawn, Raven eased the door open a crack and listened for voices. Not hearing anything, he opened the door far enough to see around the room. Satisfied it was empty, he motioned for the other two to follow him and then stepped out of the basement.

They made swift time across the room toward the door leading into the hallway. He listened for any noises before stepping through the doorway. It was then he heard Shadow's voice coming from the sitting room. He sighed in relief when he realized she was well and talking.

With their back against the wall, they moved on silent feet toward the closed door. Raven laid the side of his head against the door and listened. His heart almost stopped when he heard the distinct voice of Collins coming from the other side.

Shadow's Justice

Raven turned and mouthed the man's name to the other two who understood and responded. Bob rushed to the other side of the door and stood ready. Paul slid to the other side and did the same. Raven stood facing the door with his gun positioned in both hands.

On the silent count of three, he reached out and turned the doorknob and swung the door open in one fluid motion. All three men rushed the room.

Everything after that seemed to happen in slow motion for Raven. Paul yelled out, "Police. Freeze. Throw your weapon down, Collins."

He heard Rose and Carol screaming. He saw Collins turn with a fiery rage and begin shooting toward them. Raven dove to the floor, rolled and came up beside Collins just in time to see Shadow jump on the man's back, keeping him from getting off a clear shot at Collins.

Raven grabbed for the gun at the same time Collins swung around to knock Shadow off his back and his gun slammed into Raven's cheekbone. He felt himself fall backwards into oblivion.

Five minutes later, Raven moaned and opened his eyes. Collins was standing over him with a gun held to his head.

"Get up and get over there with the rest of them," he ordered.

Raven hesitated for a second before doing as he was bidded. He moaned as he stood and then walked to stand beside Shadow. Blood was seeping from the cut on his cheek. He glanced around the group to make sure everyone was alright. "What happened?"

Shadow reached for a tissue off the end table and began wiping away the blood from his cheek. "He

Shadow's Justice

grabbed Rose and held the gun to her. Everyone had to back off. Are you okay?"

Raven nodded to assure her. He wrapped an arm around her waist before turning back to Collins.

"Why are you doing this?"

Collin's words were as cold as his gaze. "You're a threat to me, Deveroux. You need to be eliminated."

CHAPTER TWENTY-FIVE

Raven controlled his fear for himself and the others and tried to rationalize with an insane man. "I don't understand. Why am I a threat to you?"

"Ah, I see. You want to talk to give yourself time to think of a way out of me blowing your brains to smithereens." Collins shrugged. "I'm in no hurry. I guess you all deserve to know the reason I have to kill each and every one of you."

"Tell us, so we will understand."

"You're a lawyer, Collin's. I don't need to tell you everything you say can be held against you in a court of law." Paul warned.

Collin's burst out laughing in hysterics. "Like that's going to mean a fucking damn to me. Get real, Paul."

He waved his gun at the group. "You men, pull up some chairs beside the divan. Everyone might as well be seated. It's a long story."

When everyone was seated, he began his story as if he was telling a tale across a campfire. His mind flashed back to the past and the words he'd held in place for half a century poured out.

"My living hell began fifty years ago that summer at a party given by a girl we went to school with. B.J. Adams and I met our friend Bubba Walker at his home and we walked to the party from there. Bubba, or Ed Walker as you know him had stolen a bottle of whiskey from his father and the three of us were well on our way to being drunk by the time we got there.

A young girl who visited her grandparents every summer was there when we arrived. B.J. or Ben, whichever you want to call him, had a serious crush on the Jacobs girl, but she hadn't wanted anything to do with him the summer before. That made him want her even more."

"So, you three were at the party and knew the dead girl?" Raven asked.

"Yes, we were there. Wish to God we hadn't been. My life might have turned out a lot different. Anyway, to continue, Ben was drinking heavy and he started making lewd suggestions to the girl. She became upset and left the party early to walk home, instead of waiting on her grandfather to pick her up.

Everyone else at the party was having a good time and no one saw Ben follow her outside, still talking trash. Ed and I went after them. We were drunk and we began taunting Ben about catching his girl and kissing her into being more agreeable. How more damn stupid can sixteen and seventeen year old boys get? What happened next became a living nightmare. I can still see it so clearly in my mind.

Pressured by our teasing, Ben became more aggressive with Karen. When we were about a mile away from the party, he started grabbing her arm and pulling her to him, trying to kiss her. She was hysterical, crying and fighting to get away from him, but the struggle only managed to anger and excite him.

Ben backhanded her and she fell onto the gravel road. The fall knocked her out. He raised her up and hooked his arms beneath hers and drug her into the woods.

Then, he raped her, while Ed and I held her down. When he was finished and crawled off of her, Ed and I took our turns raping her. I was the last one with her."

"Oh my God! Oh my God!" Shadow muttered over and over. Her trembling fingers pressed against her lips in horror. Rose and Carol cried.

Collins glanced over at Rose. "I'm sorry, Sweetheart. I really didn't want you to know all of my sordid past."

"Your bastard. I hope you rot in hell." Rose told him with cold venom shooting from her eyes.

"I'm sure I will." His dismal tone promised her his fate. He tore his somber gaze from Rose and turned back to Raven.

He continued in a quiet voice. "She was conscious the whole time and struggling for her life. She screamed to high heaven and her fingernails scraped down my face, drawing blood. I became enraged. It was good and dark by then, but I was still able to see a large rock on the ground beside her. With anger and alcohol raging through me, I picked up the rock and struck her several times with violent blows to her head. Ed and Ben pulled me off of her, but by that time, she was dead."

"You killed her?" Paul lurched toward Collins, but sat back when the gun swung toward him.

"Don't force me to kill you first. My quarrel's not with you," he warned.

"Let him finish, Paul. I want to know everything." Rose said. Her eyes were glazed with hatred.

Collins lowered his gun. He continued as if he

hadn't been interrupted. "We panicked. Ben wanted to leave her lying there, but I was too afraid of someone finding out. I remembered Old Man Fletcher was building a new cabin for his bride on some land right down the road from where we stood. We decided we would bury her in the spot where the new ground was already broke up for the cabin's foundation.

We carried her there and found a couple of shovels on the site and dug a deep hole. We buried her and filled in her grave with the dirt. We stood over her grave and made a binding pact between the three of us that we would never tell a living soul about what happened that night. We pledged we would always protect one another. We gave ourselves the name of "The Brotherhood of Silence".

"So, now we know the names of the 'Brotherhood'." Bob stated.

"Yes. That was us. We hightailed it home after that. We breathed a sigh of relief a few weeks later when Fletcher's newly built cabin covered up our sins.

The three of us got on with our lives. We all became honorable and respected citizens of McClane Ridge.

Then, a few years ago, all hell broke loose threatening to destroy our hard earned image. Judd Tucker tried to blackmail us. His bank was going under and he needed money. He said he knew what happened that night with the Jacobs girl. He'd followed us from the party and witnessed everything. He'd been too frightened and distraught by what he saw and he'd blocked everything from his memory.

Images of that night slowly started coming back to Judd about a year before he contacted the three of us.

He said he would go to the cops in another state with what he knew if we didn't give him two hundred and fifty thousand dollars. He told us he had guaranteed his safety by recording everything he knew on tape. He said he was writing a letter to his friend, Jack McClane that if anything happened to him, he would give him the authority to open up a safe deposit vault which held a tape with important information. He wanted Jack to take the tape to a police station out of state."

Shadow drew in a sharp breath. She didn't know if she could stand the pain of hearing what was coming next. She felt Raven's hand close over hers.

"Ben, Ed and I knew what had to be done. Ed broke into McClane's home that night and stole a pistol out of his guncase and brought it to me. The next evening, I hid inside the bank until closing time. When everyone was gone except Tucker, I pulled on a pair of gloves and walked into his office. I let him know I was there before I shot him point blank in the head with McClane's gun. I dropped the gun on his desk and found the letter written to McClane still lying in his out-mail slot. I grabbed the letter and walked out."

Shadow screamed out and flung herself at Collin's. Her fists beat at his face and her nails ran down his cheeks. Collin's knocked her backwards.

Raven moved to tackle Collins. He lashed out in anger. "I'm going to kill you, you bastard."

Collins fired the gun over Raven's head and plaster fell. "I'm not ready to kill you just yet, Raven. So, shut up and sit down."

The women screamed and cried harder.

Raven sat back down and drew Shadow's shaking

body into his arms. His jaw clenched with fury. "You'll pay for this." He promised.

"I'm sure I will, but for now I'm going to finish my story." Collins relaxed. "The crime lab found McClane's fingerprints on the gun and Ed arrested him for murder. The hilarious part was that Rose and Jack turned around and hired me as his lawyer. I'm sorry, Rose. We didn't mean to hurt you. We were only trying to save our skins."

"I hope to hell you're not asking for my forgiveness." Rose ground out through clenched teeth.

Collin's shook his head with a sadness. "No, Rose. I know it's too late for that, but please believe that I'm truly sorry."

"Go straight to hell." Rose screamed out through her sobs.

"I'm sure I will." He bowed his head for a moment before continuing. "No one, other than the Brotherhood, knew how I hid the evidence over the years that might have gotten McClane off or how I planted damning evidence that convicted him. Jack had his day in court and was found guilty. Judge Ben Adams announced the juror's decision and sentenced him to death. So easy. Everything just fell into place. Until Raven and Shadow started sticking their damn noses back into the case."

"You're gonna die." Raven stated matter-of-factly.

Collins ignored him, his mind on the past. "For years, we looked for the tape Judd said he'd made, but never found it. I even hired a private detective to watch Judd's son, Steven in case he could lead us to the tape.

Several things happened after that. Raven and

Shadow broke into my office and found the papers I had filed from the private detective. I tried to warn them to back off with a small explosion in their car, but that only made them more determined. They were making it obvious they were now suspecting me."

"Around that time, Ben got a phone call. We were being blackmailed, once again. The horrible nightmare was starting all over. The caller was Steven Tucker. He found the tape his father had made and was threatening to turn it over if we didn't pay up. He didn't give a damn about revenge, he wanted money. Ben told him he had to give him a few days to come up with that much cash."

"Ben met with Tucker two days later with a briefcase full of money in exchanged for the tape. Ben left with the tape and later that night, Ed and I broke inside Tuckers home and found him in his study. I shot him point blank to the head, just like I did his father. Ed grabbed the money still in the briefcase beside his desk and we fled."

"Oh my God!" Shadow cried out on Raven's shoulder.

"Ben became worried Tucker had made copies of the tape. So, I went back the next night and torched the house. If there were any copies, they went up in smoke along with the house that night.

Then, all hell broke loose, again. The McClane Construction Company was contracted to build a large hotel right on the spot where Old Man Fletcher's cabin sat. It was enough to scare Ed into having a heart attack and being put into intensive care.

That left me to take care of the problem on my own. I hired some men who owed me favors to set off a few explosions at the construction site. I didn't want anyone hurt. I just wanted enough blasts to scare the workers away for a few days, giving us time to dig up the body."

"You bastard. You almost killed my son," Rose flung out.

"No. That was his own damn fault. He wasn't even supposed to have been on one of the dozers," Collins lashed back before continuing. "I went to the hospital later that evening to check on Ed. Unfortunately, the stupid bastard had become righteous when he thought he was dying. He told me he wanted to confess everything to cleanse his soul. I couldn't let that happen. Killing my best friend of sixty years, a member of our 'Brotherhood' was the hardest thing I have ever had to do in my lifetime, but I didn't have a choice. Ben was behind my decision, one hundred percent.

That night I met my hired men at the site. The security guards made it a little more difficult, but my men still managed to sneak into the cabin and get the boards from the floor pulled up. They dug some, but were unable to find the body. The next night, we went back to finish the job. I should've known something was up when I noticed the security guards were gone. We were set up.

Then Paul, Raven, Shadow and Bob stormed in on us while my men were digging. They never saw me. I managed to get behind them and get a shot off at Raven, allowing us time to escape."

"You're fate will be much worse." Raven promised him.

Collins ignored him. He was too far into his story. "The next day, the construction crew dug the body up. I almost gave up then, but then I decided it was time to come up with another plan.

I called Ben to meet me at our usual place, outside of town at the bayou swamp. I had been drinking, trying to calm my nerves before Ben got there. As soon as he arrived, I told him about the body being found. He started harping on my drinking and incompetence. After all I had been through, my mind snapped. I pulled a gun out of my jacket and shot him in the head as he drove off. His car ended up submerged in the swamp. The alligators were swarming his car when I left.

Then that left me, the only surviving member of the 'Brotherhood'. And Raven, you were closing in on me. You flaunted a cufflink in front of me that you found on Tucker's lawn. You knew it belonged to me and knew when I'd lost it. You only had to prove it."

Collins raised the gun, the barrel pointed to the center of Raven's head. "I have to stop you, Raven. My only chance is to kill you."

CHAPTER TWENTY-SIX

Raven didn't give Collins a chance to pull the trigger. He dove head first into Collins's midsection knocking him backwards. They both hit the floor rolling.

Raven grabbed for the gun, but Collins held on tight. He was fighting a man who had nothing left to lose. His fist drew back and slammed into the lawyer's face knocking his head back hard against the floor.

The man, twice Raven's age fought him off. Collins swung his fist holding the gun. The butt of the gun smashed against Raven's cheek. Raven groaned and fell backwards, blood pouring from the cut.

Raven shook his head to fight unconsciousness. Out of the corner of his eye, he saw Paul and Bob tackling Collins, attempting to take the gun away.

Collins fought them hard and cursed them all with every breath in him. He was outmanned and losing strength. His battle was almost over.

Then, as if the events were playing out in slow motion, Raven watched in horror when Collins broke away from the two men. He screamed out, "I have to make the screams stop!" before he raised the barrel to his own temple and pulled the trigger.

* * *

Shadow screamed with hysterics over and over as

Collins's blood splattered across the room. She felt Rose's comforting arms go around her. They held each other tight, weeping out of control.

Long seconds passed as Paul called the proper officials and then talked in a quiet voice to Raven and Bob.

Shadow pulled away from her stepmother as Raven approached and put his arms around them both. She naturally walked into his arms to be held and comforted by the man she loved as she cried her heart out.

"Shhhhh. Shhhhh, baby. It's over. He can't hurt us any longer," he told her over and over as his palm rubbed up and down her spine in a soothing motion.

When her sobs turned silent, Raven insisted on leading the three women into the kitchen, away from the gory scene. He stayed long enough for Carol to doctor the cut on his cheek before rejoining the men in the sitting room.

Shadow remembered someone saying later that the coroner had arrived, but she wasn't observant to anything happening around her.

Her mind kept replaying, like a broken record, everything Collins had confessed. So many lies. So many deaths. All because of three young boy's corrupted desires.

Her world had been turned upside down because of what had happened fifty years before. Her father had been innocent, but was sentenced to death just to keep their countless secrets hidden. His good name had been tainted as a murderer. Now, she vowed the whole town would know the truth.

Steven Tucker's son would grow up knowing the partial truth about his father's death. She would make sure Steven's son nor his wife, would never learn the horrible details about his blackmail attempts leading up to his death. They had enough pain to live with for the rest of their lives without knowing about Steven's one time fall from Grace.

Shadow raised her face toward Heaven and whispered, "God forgive me, but I pray you send Collins straight to hell for what he's done to my family and the others."

* * *

Raven's hand shook. He couldn't bring himself to take another look at the insane man lying dead on the floor. He was so freakin' pissed that he couldn't kill the bastard himself.

He cursed and ran his hand across the top of his head trying to calm his anger. He felt Bob's supportive presence beside him as he moved aside to give the men room to remove the body.

Raven sighed and glanced up at Bob. "Guess it's finally over."

Bob nodded. "Paul needs us to follow him to the police station to give a statement as witnesses. I let the women know we were going."

"Okay. Thanks." Raven turned and without another word, walked out of the house. When he stood outside, he leaned over with his hands on his knees and took several deep, cleansing breaths.

Nothing in his life, not his military experiences or his mercenary business had ever prepared him for this horrible, gut-wrenching fear. Rose and Shadow could have been killed earlier and snatched from his life by that maniac before he had a chance to tell Shadow how much he loved her.

* * *

Shadow's Justice

Shadow paced the floor. Her turmoil thoughts drowned out her stepmother and Carol's gentle weeping from across the room.

She could hear muted voices down the hall. Officials were leaving one by one. They had taped off the sitting room and locked the door going to the crime scene. She didn't know if she would ever be able to go back into that room, again.

Shadow stopped in front of the large windows overlooking the front drive for at least the hundredth time. Pulling the curtains back, she watched for Raven, but with no luck. With a sigh, she let the curtains drop back into place and resumed her pacing.

She rubbed her shoulders trying to rid herself of the shakes still racking her body. The past few nightmarish hours had been relived over and over in her mind. They had all come so close to being killed.

She needed to be held by Raven. She needed to feel his heartbeat against the palm of her hand as a reminder that he was alive and well. Fear like she had never known paralyzed her mind while Raven was in danger an hour before. She'd watched Raven try to wrestle the gun from Collins, not knowing whether he would live or die.

It was vital to her to feel the comfort of his arms before she would finally believe all the pain and terror would stop with Collins's death.

Shadow's thoughts were interrupted by the sound of a car's engine. She ran to the window and looked out. Her disappointment could be heard in her sigh. It wasn't Raven driving up like she'd hoped, but it was Stacy, instead.

She was still happy to see her friend and greeted her warmly at the door with a hug.

Shadow's Justice

"I'm glad you came."

"Shadow, what's going on? I heard on the police scanner where everyone in the household was being held at gunpoint. Is everyone okay?" Stacy's voice shook.

Shadow nodded and drew her into the kitchen where Stacy greeted Rose and Carol. "We're fine." Shadow filled her friend in on the past few horrifying hours.

Fear and worry showed on Stacy's face as she sat in stunned silence. In the end, her only words were, "Bob was here, too?"

Shadow glanced at her friend as understanding dawned on her. Stacy's concern for Bob ran more deep than that for just an acquaintance. Stacy was in love.

Shadow smiled, too weary to delve too deep into the affair, at that moment. She gave her friend a hug. "We'll talk later. I can't wait to hear how this developed."

"What?"

"Don't play innocent with me. I'm so much in love with Raven that I can easily spot your love for Bob a mile away. Am I right?"

Stacy's grin gave her away. "You know me too well. We worked on making our love even stronger between us last night."

Shadow laughed out loud. "I bet you did." Then the deep pain crept back into her voice. "Raven, Bob and Paul drove back to the police station to take care of all the phone calls and paperwork involved." With tears falling down her cheeks, she walked back to the window and looked out.

Shadow felt Stacy's hand on her shoulder. She

turned back to her friend with urgency in her voice. "There's someplace I have to go. Will you tell everyone I'll be back in a little while?"

"Sure. Do you want me to come with you?" Stacy asked in concern.

"No. Thank you, but this is something I need to do by myself."

* * *

An hour later, Raven found Shadow sitting at the foot of her father's grave. He'd known exactly where she would be.

Her tear-ravaged face played witness to her pain. A bundle of fresh flowers lay across the mound.

He stood in silence beside her as she finished telling her father how much she missed him and loved him. He gave her the time to tell her father goodbye in her own way.

Finally, she turned her face upwards and smiled softly at Raven. "I wanted Dad to know his name has been cleared and to know how much I love him. I really believe he heard me."

Raven helped her to her feet and drew her into his arms. "I know he did, sweetheart. He will always be with us and listen to us as he did when he walked this earth."

Raven grinned and continued. "Knowing your father, he's in heaven right now dancing the jig and has one foot at the Pearly Gates raised in eagerness to kick Collins straight back to hell if he dared to arrive."

Shadow laughed out loud. "I wouldn't doubt that for a minute."

Raven sobered. He looked down at her tear-streaked face. His fingers moved across her skin to wipe away the moisture.

Shadow's Justice

He looked deep into her eyes as he confessed. "I love you more than I could have ever thought possible, Shadow McClane. I was so damn scared when I thought I could've lost you back there. I kept thinking my life would have been over if Collins had killed you."

Raven glanced away for a moment to gather his thoughts and then looked back down at Shadow. "I have decided to give up my Mercenary business."

"No." Shadow shook her head.

"Yes. I am. It dawned on me that if I kept the business and went out on my missions, you would be here at home going through the same gut-wrenching fears I was experiencing a few hours ago, when I thought you were in danger. I never want to put you through that hell."

Shadow's love for Raven shined in her eyes as she gazed up at him. "Don't you know you have proven over and over to me that you are more than capable of taking care of yourself and everyone else around you? I have every confidence you will always return home safe to me. Being a Mercenary is part of who you are and a big part of who I love. I could never ask you to give that up."

Raven smiled. "You never asked that of me, but I am willing to give it up for us. Besides, those two stepbrothers of yours will need all the help they can get if we plan on making your father's business a mega-million empire in the future for our children."

Shadow's laughter rang out. "Mighty big plans there, buster."

Raven grinned and then sobered as he gazed down at the face he loved. "I want you to be my wife, my life's partner and the mother to our children. You will always have my heart. I love you, so much. Will you marry me?"

This time it was tears of joy that ran down her face. She cupped his cheek with one hand and laughed out loud. "Yes. Yes. I will marry you. I love you with all my heart."

Raven pulled her into his arms and kissed her until they were both breathless. He pulled back and whispered, "I need to be alone with you right now, more than anything in this world."

He brought his lips back to hers, again pouring every ounce of his pain and insecurities into the kiss.

He broke off the kiss and leaned his forehead against hers. "Will you go with me?" he whispered.

Shadow nodded and leaned into his arms as they walked side by side back to their cars.

EPILOGUE

Shadow lay naked on the bed inside their get-away cabin in the woods. Her arms reached out to pull Raven toward her for another earth shattering kiss, but he resisted. Her arms fell back to her side.

Raven's lips on her stomach felt more luscious and soft than the silky sheets beneath her. She moaned out loud as the silkiness kissed one breast, leaving the other one aching for the same.

His hands roamed free across her body, not leaving one sensitive spot untouched. He knew her body like a road map and he took his sweet time exploring the highway.

"Raven, please," she whispered in between her moans.

She could not remember anytime in her life when she needed anything more desperate than she needed Raven, right now, right this second.

Thank God, he felt the same way, she thought as he moved to cover her with his body. She cried out his name over and over as the pleasure became pure and explosive. They each soared in ecstasy before spiraling back to contentment.

Breathing heavy, they lay side by side, holding each other tight until the tremors passed. Raven planted gentle, sweet kisses across her face while whispering love words between each kiss.

Shadow absorbed into her mind and heart, every touch and every word he expressed from deep down in his soul. She raised herself up on her elbow and leaned over to give him a long, lingering kiss, one born out of a timeless love instead of passion that would disintegrate as soon as their bodies separated.

Shadow wiped away an emotional tear and gave him a saucy grin before leaning over to kiss him. "Now, can we have that little talk about why you pushed me away at sixteen? Just look at what you've been missing out on all these years. It's a good thing you have a lifetime to make it up to me."

"Oh, believe me, honey. I'm looking forward to it." His voice held a promise and a pledge.

Connect with JERI LYNN STONE

I really appreciate you reading my books! I write for you and for my sanity. I would love to hear from you.

If you enjoyed reading Shadow's Justice please take a moment to leave an honest review on Amazon at:

https://amazon.com/author/jerilynnstone

Here are my social media coordinates:

Friend me on Facebook:
http://facebook.com/jerilynnstone
Follow me on Twitter:
http://twitter.com/jerlynstone
Subscribe to my blog:
http://www.jerilynnstone.blogspot.com
Subscribe to my newsletter:
http://www.jerilynnstone.blogspot.com